A Small Favor

"Melanie has outlined what we'd like you to do for us," the Professor said; it wasn't exactly a question.

I nodded slowly.

"At ten-thirty AM, Thursday, September 23, 1971, the mother of the Appointed One should be under the statue of Goethe in Lincoln Park."

"You can pull the chronalcage in there," Melanie said, a fierceness to her voice, "kill her, and be gone before anyone even sees you."

"It will be just another unsolved murder," the Professor said. "Chicago had a lot of them then."

"But . . . I'm not a cold-blooded killer," I said. "And even if we knew it could be done, if the laws of chronal travel would permit it, I couldn't just . . ."

"Do you realize what this could mean, Stillman? You have the power to rid the world of the Appointed One, to see that he was never born. Stillman, don't you understand? *You could be the real savior of mankind.* . . ."

Other books by Richard C. Meredith:

AT THE NARROW PASSAGE
THE SKY IS FILLED WITH SHIPS
WE ALL DIED AT BREAKAWAY STATION

Run,
Come See
Jerusalem!

Richard C. Meredith

BALLANTINE BOOKS • NEW YORK

Library of Congress Catalog Card Number: 75-45061

ISBN 0-345-25066-4-150

Manufactured in the United States of America

Cover art by The Brothers Hildebrandt

First Edition: May, 1976

This one's for Fred and Shirley Brown

Prologue

It's quiet here and I'm not often disturbed. I have much time to reflect, to remember, much time to rebuild the past in my mind. And I suppose that's why I'm relating this story, because of the time I seem to have. Not because I think the story is very important now, not to anyone but myself, that is.

They don't care, but the machines might. The machines will be here long after they are gone. They can store it away for their own electromagnetic purposes. Someday, perhaps . . .

1

Cold and quiet.

Those were my impressions, my sensations, my total perception of reality: cold and quiet.

The pain hadn't come yet. I was still too shocked for that, too numbed to perceive the pain, though dimly I must have been aware of it, aware that it would come, for there was blood on the seat, the belts, the canted deck, the control panel before me; and some portion of my mind registered that fact and the fact that the blood was mine. It could have been no one else's.

But at first it didn't seem important. Not much of anything seemed important. I was too numbed, too stunned to care.

After a while I moved, slowly and carefully, as if I were made of eggshells and china so thin you could see through it and poorly finished papier-mâché and would crack and shatter if I moved too quickly. Maybe I was.

Then I finally made a conscious effort to get my eyes to focus and see what there was about me. It was the first flickering of curiosity I'd had in a long, long time.

Far *longer,* in a sort of reverse way, than I knew at the time.

Slowly, as though my inner ears were as sluggish as the rest of me, I realized that I was sitting at an improbable angle, tilted forward. The belts that crisscrossed my chest and that went around my waist were holding me into the seat, and if they hadn't been I would have been pitched headlong across the panels in front of me and

1

have smashed against the cage's bars some meter or so beyond the panels. As it was my head, my face had battered against the controls, anyway. That's where the blood had come from: gashes on my forehead, cheeks, nose, chin. Nobody'd ever thought to pad a chronal-cage's control panel; but then maybe there had never been a reason before.

Through the cage's bars I couldn't see much besides a blank, almost smooth, flat whiteness, a blanket laid over the landscape that was broken here and there by clumps of gray-brown twigs, the tips of some tall grasses. Not far from the corner of the cage, as it appeared from my perspective, were tiny, three-toed indentations in the whiteness: paths, trails made by some small animal.

Small animal? I asked myself slowly, carefully shaking my head to clear it of cobwebs, but still fearing that it might break open like a rotten egg and spill what was left of my brains. And then told myself: yes, small animal. Foot-, pawprints. Cat? Dog? What?

I could see little else without raising my head, and because of heavy, dull aches I began to feel running from the base of my fragile skull down my back, knobby with the bones of my spine, I didn't want to raise my head. My curiosity wasn't that great, was it?

It was.

With an effort that I thought to be little short of superhuman, I lifted my head enough to find the horizon, which consisted of more whiteness, stretching some distance away, undulating slightly, then broken by rises of trees—a thin forest of conifers, I thought, pines, maybe, and firs, and some broadly branching, leafless-limbed hardwood trees. A north temperate zone forest, some more academic portion of my mind said, though I really didn't give a damn right at that moment.

If I turned my head slightly to the left, I could see that the forest was thicker and nearer in that direction, dark in shadow under a sunless, cloudy sky. It was too much effort to turn my head to the right.

I let my head slump forward again, my chin resting on my chest, a slow, viscous trickle of blood further staining my gray jacket and the white shirt under it where the jacket opened at my throat. I would have to account to Maughton for that jacket, that shirt, I thought, for I was reminded of him by the stylized sundial embroidered on the jacket above my heart. I'd have to tell him how they got ruined and he'd probably dock me for them. My clothing allowance didn't include ruining issue uniforms with blood, did it? I couldn't exactly recall, but it seemed unlikely.

Maughton. Dr. Jerald Maughton. My mind ruminated slowly over the name as further awareness came to me that I had been injured. My left wrist was beginning to feel as though some expert in Oriental combat had taken it carefully between his two hands and tried to wring it from my arm. Now, why should it feel that way?

Then I found myself almost making sense: why should any of this be so? what's happened to me?

I guess that's when I fully regained consciousness and all the pain came to me, all the pain and the anger and the fear; and I think I tried to curl into the fetal position despite the straps that held me in the seat; and I believe that I moaned aloud and tried to cry like a baby, though when the tears came they were terribly cold against my cheeks, scratched and cut as they were, and I quickly wiped them away with the back of my hand. That's how I discovered that I could still use my right hand.

When the wave of pain and fear left me, when I found that the pain wasn't so great that I couldn't live with it—no serious injuries, I thought, just lots of little cuts and bruises (and I found that the anger was rather pointless right then, and that the fear could be held in abeyance because I was in no *immediate* danger)—I also found that I could almost laugh at myself for wondering how I was going to account to Jerry Maughton for the soiled jacket and shirt. A few ruined garments were the very least of the things I had to account for.

I was an enemy of the Church and the State. I was a heretic already presumed guilty of crimes in thought and action. I could be shot on sight.

If anyone ever sighted me . . .

I held myself as still as I could, uncomfortable as I

was, pitched forward against the belts that were cutting into my chest and abdomen despite the clothing I wore, and made a very determined effort to get my head together.

They say that your mind works better in cold weather. If that were so, my mind ought to be functioning like a fifth-generation ASN-HB computer. *It was cold!* The air was hardly stirring then, yet the faintest breeze came cutting through my shirt and jacket, through my trousers like razor blades. My blood and tears ought to be freezing to my skin, not drying, I thought.

Yet, I told myself, I really should be giving myself some congratulations. I was alive, wasn't I? And considering the way things had been going not so very long ago—not long ago as I measured subjective time, though in calendar, in solar, in stellar terms . . .—I was rather damned lucky to be in even the sad condition I was. Better freezing my ass off *out here* than in a Min-Sec "Instruction Chapel." And my injuries—well, they were rather minor compared to what the blueshirts or the MinSec Proctors would have done to me if I hadn't gotten away when I did. It's said that the Lay Brothers of St. Wilson have some rather unpleasant ways of dealing with heretics—or whatever the hell they officially call people like me nowadays.

Nowadays . . .

The word triggered something in my mind, another train of thought that should have come to me sooner, would have come to me sooner if my mind had been as clear as I wanted to think it was. I began searching with my eyes across the controls before me, trying to get them to focus and read the dials and the meters in the panels and get some kind of intelligence out of them. But they didn't make any sense, those readings. The digital readings of one meter did not seem to register with those of another. While the BVP gave me a reading of .00009, which should have indicated fully operational status, the IRM said just the opposite and the Rydberg Monitor gave out something in between. From no two of them could I get any kind of agreement, but then I wasn't a chronal engineer. Maybe I didn't know how to interpret the readings as well as I thought I did. Some kind of dodo, me?

Apprehensively, as though I were afraid that someone might be sneaking up on me across the snow-covered landscape, I raised my head again and looked out through the bars that surrounded me on three sides; the rear bulkhead of the cage wasn't transparent, was solid, gray, unyielding metal. Outside: snow and trees and some underbrush. That was about all I could see. Cloudy, gray sky above, remotely illuminated by an invisible sun. Eyes back to earth: maybe there was some movement among the dark, distant trees, the thicker ones to my left, but I couldn't be sure of even that. I was alone. Of that I was rather certain.

I found my right hand could reach the computer keyboard that was, awkwardly, situated to my left—and, not for the first time, silently cursed the engineering genius who'd put it there—then with numb, clumsy fingers, I tapped out the code characters that should ask the computer to give me my chronal/geo position.

The computer, a dumb little thing that wasn't as bright as a superchimp, though it could add and subtract a lot faster, hummed and chattered stupidly. Its cathode ray tube, a long, narrow window marked with grids and numbers, lighted up in green phosphorescence and characters began to be displayed across it. (This computer couldn't even talk!)

INSUFFICIENT DATA AVAILABLE TO MAKE CHRONAL/ GEO DETERMINATION, it said without a sound.

The green-glowing letters faded away to be replaced by: CERTAIN SYSTEMS IN STATE OF SERIOUS MALFUNCTION.

Dammit, I know that!

Then: CHRONALCAGE IS IN NEED OF REPAIRS. SUGGEST IMMEDIATE RETURN TO . . .

With that the CRT display faded and all my punching of keys could get no further response from it, though the computer continued to chatter away for a while as if it were making some kind of sense.

Silently, to myself, I cursed the universe for allowing this to happen and the chronal engineers for not having made the cage more durable. Then I cursed myself, for I was the one to blame, and wondered just how much damage I'd caused to the chronalcage. Too much, I figured. But then, had I had any choice? Back then? I'd escaped with my life. Hadn't I?

But what about Melanie?

Better not to think of that. Not now. Not yet.

Maybe never.

My right fingers were still as numb as ever as they began to key other controls. The delivery systems of the chronalcage were obviously badly damaged, but they consisted of the circuitry in the left-rear console, and they would have probably received the most shock in the kind of "landing" I'd apparently made. But maybe the backups in the return systems weren't as badly off. A new set of lights began to come on in another portion of the control panel, those that should indicate the status of the return systems, but some of these lights didn't come on at all, and when some of the others did, they were red, not green. There weren't enough green lights coming on to do me a damned bit of good either. The chronalcage delivery and return systems both were damaged, far too damaged to ever get me into chronal "motion" again.

I slammed my right fist against the panel and got only the satisfaction of adding to myself another bruise and an additional degree of pain.

Dammit! Dammit! Dammit!

Then I didn't know where I was, when I was; and that damned, stupid computer didn't know either, and maybe couldn't have told me if it had known. I could be anywhere, anywhen—but, at least, I tried to tell myself, I wasn't in the hands of the Lay Brothers of St. Wilson or the MinSec Proctors.

And, well, maybe things were not really as bad as they seemed.

Maybe I wasn't as far from *home* as I feared I might be.

It was with mixed feelings that I realized that I probably wasn't totally lost in time/space. Despite what had been going on at the Project when I'd made my rather

sudden departure—under circumstances I hadn't fore-
seen(though maybe I should have foreseen them)—they
would have all the readings there. They'd know exactly
how much energy had been consumed when I'd timed-
out, and from that they could pretty well compute just
how far I'd been displaced downtime. They would know
where I was, even if I didn't, and they'd be sending
somebody down after me—probably somebody in a blue
shirt and blue trousers with a white cross embroidered
above his heart where I wore a sundial, and with a needle pistol tucked inside his waistband. Deacon Carl Fulford or one of his ilk would be coming after me, fully
warranted by the MinSec and the Rector-for-Life, I had
no doubt of that, and I didn't figure that it would exactly
be a mission of mercy.

" 'Mercy is mine to extend,' says the Lord," the Book
tells us. " 'Men are to exact only justice.' "

I remembered my catechism.

And I'd be pretty stupid to be sitting here waiting for
them, belted into the cage's bucket seat, trussed up like
an asylum inmate waiting for them. I'd better get my ass
out. Soonest!

As I began fumbling with the straps, finding that my
left hand, despite the aching of my wrist, would work almost as well as my right—which wasn't worth a damn
because of the cold—I began wondering just how close
they would be able to pinpoint me. To the year, certainly. To the month, maybe. To the day, never.

They'd have to do some searching.

And since they hadn't been waiting there for me when
I woke up, I was certain that they weren't downtime
from me. They would be coming in uptime, in the future, but how far in the future I didn't really want to
guess.

Not likely within hours, though it was possible.

But certainly within days.

Getting out of the belts that held me in the seat was
not quite as difficult as I'd expected, though when I finally released the last catch with my left hand, it was all I
could do with my right hand to keep myself, head and
shoulders, from smashing headlong into the control pan-

el. As it was, I held myself away from the panel just enough to cushion my fall against it. I did bump my forehead again, bringing a fresh flow of blood from a set of lacerations already there, but the blood soon clotted in the cold breeze that had now begun to blow from the direction I had tentatively identified as north, without really knowing why.

Out of the seat and on unsteady legs, I turned to look back toward the rear of the cage and then saw what had caused all the damage.

My guess was that the cage's delivery systems had somehow failed to make full geo compensation—which wasn't too surprising, circumstances considered—and that the cage had probably "materialized" at some meter or two above the surface, maybe farther, and had fallen under normal gravity the rest of the way, some three-tons-plus of metal and ceramics, silicon and glass. It had never been meant to timein like that. It—the chronalcage—was never meant to move in "space," at least not relative to any firmly existing, time-encapsulated world. Geo referencing of a chronalcage is not done with any conventional form of locomotion, but through another aspect of the Inatusta Effect, the phenomenon that makes "time travel" itself possible. But I won't go into all that now.

However, a drop of a meter or two to a fairly level surface probably wouldn't have done all that damage. What had done it, or completed the work begun by the fall, was the tip of a buried granite boulder that protruded above the earth and snow by some half a meter or better, rounded by wind and weather, though now cracked and fragmented to sharp edges of stone. The left-rear corner of the cage, the section that houses some of the most critical circuits and systems, had struck that boulder. Metal had bent and torn; delicate circuits had ruptured; crystals and wafers and glass had shattered. And then, probably perched at an even more precarious angle than it was now, the chronalcage had slid off the boulder, some three or four meters down a slope, and the right-front corner of the cage had smashed into another protruding boulder, which had brought it to a stop.

I didn't remember any of this. I had probably already been unconscious upon arrival—sudden and particularly long-range timingout can sometimes do that, put you out for minutes or even hours. But the gouges in the snow and frozen earth, and the shattered stone, were evidence of what had happened. And that's how I'd gotten all my cuts and bruises. I didn't doubt that the cage, delivery and return systems both, were damaged beyond my meager ability to repair. As I told you before, I'm no chronal engineer.

Though my intellect told me that Carl Fulford and his blueshirts weren't likely to come for days yet, maybe longer, underneath I wasn't convinced. I expected to see another boxy chronalcage come shimmering, screaming out of time at any moment, its occupants armed and ready to needle me out—if not kill me outright—and take me back to stand trial before a MinSec judge and jury for a list of crimes I could not even begin to enumerate. I was close to panic, but I held it in an unsteady check and told myself I'd better begin doing what I had to do to stay alive until . . .

As I rose from my kneeling position on the front "porch" of the cage, I happened to glance to my right, the direction my instincts told me was south or southwest, and saw marks in the snow that I hadn't noticed before, hidden from me earlier by a slight rise in the ground. I still didn't have a clear view of the marks, but what I could see told me that something had been there, recently; something big and heavy had, for a time at least, occupied a spot in the snow no great distance from where my ruined cage now sat—something big and heavy and artificial.

Moments before, I had told myself that I wasn't even going to think of stepping off the cage until I was armed and dressed in something more suitable for arctic conditions than my uniform jacket and slacks, but the sight of those marks in the snow forced such reasonable considerations from my mind.

Without thinking about it, I was leaping from the cage's "porch" and my feet were crunching on the hard white surface. I didn't have far to walk, though before I got back to the cage I learned to appreciate that even its meager shelter had been some protection from a breeze that seemed to grow brisker and colder with each passing minute.

A chronalcage, at least the Mark III unit I was using, is shaped something like an open box, about four meters on a side, with no top, but with a rear bulkhead about two and a half meters high; two consoles set into the rear extend forward to form sides running about halfway toward the front, both right and left. The remainder of the sides and the entire front of the cage is enclosed only with vertical bars, from which it gets its name "cage." Between the rear consoles, against the bulkhead, sit the lockers. Across the front is the control console, behind which sits the cage's single seat, a not uncomfortable bucket-like affair. Protruding from the front and rear are the "porches," actually more instrument housings than the steps for which they are often used.

All this is a preface to this: the base of a chronalcage is a square, four meters on a side, supported by four parallel "skids" and four "parking jacks," one on each of the four corners.

If a chronalcage had set down here in the snow and then departed, without having moved in this geo framework, it would have left marks exactly like those I found in the snow less than a dozen meters from my own cage!

I stood in frozen amazement for a moment, looking about myself in every direction. Then I looked back at the marks in the snow: four grooves for four skids; four craters for four parking jacks.

A chronalcage had been here, and recently.

How long it had been since the last snowfall I couldn't guess. Hours or days, even longer. But since the last snow, *someone* had been here and left. Someone looking for me? Someone who'd come, downtime of my arrival, found I wasn't here, and then had gone on, uptime, searching for me? How far uptime? Hours? Days?

I could visualize Carl Fulford's sullen face gazing out

across this snowscape, searching for signs of my presence, then ordering his chronalnaut pilot to move uptime a bit and look for me again.

They could be timingin just about anytime.

I was suddenly more scared than I'd been before. I had no time to lose, no time . . .

But I wasn't so scared that I failed to notice something else that had not caught my eye at first—spots not far from where the cage had been, spots frozen into the crust that were bright in contrast, a redness that pocked the snow with tiny craters, as if some warm liquid had fallen onto the snow, melted it, and then frozen back into the crusty surface.

A warm liquid with the redness of blood.

Had it been 98.6° F. when it hit the snow?

Was it blood? I asked myself.

And if so, why? Why blood? Whose blood?

I gave myself no more time for pondering. If they came now I'd be caught flatfooted and defenseless.

To hell with it, I told myself, and hurried back to the cage, shivering in the rising wind.

To the rear of the cage's single bucket seat, as I said, were the supply and equipment lockers, nestled between the two major consoles that had given life to the "time machine" not so long before. As I reached those lockers I found myself very grateful that Jerry Maughton and Welles Kennedy had been able to ram home their contention that chronalnauts should be provided with facilities for every eventuality. The MinSciStu Proctors hadn't wanted to go to the added expense, but the Chronal Project's secular head and his chief assistant, backed by the chief of BuChronRe, had threatened to resign unless *full* safety precautions were taken, as full as the state of the art would allow. The MinSciStu Proctors had finally, grudgingly, agreed. And the lockers that I began to open held not only clothing of the late Elizabethan period, which had been my destination not so very long ago as my internal clocks measured such things, but a wide range of other garments, including a heavy parka of chronal gray, thermal boots, snow goggles, snowshoes, and just about everything else I needed to stay alive in this environment until I found out where I was—and how the hell to get to someplace else, warmer and more nearly civilized.

Another locker, marked SURVIVAL GEAR in yellow stenciled letters, disgorged a long, ugly, ornately decorated 8.5mm Weatherby Magnum semiautomatic rifle (2010 model), a good supply of ammunition, and a snub-nosed 4mm Colt Special needler.

Within a half-hour of opening the first locker, I'd bandaged the worst of my injuries, taken pills that seemed to clear my fuzzy brain and dull the pain of the cuts and bruises, and was clothed in garments that kept out the cold wind that now came whistling out of the trees north of me, sighing in their branches, giving some sound, if an alien one, to the terribly quiet, cold, white world around me. Then I stacked emergency rations, along with the first-aid kit, on the canted deck, placing them against the back of the seat to that they wouldn't slide too far.

When I had gotten everything out of the lockers that I thought I would need in the immediate future, I began to wonder just what I was going to do with the stuff. I couldn't just leave it sitting there on the deck of the open cage. *I didn't plan on staying there.* Exactly what my plans were, I didn't know yet, but I figured that I'd better start preparing some kind of reception for the committee of blueshirts when they came after me. They weren't going to take me easily, I vowed to myself.

I tried not to think of Melanie and how they'd taken her . . .

After giving my situation a little thought, and finding that thinking didn't come to me as easily as I thought it should. I decided that I'd better do a little scouting of the territory and see if I could find myself a place of shelter, someplace out of the wind where I could build a fire and wait until someone came. I didn't intend to do much exploring at any great distance. I had the feeling that there really wasn't much in this "world" that I would find too interesting from another, other than from an academic standpoint—historian though I may be by

profession, other things were of greater consideration at
the moment. Furthermore, a check of the various bands
of a miniaturized transceiver which had been in the
locker, nestled between boxes of 8.5mm Magnum shells,
seemed to reinforce the idea of limiting my exploration:
if there was anyone in this when-and-where using radio,
they weren't doing it on any of the wavelengths that this
set could receive, and that was most of them below
microwave.

(I mentally noted that this put me in time somewhere
before the twentieth century, not that this was any great
deduction. I was certain that I was even prior to the ear-
ly-seventeenth-century target date I'd originally had,
before . . .)

With the parka's many capacious pockets stuffed full
of items I thought I might need, including a few candy
bars, a flask of water, a compass, the Colt needle pistol,
a box of 8.5s, and with the Weatherby hung across my
shoulder by its decorated sling—an American eagle with
a fistful of arrows was embossed on the buckle—I awkwardly clambered down the deck of the cage. Placing
my feet on the "porch," I jumped down to the snow-
covered earth, feeling a twinge of pain shoot up from my
right ankle, which must have been twisted and bruised during the course of the cage's coming to rest. It wasn't so bad
that I couldn't walk on it, though I certainly wasn't up to a
cross-country hike with full field pack.

The cage sat so that its front faced roughly southwest,
and behind it, where I hadn't been able to see from inside the cage, were more trees, conifers and hardwoods.
These gave way to ragged outcrops of stone that must
have been the beginnings of foothills of mountains
I couldn't see because of the distance and the cloudy
haze that had come with the rising wind. And although
the boulders on which the cage had come to rest seemed
to be of granitic, igneous rock, what I could see of the
stone tiers rising to the northwest appeared to be composed of sedimentary rock: shales, sandstones, perhaps
limestone. If that were so, it seemed that I might stand a
good chance of finding shelter among them, niches, even

caves weathered out. I set out northwest, fixing my position as well as I could, locating landmarks so that I could hopefully find my way back to the cage without too much difficulty.

Wherever I was in geo terms—I told myself, my feet crunching loudly in the frozen snow, listening to the silence of the world—it was certainly not Chicago. Nor was it anywhere near London, which had been my original geo destination, as 1602 had been my original chronal destination. At least it wasn't Chicago or London during any recent geological period. But I hadn't come back *that far,* had I? The conifers and the hardwoods told me that I hadn't, not past the beginnings of the Paleocene. There *was* some comfort in that.

During the next couple of hours I covered far less distance then I'd hoped to, but to my pleasant surprise I found exactly the sorts of things I'd hoped to find: tumbled stones, niches, cavities, shallow caves among the rock and wind-gnarled trees, and began to realize that the cage had come to rest in a broad, though shallow valley surrounded by low, stony hills.

There were birds in the air and among the trees of kinds I didn't recognize, though my knowledge of birds of any time or place is very limited. On the ground, amid the snow, were multitudes of animal tracks, from small ones like those I'd seen near the cage to some much larger ones. The largest ones, fortunately rare, were bigger than my own booted feet, pressed deeper into the snow than did mine, and showed the imprint of pads and clawed feet. Bears? I wondered. That seemed to be about the only animal that could have made tracks like these, unless I were a lot further from my hometime than I thought I was.

After seeing the first of those large tracks I kept the rifle in my hands, my gloved thumb on the safety. I had the cityman's traditional fear of large animals. I had seen a bear once, I recalled, when there still were a few of them alive in the old Lincoln Park Zoo, big and ugly to my child's eyes; and I'd been fearful of it despite the distance and the bars that separated it from me, as I clutched my mother's hand and insisted we go on to see the funnier monkeys. I must have been five or six then; my mother died when I was seven.

Close to three hours after leaving the ruined chronalcage, weary and aching in every muscle, and having made an exhaustive search of every cave and cavity I'd seen, I found exactly what I was looking for: a cave with an opening almost high enough for me to enter without stooping, which flared out into a larger room a few meters back and which was lighted, if dimly, by sunlight spilling in from outside. The cave's opening faced southeast, and if it had not been for outcroppings of rock and a rise of land I could probably have seen the chronalcage in its shallow valley from there. I thought I might be able to see it by climbing only a short distance above, on ledges of limestone that climbed toward a wooded crest some meters away.

I dug a flashlight out of one of the parka's pockets and held it in my left hand—the rifle was in my right— and slowly entered the cave. Even inexperienced as I was at such things, I rather suspected that I might not be the first to find this cave a desirable place to use as living quarters, and I remembered the footprints, big, clawed, and hairy, though I told myself that bears hibernate in the winter and if I did find one he was likely to be in the midst of his "long winter's nap."

"But those footprints are fresh, buddy," a part of my mind said, and I went into the cave very cautiously.

In the front part of the cave, where it widened out, was ample evidence that someone, something, had been there before me: broken bits of bone, fragments of furry skin, piles of dung, a heavy animal odor. I stopped, listened, waited, then proceeded toward the rear of the cave, found more bone and more stink, and discovered that the room narrowed again, becoming hardly more than a small tunnel that pushed further back into the earth and stone, too small for me to enter and too small for anything the size of the animal that had made the footprints which worried me.

The cave wasn't currently occupied. There wasn't even a bat in it, and for that I was thankful as well.

The cave's main room was roughly egg-shaped, ceiling curving upward and floor curving downward, concavely, to where stood a bowl-shaped depression filled with ice. The walls of the cave were of light-colored limestone, fragments of other stone, and shells here and there, all of which was covered with thin flowstone, which in warmer times had formed tiny projections above me that had never become real stalactites. It wasn't much of a place to call home, but it would keep the wind out.

I cleared a spot on the rough floor near the entrance, some meter or so in front of the bowl of ice, sat down, ate a candy bar, drank from the canteen I carried, felt weak and tired and had the very unpleasant sensation that I had the beginnings of a fever.

I hoped to God that I wasn't coming down with something. Shit! But half the Project's staff had been out the past few days with one sort of ailment or another—"flu," they said, whatever the hell that's supposed to mean these days. Dammit, that'd be just my luck. That was all I needed now.

Finally, after resting as long as I thought it safe, I decided that I had better get back to the cage, get my supplies and try to get them stowed. Time was of the essence, in more ways than one.

Since the day was overcast, a mother-of-pearl sky that gave no hint of the sun's position, there were still no real shadows to indicate what time of day it might be. I had the feeling that it was afternoon, but I didn't know exactly why I thought so, and how late in the afternoon it might be I couldn't guess. The way things were going, I felt I was certain to be caught by darkness before I got finished with everything I wanted to do—and without landmarks and in this cold, I didn't want to consider the possibility of dark coming on me while I was somewhere between the cage and the cave.

I got back to my ruined chronalcage, alone in the shallow valley, just before the sky faded out and left me in total darkness.

I spent the night huddled in the corner between lockers and consoles, wrapped in every garment I could find, and promised myself that before the next night came I would have a roaring fire in the entrance of that cave.

The cold and the distant, lonely, unreal cries of nocturnal animals I never saw kept me awake. I'd never really expected to get any sleep, and didn't.

2

My name is Eugene David Stillman, in case you're interested. I was born in Chicago, Illinois, U.S.A., in 1995 and, measuring the way I do, I'm thirty-seven years old. Other measurements might put me at vastly different ages, even negative ages. On the other hand, maybe I was never born at all.

I hold a doctorate in history. My thesis was on the effects of the plagues of the late sixteenth and early seventeenth centuries on Elizabethan arts; Shakespeare, Ben Jonson, and their contemporaries, to be more specific. That's not much of a background for being a "time-traveling adventurer," is it?

But my credentials aren't wholly limited to the academic world, or I would never have been inducted into the Chronal Corps. I'd served in the Infantry during the Sino-Indian War (2008–2015), had been a Ranger (I had delusions of heroics when I was younger), had received a battlefield commission (which I lost as quickly as I gained) when our company ran out of officers, and I'd gotten a Bronze Star during the assault on Nagpur after the Chinese retook it. I also got a Purple Heart out of it and an ugly scar on my right thigh that I once used to impress the girls. (How quickly a culture can return to an adoration of uniforms and war heros if it's fed the right propaganda!)

And it wasn't as if this were my first chronal displacement. It was just the first during which I'd displaced so quickly, with an unknown destination hastily keyed into the controls—and as a fugitive from the Church/State.

18

During the cold night, listening to the wind moaning in the limbs of trees and a nocturnal predator screaming over the body of its prey, the memory of that most recent displacement came back to me more fully than I might have wished.

The countdown was going quite smoothly. During the past few months, most of the bugs had been worked out of the chronal-displacement equipment and we were seldom plagued with the problems we'd had so frequently during the two years before, when displacement—timingout and timingin—was still in its infancy. I remember one situation where we'd had to hold for over twelve hours while I sat in the chair, strapped in with belts crisscrossing my body, unable even to go to the bathroom, figuring we would pick up the last few seconds of the countdown at any moment. The damned thing was finally scrubbed when we discovered a malfunction in the left propeller accelerator-calibration systems and I finally pissed in my pants. Things like that didn't happen often anymore.

Jerry Maughton, Ph.D., F.S.S., D.S.T., Director of the Bureau of Chronal Research's Project Chronos, dressed in a white smock and thick glasses, an empty, proscribed pipe clenched between his teeth, was flitting around from one console to another, checking each phase of the total activating procedure, constantly asking me through my headphone whether this or that dial or meter on my control panel agreed with his readings. They always did agree, which was good all the way around. Even though I, as mission chronalnaut, had the final control over all displacement systems, it was good that the systems—and the systems of the all-important propeller unit—were in exact harmony with mine. If they weren't—well, I might not be exactly certain *when* I'd come out, downtime.

Welles Kennedy, Maughton's chief assistant, had been the very first of the chronalnauts, the first man who had ever traveled backward in time, even if during his first trip he had only been displaced some thirty-seven seconds downtime and some nine meters in space and had been the first man ever to see a previous-self and had proved that paradoxes do exist in Time. He was now acting as power-consumption monitor, along with a dark-vestmented Proctor from the Ministry of Scientific Studies who peered over his shoulder distrustfully. I didn't know the Proctor's name. I'd made it a point not to learn it. I didn't—don't—like Proctors.

But then who does?

Other Proctors?

I doubt it.

Deacon Carl Fulford stood quietly in the rear of the displacement chamber, his arms folded across his chest, dressed in the blue uniform of the Lay Brothers of St. Wilson, white cross over his heart, black needle pistol tucked into his waistband, neuron staff dangling from its cord on his left hip. Even though his eyes appeared to be closed—as well as I could tell from the distance—I had the feeling that Fulford was seeing everything that took place in that large room, and maybe even hearing the heretical thoughts that were right then passing through my mind, thoughts of heresy and treason and assassination, fire and blood and the murder of an unborn child, a tiny fetus not yet human in its mother's womb.

I was sitting in the chronalcage's single bucket seat, strapped in securely, watching all the meters and dials and gauges, watching the digital chronometer on the far wall, matched by its miniature on my panel, counting down the last hundred seconds to displacement. I was dressed in the white shirt, gray slacks, gray jacket, black boots of the Chronal Corps; on my chest, above my heart, was the stylized sundial of the corps.

The so-called destination dials of my panel were set for an August evening in 1602, spatial location (geo reference) in three sets of digits, each ten characters long, that would read on one of our maps as an abandoned cemetery on the outskirts of London, England. William Shakespeare would be alive then, thirty-eight years old, already having written some of his important works such as "Venus and Adonis," *Romeo and Juliet,* and *A Midsummer Night's Dream*; most of his historial dramas dealing with the kings of England, and *Hamlet*; and with works such as *Othello, Macbeth, Antony and Cleopatra.*

King Lear, and the more serious comedies still before him.
Ben Jonson would be twenty-nine. And the famous Globe
Theatre, built in 1599, would have its patent granted to
Shakespeare a year later by King James I. It would burn
in 1613, eleven years away.

At last I was going back to Shakespeare's world.

As long as I'd been in the corps I had been pushing
for this assignment. This was really why I'd let Jerry
Maughton talk me into joining the corps in the first
place—though if I hadn't joined willingly, the MinSciStu
Proctors probably would have drafted me, Jerry had
said, despite my rather dubious record regarding politi-
co-spiritual matters. But I'd let Jerry talk me into it and
had joined willingly and then I'd badgered Jerry and
he'd badgered the Ministry of Scientific Studies, Bureau
of Chronal Research, until we had been permitted to
jump downtime into Elizabethan England. This one was
a purely secular trip, one of the few ever allowed. And
there wasn't one spiritual matter I was assigned to
prove, for which I was thankful. I wasn't being sent
back to holograph the Crucifixion (we'd already done
that and had been able to show it to the world with only
a minimum of editing; the gaps hadn't shown too badly,
though the sound track that went with it was wholly a
modern fabrication, which was caught by the Europeans
but roundly denied by the Rector-for-Life) or St. Peter's
martyrdom (which we never released for reasons of
"state security") or Martin Luther posting his 95 propo-
sitions on the Wittenberg church door (that one we
could use in toto) or even the christening of the Appointed One (which was always popular and was broad-
cast to the world yearly on the day we celebrated as the
birthday of God's Last Messenger to Man). No, I was
just going back to do a little research into the plagues of
Shakespeare's England—and maybe to prove or dis-
prove a few of my own private theories about the Bard's
life and times.

I'd promised the Bureau of Historical Subjects that I
would submit a revised draft of my thesis once I'd been
there firsthand. In fact, I was certain, Martin Engel of

BuHistSub had been instrumental in persuading Bu-ChronRe to allow me to make this trip.

I might have been silently thanking Marty and his staff right then, when the digital chronometers began clicking down from three figures to two, if there hadn't been so damned much else on my mind.

Things like the promise I'd made to Melanie Proctor . . .

I wasn't a member of "the Cell," as they called it. I never had been and I'd had no intention of ever being a member, but . . . Well, maybe that's one of my problems; I mean, I would seem to be unable to fully commit myself to things—to ideas, hopes, dreams, plans, even to people. Even Johanna had always said that about me. But still I agreed with them, those people in "the Cell." I thought they were right. Oh, maybe not in every respect, and I certainly didn't feel as strongly about a lot of things as they did. I had always considered myself an apolitical person—which in the world of the U.S.A., 2032 A.D., means *a*religious as well, and vice versa. And I'd never planned on getting mixed up with any of the kinds of things "the Cell" and people like that were involved in. But then I'd never planned on falling in love with a girl named Melanie Proctor either. Nor had I ever planned on anyone convincing me that I could save the world . . .

The chronometer was reading minus 90 seconds when I looked up again, out through the cage's bars, past the scattered elements of the propeller units, past the bulking consoles and the snaking cables, past the smocked and bustling figures in the displacement chamber to the small console at which Melanie sat, the console that monitored electrical-power generation from the Tokomar fusion reactor, which powered the Project from seventy-five meters below the displacement chamber. She wasn't watching her board.

She was watching me.

I knew why.

Melanie Proctor. I hadn't liked her at first, when I'd first met her at the time she joined the Project's staff some year and a half ago. Not that she wasn't young and attractive, something to look at—twenty-five years old, 170 cm, 49 or 50 kilograms, dark hair, dark eyes, a full feminine figure under the shapeless lab smock—*and* a highly qualified electrofusion technician. But maybe it was her name that turned me off: Proctor. I didn't like Proctors, not the arrogant, suspicious, holier-than-thou kind that wore the dark vestments and stood outside the laws that governed merely mortal men. And that was her name, even though she wasn't a "Proctor" of the Church/State.

And maybe I was turned off by the silvery little "VV" pin she wore, bright and arrogant and ignorant and antisex.

But later I learned a lot different.

She wasn't anything like the men and women who wore the title "Proctor" like a crown from God Himself. Maybe that was one of the reasons she hated them so much; maybe she felt they had sullied the good family name of Proctor, whose line she could proudly trace back some three hundred years. And she wasn't exactly a "Victorious Virgin," as the pin said she was. I learned that later, too.

But now—the chronometer said minus 80 and was still counting down—she was looking straight into my eyes, not begging nor pleading, nor even asking if I were going to do what I'd promised I would do, but sort of telling me with her dark eyes that she had confidence in me, that she knew I could do it, would do it.

I had decided by then that I would.

I had listened to all her arguments, all her claims, during those long evenings together, and I'd often wondered how much of her feeling toward me was genuine and how much of it faked. Had she seduced me in the first place with the aim of recruiting me into "the Cell," making me—the only chronalnaut they could get to— into their agent to carry out their plans downtime?

I didn't like to think of *that,* but . . .

The chronometer said minus 70 and Jerry Maughton's voice was speaking into my ear, "Decimal three-five-three-nine on right projection accelerator. Does that still agree, Gene?" when the doors beside which blue-clad Carl Fulford stood burst open and a Proctor bearing the brassard of the Ministry of Church/State Security came into the room like an avenging angel sent down by the Lord God of Hosts, followed by half a dozen or so blueshirts carrying 4mm carbines.

A sudden, fierce chill went through me, a spasm of stark and total fear. MinSec! What in the name of the Appointed One are they doing here?

But I knew why they were here.

I knew exactly why.

The MinSec Proctor paused as he entered the room, dark eyes scanning the displacement chamber, sweeping across the wide room, pausing for a moment when they reached Melanie's position, then coming on to reach my own eyes, stopping, fixing, staring into mine like the eyes of a hypnotic snake into those of a paralyzed bird.

I wanted to vomit.

The Proctor handed a piece of paper, stiff and crisp and official, to Deacon Carl Fulford.

Fulford glanced at it, his eyes widening as he glanced up at me and then at Melanie. Then, he nodded as if he'd been expecting exactly this, muttered something to the Proctor. The Proctor replied in low tones. Fulford's eyes went back to the sheet of paper, reading it slowly, and while he did, his hand went to the needler stuck in his waistband; an old custom, going back to the days before the Lay Brothers of St. Wilson could afford holsters for their stolen weapons, was this habit of carrying a pistol in the waistband of his trousers. Finally Fulford handed the paper back to the Proctor and yelled a command to Jerry Maughton, who wasn't yet aware of the intrusion: "Dr. Maughton, this displacement is to be canceled!"

Jerry froze in his tracks, his complexion growing even more florid with anger as he turned to face Fulford, then paling as he saw the MinSec Proctor.

"What's the meaning of this?" he demanded, speaking around the cold stem of the outlawed pipe in his teeth.

My chronometer said minus 60 and counting.

"Slap a hold on this displacement, Dr. Maughton," Fulford said, his hand still resting on his needler, taking one step forward down the low stairs toward the chamber proper.

The Proctor and his blueshirts stood where they were, just inside the doors.

"Not until you tell me what the hell's going on here," Jerry said, his anger returning even in the face of the dreaded Proctor.

"Dr. Maughton," the MinSec Proctor said in a sepulchral voice, one gained in elocution lessons from the dead, I gathered, "this is a SECURITY matter." The way he said it the word was in all caps.

"This is not a province of the Ministry of Security," Jerry Maughton said bravely, foolishly.

By now everyone in the chamber was aware of the entry of the Proctor and his blueshirts; every face was turned their way, including that of Melanie—and her face was pale now, white, bloodless with the fear of discovery, torture, and a long, lingering death. Mercy was not a grace extended by MinSec to members of heretic, treasonous groups. We all knew that.

"This is a matter of Church/State security, Dr. Maughton," the Proctor said with his dead man's voice, "and thus places even *your* project under the Ministry of Security. I must demand, in the name of the Rector himself, that a hold be placed on this displacement *now!*"

"Well . . ." Jerry stammered.

"I have warrants for the arrest of two of your personnel," the Proctor continued. "One ElecTech Melanie Proctor and one Chronalnaut Dr. Eugene . . ."

I didn't hear him say the rest of my name. I was too damned busy to listen.

Most people don't seem to realize it, but there's a world of difference between the countdown of a spacecraft and the countdown of a chronal displacement, though they both have the same basic purpose, I suppose. What I'm getting at is this: as complex as chronal displacement equipment is, it's a hell of a lot simpler than a St. James booster assembly, for example, and it's got no moving parts. Actually, a chronal countdown is mostly a matter of checking circuitry and making certain that everything's working exactly like it's supposed to work—which is why there's a spacecraft countdown, too, I suppose. But there is a big, fundamental difference. You *can't* launch a spacecraft until the countdown is completed. You *can* displace a chronalcage before the countdown is completed.

So I displaced.

The MinSec Proctor must have realized what I was going to do, for he broke into a savage scream, like one of the living dead coming out of his coffin at the fall of darkness. He brushed Carl Fulford aside and leaped down the stairs, his blueshirts behind him, startled, and maybe angry, too. He was pointing toward Melanie, who had risen from her seat and was backing toward the wall, her face stark with a fear she'd hoped would never come to her, but he was looking at me. Two of his blueshirts, following his unspoken command, dashed after Melanie, while the rest of them followed the Proctor in his leaping run across the chamber, yelling at the top of his lungs now: "Stop the displacement!"

Melanie had begun to yell, too. "Gene, do it! For heaven's sake, go back and kill Dover!"

And I was throwing this switch and pushing that lever and seeing a bank of lights come to green life, and then I was throwing one after another in a long row of toggle switches.

Jerry Maughton, knocked aside by the blueshirts, his battered old pipe lost in the scuffle, was yelling too. "Don't do it, Gene. Displacement's too dangerous now."

But I was coming to the end of the row of toggle switches . . . and Melanie had apparently opened her board up all the way before she'd backed away from it . . . and Welles Kennedy and the Proctor who supervised him apparently hadn't thought to cut power through his board and . . .

There was a great screaming whine as the generators in the propeller units came to life—not mechanical life but electrical, and something more—twisting into the very fabric of time/space, bringing into action the Inatusta Effect that opened up the substance of Continua. Why they screamed like that nobody's ever quite figured out, but when they reach chronal potential they always do.

"Stop him! Stop!" the MinSec Proctor yelled, his voice even louder than the screaming of the generators, now almost near enough to the cage for him to grab its bars with his outstretched hands . . .

"Gene!" Melanie was screaming as the two blueshirts reached her, grabbed her arms, twisted them behind her back.

God! Am I that big a coward! I'd said I loved her, but I was going to go off and leave her in *their* hands. I . . .

Then the earth fell out from under me, away from me and from the chronalcage, and I and it were falling downtime through the blackness, the absence of *anything* that's always there, and into another sort of blackness that is unconsciousness.

3

With the first signs of dawn in the sky, my stomach hot and lumpy inside me, sweat on my forehead that I couldn't account for, I shivered my way out of the bits and pieces of clothing I'd used to blanket myself against the cold during the long night and began wondering just how I was going to manage to take all the supplies I'd gotten from the lockers with me to the cave. I probably had a lot of stuff I would never need, not if my stay there was as short as I thought it was likely to be, but on the other hand the future was a very uncertain thing.

The thought had crossed my mind more than once during the night that I might be a good deal further into the past than I'd wanted to think at first. I *might* be somewhere in North America in the eighteenth or nineteenth century, or maybe even in the early twentieth— but I could just as well be in, say, middle Europe in the Paleolithic or even prehuman times. There were *lots* of cold spells during the Pleistocene . . .

A funny thing about time travel—chronal displacement, to use the more proper term—is that the greatest difficulty is in getting out of the present, the Now. That takes one hell of a lot of energy, and it was years after the discovery of the Inatusta Effect and the development of all the chronal-displacement theories before anyone found out just how much energy it did take. But— and this is the important point—once displacement has taken place, very little more energy is required to extend the length of one's trip downtime. There's a sort of inverse-cube-of-the-chronal-distance law that governs time travel, one that allows travel for great time distances. Once you've made that important leap out of Now, you can travel into the past a year for only a fraction more energy than it takes to travel downtime an hour, and the further you go into the past the cheaper in energy it is to go per year. Like sliding downhill, so to speak, gaining chronal inertia as you go. Follow me?

What I'm trying to say is that it wouldn't have been very much harder for me to have gone back to the Pleistocene than it would have been for me to have gotten back to the early seventeenth century. I don't know exactly how you would express it in terms of ergs or something, but the power had been available—if I'd wanted to and had had the opportunity to—to send me all the way back to the Jurassic period. I was glad I hadn't gone back that far: dinosaurs would probably frighten me even worse than bears.

(Let me throw in another point or two here, since it seems appropriate: the Now that it's so hard to bust out of is only the Now of the beginning of the journey; in this case, 4 March 2032. Once downtime, out of that Now, I would have had more than ample energy available in the cage's power cells to go hopping some distance up and down time, if the cage hadn't been damaged. Only by going back to the Now of departure, 4 March 2032, would I have been putting myself into the Now that requires vast, and I mean really vast, sources of power to achieve displacement.

(*And* that Now—the now-future Now of the journey's beginning—has another significance: that's as far as I could have gone into the future—right back to the moment from which I left. I couldn't go past it. I couldn't have gone to 5 March 2032, or beyond. The theories that explain the Inatusta Effect say that travel into the future, beyond that Now, ought to be possible, but so far, as of 4 March 2032, no one has ever achieved it. Maybe it's just a matter of having sufficient chronal power, or of applying it in some different way, that would let us go uptime from the Now. But if that's the case, the mechanics of it haven't—hadn't—quite been worked out. Okay?)

But—to get back to where I was—*if* I were some-where back in the Pleistocene, back in the time of the Neanderthalers or before, the MinSec Proctors might just figure that I'd gotten what was coming to me and leave me here to find whatever fate was in store for me. They certainly would if they knew the condition of my cage now. And maybe they would shortly.

But I liked that idea even less than I liked the idea of Carl Fulford or a MinSec Proctor coming downtime for me. With them, well, I just might have the chance to get my hands on another cage, if I were smart enough and quick enough and—well, ruthless enough.

Finally, when the sky had turned again to a mother-of-pearl grayness that spilled enough light to get around by, I decided that I'd better take everything I could with me to the cave. To do that I was going to need some kind of transportation.

Since I had no wheels—I *was* that far back in time, I thought then—what I ended up with was something like what the Plains Indians of North America used to use, a travois, or dragging litter, so to speak: two long poles I'd cut from hardwood saplings not far from where the cage sat, crossed by shorter ones made from limbs. I then stacked my supplies and equipment on the platform made by the poles and tied them in place with lengths of rope. I could lift one end of the rig by the longer poles; the other end would drag on the ground.

That's exactly what I did: I started pulling, dragging the travois along behind me with some forty-odd kilograms of food and gear. It wasn't elegant or speedy, but it was better than trying to pack all the stuff all the way on my back. I hadn't done that sort of thing in a long time, and I didn't intend to start now if I could help it. I never had liked the Army.

It must have been close to three hours later when I got far enough into the rugged stone hills that I could no longer drag the travois over the stones, but by then I was close enough that I could almost see the cave. It had been much easier to find, the second time around.

During the trip I had constantly looked back over my shoulder into the shallow depression where I could see my cage and the impressions in the snow made by the arrival and departure of an earlier chronalcage. They had not yet come into my real time, whoever it was that was after me. But they could anytime. (I wondered about the spots that looked like blood on the snow near the impressions, but I couldn't imagine why there should be any blood there, if blood it were.)

The tracks of my feet and the trail left by the poles of the travois in the snow would be a path leading anyone directly to the door of my cave. I didn't much like that, but I wasn't sure what I could do about it. The crust on the snow was too hard for the wind to scatter other fallen snow over the tracks or for me to try to cover them over. I could only hope that a new snowfall would come to cover them, and from the looks of the sky that didn't seem to be an unlikely thing. But until snow did fall to obliterate the trail, I would just have to be ready for someone to come following it.

I made four trips from my stopping place to the cave; for the first one I was loaded lightest and held the Weatherby at the ready. The cave was still empty, but I had the sensation that the animal odor in it was stronger than it had been the day before—fresher, perhaps, still warm from a living body. But I found no real signs of an animal having entered during my absence.

In the remaining three trips I completed transferring my supplies to the cave.

By the time I was finished, I was tired, feverish, nauseated, yet starving and feeling as if I were about to die of thirst. I forced myself to eat some of the emergency rations which, washed down with water, settled into an unwilling stomach. Pulling blankets over me, I lay down to take a short nap. After I had rested some, I told myself as sleep began to come over me, I would gather firewood for the night and take a climb to a higher spot to see if I could really see the damaged cage from here.

Then I slept.

I consider myself lucky to have ever wakened up, but I suppose that's something of an exaggeration.

I'm not usually a very sound sleeper, but fatigue and

lack of proper rest the night before must have put me into an unusually sound sleep, for I didn't awaken until the bear was almost into the entrance of the cave.

I'd been sleeping on my side, facing the flowstone that covered the cave's walls, when sounds disturbed me and I rolled over to see if it were someone stumbling in late at night, coming noisily and maybe drunkenly—bootleggers do prosper in my U.S.A.!—into the wrong room in the chronalnaut dorm near the Project Center, downtown Chicago. Then I saw it was daylight and that the stone of the cave's walls was certainly not anything like the walls of my cubicle.

I think I let out a startled scream, for the bear didn't seem to be aware of me until I did. It stopped, its furry head inside the opening of the cave, its big, bright, brown eyes startled, its mouth open, its tongue lolling out, dripping saliva that steamed in the chilled air. For a moment the bear looked at me as if wondering whether it was coming into the wrong cave, one occupied by some strange bear of a tribe and race it didn't know.

After a moment of frightened stillness, I remembered where I'd left the rifle, near at hand in my novice's fear, grabbed for it, snatched it up, clicked off the safety with clumsy fingers.

The bear—a male, I supposed—growled, deep and guttural, his breath a fog deeper than my own as if he had a body temperature higher than mine, but made no menacing move. He continued to look at me, now seeming to be trying to stare me down, to make me rise, bolt, and run, and leave the cave to him.

I don't know much about bears and hadn't seen one since I was a small child. There just weren't any left in my world uptime. Our ursine brothers had gone the way of so many of the animal species that had once populated the Earth—before there were just too many people to have any room for useless creatures lower on the evolutionary totem pole than we! But I'd read a few books and had a course or two in zoology at the university, and this bear didn't really look to me like any that had lived in recent times—like, during the era since the retreat of the ice at the end of the fourth glaciation.

He was big, maybe three meters tall if he stood on his hind legs, and must have weighed a hundred and fifty or two hundred kilograms. His fur was long and shaggy, more so than that of any bear I'd ever seen a picture of, and his ears did not look like those of a bear at all; more like those of a sheep dog, perhaps—long and floppy. His color certainly wasn't the white of a polar bear, but it wasn't quite black either; more of a silvery gray, with spots here and there that were more brownish. And his mouth was big and wide and full of very large, very sharp teeth; his paws were just as well armed with claws.

Somewhere I had once read about something called a cave bear, which had lived during the Pleistocene; and though I knew nothing more than that about it, I was now very convinced I was meeting one in the flesh, in the fur. That confirmed several things I'd begun to suspect, though I didn't have the time to give them much consideration right then.

The big, shaggy bear stayed where he was, only partly into the cave, but was seeming to become more and more convinced that he had, in fact, come home, to his own cave, and had found a stranger there. His growls grew louder and deeper, and finally he took a tentative step toward me.

"Get back!" I yelled. "Back. This is my cave."

I seriously doubt that he understood the words, but he got the message. And he didn't like the idea. Not at all. He stepped forward again, his paws looking the size of old-fashioned picnic hams, growling louder still and showing me every one of his many teeth.

I had absolutely no desire to shoot the bear, not if he would leave me alone—and I had no idea how to prepare bear steak, even if I'd the practice of eating meat —so I aimed the rifle above his head and fired a warning shot.

Startled, he took a few steps backward, then seemed to realize that the noise had done him no harm. More angry than ever, he started into the cave once more, growling loudly again. I put two more rounds from the 8.5mm into the stone above his head, showering him with chips of rock and a ricochet bullet that did no more than graze his shaggy fur.

But apparently that was enough. Some of the stone chips had been sharp. He quickly backed out of the cave, continuing to growl, but not so forcefully as before. Outside he stamped around in the snow, muttering to himself for a while like an old man trying to remember if he'd left anything important behind in the cave, apparently decided that he hadn't, then shuffled off to the south, maybe with another, less desirable cave in mind.

I decided that it was safe for me to start breathing again.

It wasn't until almost dark that I worked up the courage to go outside for firewood, and probably wouldn't have then if I had not been afraid that he might come back for me after dark and really get into the cave if no fire was there to block his way.

He didn't come back that night, though I didn't sleep as well as I might have hoped I would. I kept *thinking* that bear was returning . . .

It wasn't until the next morning that I went to higher ground to see if I could spot the chronalcage from there —and to see if I yet had companions from my own time.

4

Allen Howard Dover, to whom the faithful refer as the Appointed One, was born in 1972 and died when I was nineteen years old; and, as fate and he himself would have it, he died a martyr's death. Some say that he had his own assassination arranged when he felt his powers begin to fail him (he was only forty-two, but, like Alexander, "his youth had been marked by glory seldom achieved by men far older"; rumors that still circulate say that he was dying of some form of uncontrollable cancer, maybe that of the lungs). But stories of his self-arranged assassination and of his physical limitations are seldom told any longer; doubt of the semidivinity of the Appointed One is heresy, too, you know.

I can still remember as a boy, though older than I was when I met my first bear, when Dover's followers were in the minority and the more orthodox considered them an ignorant rabble clutching at false gods—one of the many cults of Southern California to spring up and die as the twentieth century closed and the twenty-first opened to find a world with too many people—and no easy answers to their problems. But as Jesus had his Paul, Allen Howard Dover, God's Last Messenger to Man, had his (St.) Wilson Burnette Daniels, who repackaged his products and sold them, with all the persuasiveness of Madison Avenue, to an ever growing, ever more desperate, ever more gullible public.

My father, who was a Methodist minister of the more liberal persuasion, once said that the Church of the New Revelation (as it was called in its earliest years during

Dover's lifetime on this Earth) was "a blend of High Anglican ceremony and Fundamentalist Baptist theology with just enough thrown in from Oriental mysticism to make it sound intellectual," but he said this when his own congregation was growing smaller and smaller and those of Dover and Daniels were growing larger and larger.

Though I don't pretend to begin to understand all of the theological ideas/theories expressed by the World Ecumenical Church of the Newest Testament (as Daniels renamed it after Dover's death, never minding the redundancy when it had a nice ring), I do think my father was selling them short. Dover himself, the Appointed One, had gone far beyond the bounds of traditional Christianity even in his own later preachings and had freely stolen ideas from the Koran and from a number of religio-philosophical writings of India, China, and Japan; from the Vedas and the Upanishads, from the *Bhagavad Gita* and the *Yoga of Patanjali,* from the *Pao-p'u Tzu* and the *Tamakushige.* He began, if one accepts as truth the official histories, by writing an addition to the standard New Testament that related God's further revelations to mankind and His plans for the final establishment of the City of God. The Newest Testament was completed after Dover's death by W. B. Daniels, who was also inspired by God and was in direct spiritual contact with Dover's soul (and was probably aided by a staff of writers comparable in size to that of the *Encyclopedia Americana's*). It was this book which finally became the standard text of the W.E.C. as it completed its conversion of America.

Despite its being a horrible mismash and even more full of inconsistencies and contradictions than the older books of the Bible, the Newest Testament *is* well written and contains a lot of ideas that seemed to grab the hearts and minds of a disillusioned people dissatisfied with traditional Christianity and its preachings, and fearful of a world and a century they couldn't begin to understand. But I really hadn't intended to write the definitive history of the rise of the World Ecumenical

Church of the Newest Testament. Not now. That seems foolish now.

So I'll try to keep my observations short, though I do want to try to sketch in some of the background for you.

God's Party, the first really successful third political party in America in decades, was formed before Dover's death. When I was still a middle school student it was active in the Southwest and managed to pick up a dozen or so House seats and three in the Senate in the election of 2012, but its time as a major national force in American politics did not come until the fiasco in India, during which the United States got its soundest military licking since Vietnam. When we turned tail and ran home, leaving two-thirds of India in Chinese hands, Daniels and his followers blamed it on the stupidity of the Livingston administration and the wrath of an angry God. A lot of people must have believed them. In the next election, Daniels' people took a third of the House, twenty-six Senate seats, and forced the new, Democratic president to put two "Doverites" in Cabinet positions, Aerospace and Interior, I believe. The W.E.C. was not yet the *official* state church, but it was way ahead of whoever the hell was second.

I was a very junior professor of history at the University of Chicago when the Reverend Archibald V. Larch, Daniels' chosen successor, was elected President of the United States. That was A.D. 2020.

It wasn't until Larch's second term, right after the Lunar Crisis and the Five-Day War, that things really got bad—that is, bad within the U.S. as well as outside it. During the last hours of the Five-Day War, when it looked as if our defensive systems were going to fail us and nuclear weapons were going to wipe out what was left of America's cities, Larch proclaimed martial law and suspended the Constitution. Within days, despite our unexpectedly successful conclusion of the war, he had reformed the government along theocratic lines, established an office called "President" that was nothing but ceremonial and placed Gilbert Gunness in it, named himself Rector-for-Life and the true power in Washington, installed his not-so-secret police of Proctors, and finally unleashed the Lay Brothers of St. Wilson—the Church's paramilitary arm—to stamp out any opposition to his rule.

It's totally untrue that Aerospace Force Chief of Staff General Nathaniel Blake committed suicide out of fear of the discovery of secret sins by the newly appointed Proctors. The fact is that he was murdered by them when he attempted to stage a palace coup to restore democratic government. Blake wasn't the only one murdered by Proctors and blueshirts during the summer of 2025, but not many of them were national heroes of his standing. And, needless to say, there are no public memorials erected in *their* honor.

By the time that Wilson Burnette Daniels was translated to heaven at the age of sixty-two (some say his "translation" was effected by a very subtle poison administered to his food by cronies of Rector Larch, but I'm not certain), the United States of America in which I'd been born only thirty years before existed in name only. It was now the Church/State in everything excepting only the most official and diplomatic documents, and you were a Doverite or you weren't a citizen. I joined the World Ecumenical Church on my thirtieth birthday, feeling that if there were really a God in His heaven (which by then I had begun to seriously doubt), He'd damn me to hell for hypocrisy. All I wanted was to be left alone and play at being a student of history, but right then the world didn't work that way—not for anybody.

They'd been calling America an imperialist power even back in the middle of the twentieth century, and I suppose there was some truth in that, if I read my history correctly, but truly imperialistic moves by the major power of the North American continent didn't really begin until after Larch had proclaimed himself Rector-for-Life and then tried to annex Canada and Mexico. The bastard was successful! Nuclear threat was sufficient.

So the empire had begun gobbling up the world in the

name of the Lord God of Hosts and His Last Messenger
to Man, Allen Howard Dover, the Appointed One.

But a lot of the world didn't want to be gobbled up by
the newly reformed Giant of the West. We've been at
war, on and off, ever since.

The cataloging of these short, nasty, ugly, bloody
wars might be a bore to both me and you.
Nevertheless . . .

The Japanese bombed Hawaii (again!) and got
themselves all but annihilated by thermonuclear bombs:
we thought we had defenses against their bombs, and we
did; they thought they had defenses against our bombs,
and they didn't.

We fought China over the ruins of Japan and got them
after we'd sown a hundred new diseases on the Chinese
mainland. Then we used nuclear and more biological
weapons to get back India, what was left of it by then.

We used biological weapons and the threat of orbiting
bombs to get South America to call us Protector of the
Americas (the Monroe Doctrine back with a vengeance!) and to pay us "maintenance allowances" to support the troops we quartered in their cities and the ships
we stationed off their coasts.

We used the threat of nuclear and biological weapons
to force EcoEurope to cut back on arms production and
sign with us some very disadvantageous "nonaggression
pacts."

And, of course, few people doubt that we sent the
seeds of the plagues that had decimated Russia from the
Ukraine to Moscow in 2025, though nobody could ever
prove it. Soviet experimental viruses *could* have gotten
loose accidentally and killed those millions, but I doubt
it.

Not that we didn't have our share of troubles at
home. San Diego was never rebuilt after the second nuclear strike and it's still nothing more than a water-filled
crater on the Pacific into which many fish venture but
from which few ever return. They say you can still smell
San Diego from as far away as downtown Los Angeles
when the wind is right, but I doubt that, too. Who can
smell *anything* in that smog?

Tucson *was* reinhabited after nerve gas wiped out its population, but they say that there's still a feeling of death about the place and it's not very popular these days.

The cities along the coast of the Gulf of Mexico were mostly rebuilt after the gigantic tsunami caused by a multi-gigaton thermonuke washed over them, but there's not much left of the western end of Cuba and not very many people ever mention Havana anymore. It's not a very pleasant thing to think about.

And then there are the "Rehabilitation Camps" in the Midwest and the "Racial Study Centers" in the South and a lot of new "correctional institutions for the spiritually unsound" all over the nation, but not very many people like to talk about them either. It tends to be dangerous to your health.

The depression that followed the breakdown of most of the governments of Asia hasn't missed the U.S., though it has not hit us as hard as it did EcoEurope and South America: our "defensive posture" and "war footing" have kept some segments of the American economy going at rates even higher than before Larch was elected President for his first term, although there now seems to be a greater gap between the incomes of the very rich and the very poor. The New England food riots of last winter seemed to prove that, as do some unofficial figures about the increasing disease rate ("pandemic," some say) along the entire Eastern Seaboard.

Other figures, equally unofficial, say that the U.S. in 2032 has the highest rate of nervous breakdown of any nation in history, both in raw figures and in percentages of the population—in all age groups and social levels—but the government denies this, says these figures are just lies told by atheistic foreign infiltrators.

Even with desalination of seawater, we're still a nation slowly dying of thirst, though the White House claims that it's a short-term trend about to be reversed.

And deny it though it will, the government cannot hide the fact that the society of the United States of America in 2032 is one ridden with drugs and alcohol (both illegal, but available) and with crime. The fact that there's a policeman on every corner, sundown-to-sunup curfews in the cities, frequent identity checks (we've got photos on *everything* now), and even some direct control of individual thought processes doesn't seem to help at all.

So maybe you'll understand why I jumped at a chance to travel into the past when Jerry Maughton asked me to join the Chronal Corps.

I don't much like my world, the one I started out in.

But then Melanie later convinced me that I could do something about it.

5

Above my cave ledges rose like the steps of a giant's staircase, rugged and crude, but not bad climbing if I favored my sore ankle and wrist. From the top of them, crouching beside a gnarled oak tree twisted by the wind into a dark, evil, and monstrous shape, with a pair of binoculars pressed against my eyes as they watered from the cold, I could see down into the shallow valley where the chronalcage sat, bent and twisted like the oak, snow beginning to pile up on the windward side of it, for there had been a light snowfall during the night, enough to cover my tracks I hoped.

If it hadn't been for the impressions I'd seen in the snow that proved another chronalcage had come into this time, I wouldn't have been certain that they would even be coming back after me. I no longer doubted that I was somewhen/somewhere back in the Pleistocene. The bear and some other animals I'd observed gave me a pretty good idea that I was. A good look at the stars, and a comparison with sky charts I had, told me that the season here was autumn, early autumn, and a sextant (which I think I used correctly, all limitations considered) told me that I wasn't all that far north. These two things I did some days later, when the weather had cleared.

So, in geo terms, I decided, I had hardly moved at all —the future site of Chicago might only be a few hundred kilometers away. Only during the Ice Ages did this part of North America (as I felt certain it was) get so cold at this time of year.

So . . . I was so far back, downtime, that despite the evidence I'd seen that another chronalcage *had* been at this spot and no doubt would come again, a little further uptime—*my*time—I feared that they just might leave me to my own devices and say good riddance to me. But I hoped they would come. I needed them to come.

When I'd first made the promise to Melanie, I hadn't really believed that I would do it, but later I did. And since the arrival of the Proctor and the blueshirts at the displacement chamber, and since I'd come downtime, I was more convinced than ever to do it if I could.

I remembered the night Melanie first put the idea into my head. It had scared me then, when I realized that she wasn't joking or talking about hypothetical possibilities, and it still scared me now, but I knew what kind of a world it was uptime and I knew what the MinSec Proctors and the blueshirts had probably done—would do, are doing, have done—to her.

I had been seeing her for several weeks then. We were going out two or three times a week, having dinner at one or another of the small restaurants around Highland Park Lake, the lake that Melanie had once, in a voice that was cold and unhappy, called the ghost of Lake Michigan; I remembered Lake Michigan, as foul as it had been, and Highland Park Lake wasn't even a ghost of that. And we would go to one of the permitted shows, one of those light, meaningless musical comedies that had no relationship to any world that I knew—escapist, maybe, if you lowered your mind to imbecile level. We'd do things like that, all pretty innocent at first, but after a while she quit wearing her VV pin when I was with her and over drinks in a Cicero speakeasy she gradually, bit by bit, allowed me to find out what she really felt about the Church/State, while I admitted that I felt pretty much the same.

Then one night we made love.

Officially Melanie lived in a dorm for unmarried women, one maintained by the Victorious Virgins. But unlike so many others of her age and sex in Chicago, circa 2032, she was gainfully employed, even made good money, in her position at the Project, and could afford to rent a second, private, apartment in Oak Park—apartments were going begging and many of the landlords weren't too curious about the credentials of those who rented them. Melanie described the old man who gave her her lease as a grubby character who always needed a shave and wore a "Bachelors Forever" button pinned to the front of a dirty gray shirt that had once been white. He hadn't even glanced at her single-occupancy papers, though he had looked lasciviously up and down *her*, and almost watered at the mouth when she counted out the five one-hundred-dollar bills that paid for her first month.

That's where we went, to Oak Park and a high-rise apartment building that must have dated from the 1980's, up a rumbling, creaky elevator with tarnished chrome and brass and greasy, finger-printed glass to the eighteenth floor.

Even as I followed her down the hallway, across worn carpeting and under flickering fluorescent tubes, I felt twinges of guilt. It wasn't that I hadn't done this sort of thing before—I'd even had my own "priapts" for a while, as a "swinging bachelor" and as a briefly married man, but I'd been much younger then. And it wasn't exactly that I'd been raised a puritanian—as I said, my father was a *liberal* Methodist. But I had lived under the Rector-for-Life in the Church/State of the United States of America, and more of the puritanism of its pseudo-culture than I liked had rubbed off on me. Some primordial element of my intellect told me that sex wasn't evil, but overlays of emotionalized antisex propaganda, and reflexes conditioned by too many hours of HV shows extolling celibacy, told me different.

The apartment was not exactly shabby. Melanie had done her best in what time she'd had free from the demands of her work and those of the Victorious Virgins and the Lay Sisters of St. Arnold the Martyr and their good works for the poor and the fallen and the unenlightened, to make it into a livable place. But she'd been fighting decades of neglect and there was a limit to what she could hope to accomplish.

At one time, I suspected, the decor of the rooms had been Neo-Elizabethan, so popular in the 1980s and '90s, though elements of Rock Years Ornamental and New Century Basic were scattered here and there, a gaudy glass-and-chrome chair of the latter style being one of the living room's most prominent, and ugly, features. She'd decorated the walls with prints of old masters and several contemporary holograms, though they did little to relieve the sensation of gloom that continued to fill the room. Nor did the HV, switched to null-channel, displaying no more than a three-dimensional show of shifting, variegated fogs. She'd probably put more money than she could afford into the multichannel musicgear that was the room's second most prominent feature, but she had a taste for music and said that she couldn't live without it.

As we entered the room, I for the first time, she went at once to the musicgear and produced a molysphere that immediately began to play Sibelius' *Finlandia*. I really wasn't familiar with it—I'd been exposed to little good music since leaving my father's home—but I soon learned to enjoy it and other examples of Melanie's excellent taste in music.

She at once ducked into her bedroom and doffed the dull-colored, floor-length dress she had worn, one that bespoke too clearly her position and status in society: female technician second class, upper-middle social stratum. She replaced it with a dress considered skimpy, scandalous by contemporary standards, a bright and colorful thing that could have come from the early 1970s. She was very deep into the '70s she told me once; it was just about her favorite period, though she wasn't exactly an Anachronist, like so many people. I never could understand why she favored the 1970s so, but then there were a lot of things I never understood about Melanie.

She got a bottle of wine, French, old, and very expensive, which she said she'd been saving for a special occasion and this was certainly one. She never did tell me how she'd gotten a French wine, and I never asked.

As I said, we made love. After the wine. With the music.

I wasn't a virgin—despite the official statistics, not very many men in their thirties are. In fact, I'd even been married once. That was shortly after I'd gotten out of the Army, returned to school, and finally gotten my degree. I was a very junior professor and she was a very lovely grad student. We fell in love—or thought we did —within a week of meeting and were married within a month. But it didn't work. Maybe it was my fault. God knows, Johanna tried hard enough. But I guess I just wasn't ready for marriage, or something. Maybe I'm not the kind to accept the responsibility of a wife and children and all that goes with them. Anyway, after a little more than a year Johanna applied for a divorce and got it.

Something I'll say in favor of the World Ecumenical Church is that it's a bit more liberal in some respects than you might expect it to be. Or maybe it's that the people who founded it and run it, and now the whole country, are just realistic enough about human nature to allow some compensations, such as easy marriage and easy divorce, as long as they aren't too frequent and as long as both are performed under the aegis of the Church/State.

And maybe realism about human nature is why underground prostitution is allowed to flourish in all the country's major cities; Chicago's got some of the biggest, most elaborate cathouses the world's ever seen, but the madams and the pimps and the girls are quiet about it and don't bring themselves to public attention very often. Of course, the pulpits and the judges' benches condemn the brothels and the speakeasies as the "wickedness of Babylon" and all that crap, and the police and the Lay Brothers of St. Wilson make their occasional raids; but, all in all, the houses and the speaks are allowed to operate if they pay their squeeze, and the men and women in the street can get some of the release they need. They're pressure valves, I suppose, and without them the Church/State would probably have a lot more opposition than it does. The system seems to work, damn it!

But as for Melanie and me: we made love after the

wine and to the music, and I'm afraid that I showed her that, despite my youthful marriage, I wasn't very experienced sexually. Melanie was, but I didn't ask her about that either. I just accepted the fact and enjoyed it and let her show me things that I'd only experienced in my imagination before.

Afterwards, as we lay side by side in the dark, smoking the expensive black-market cigarettes that are a weakness of mine, she told me she was a member of a group that called itself "the Cell," and she felt that I should join them. Their goal was the overthrow of the Church/State.

I had known there were such organizations around, but I'd never met anyone before who would admit to being a member. The ones they'd shown on HV after successful manhunts or while undergoing public trial for treason had always been dirty, brutish sorts who had lusted for the blood of righteous and God-fearing folk. Popish rapists and murderers, they had been, bomb-throwing drug users. I had the impression that Melanie wasn't that sort.

And neither were the others who were members of "the Cell." They were intelligent, reasonable people, Melanie said, who loved America and what it had been in the past; who wanted to see constitutional government and democratic procedures restored; who wanted to see an end put to perpetual worldwide warfare; who wanted nothing more than freedom for themselves and their children. Those who wanted to join the World Ecumenical Church, or any other religious body, should be allowed to do so, they said, but those who didn't want to should be allowed the freedom to choose their own God, or lack of Him.

As a historian, a lot of that sounded familiar to me. But I knew how they felt. Hell, I felt the same way! Didn't I?

I can't really say why—maybe it's a fault of my character, maybe *that's* why my life had always been so, well, empty—but then and later I refused to fully commit myself to Melanie's "Cell." I suppose I'd have done just about anything else for her, after that first night in bed with her, but I wasn't going to join. Maybe it was just the realization that, although I agreed with her intellectually about the Church/State, I didn't have the kind of emotional setup it took to hate it as much as she did. I didn't join, but I suppose I was a fellow traveler.

One night—or, rather, early one morning, an hour or two before dawn—we lay in the darkness on her bed in the Oak Park apartment. We had watched the moon, more scarred and pocked than it had been in my childhood, set through a window of her bedroom that looked to the west over the city and the twisting serpent of the New River (really a canal). We'd lain there not speaking, but without sleeping either, while the clouds moved in on schedule and the morning rains fell as they always do, clearing for a while, at least, the air of the smog and haze that lay over the city. Now the sky was clearing, and we could see a few of the brighter stars despite the brightness of the nocturnal city. Tomorrow was the Sabbath, and except for the required church service, we neither had commitments. We could sleep away most of the day, if we wished—and, well, there seemed to be a kind of tension in Melanie that kept her from sleeping and kept me awake, too. Finally, after what seemed like hours, she spoke.

"Gene," she began softly, speaking to me through the silent darkness, for despite its shortcomings the apartment was high, soundproofed, and silent except for the ticking of a clock and the humming of appliances, "Gene, have you ever thought about changing the past?"

"Sure, who hasn't?" I asked. "If I had my life to live over . . ."

"No, that's not what I mean. I mean really. Have you?"

"I don't get it."

"Well," she said slowly, "it's true, isn't it, that the past can be altered?"

"You mean the historical past, downtime?"

"Uh-huh."

"Nobody really knows."

"But you have indications, don't you?"

"Yeah," I said, "mathematical, theoretical ones.

That's why we're not allowed to involve ourselves in any active way with the past. We go downtime strictly as observers. We take pictures, make recordings, that sort of thing, but we do our damnedest to stay out of everyone's way. I don't even like to be seen when it can be avoided. It's fear that even our very *presence* can change things. Heisenberg's uncertainty-principle-sort-of-thing, you know. But you should know all the rules; they're posted everywhere in the Project."

"I know that. But you *could* change things?" she asked, seeming to want a definite, unequivocal answer from me.

"Like I said, nobody knows for certain. It's not something we can even get empirical data on, you know—or would want to try to get empirical data on."

"Why?"

"Oh, call it a 'time paradox,' if you like. I suppose that's the popular term."

"I think I know what you mean," she said, "but I'd like for you to go over it again. I'm not certain I really follow it."

"Does anyone . . . ? But, okay. Let's say that I wanted to go back and do something noble, say, keep Lincoln from being shot, okay?"

"Okay."

"And say I do. I timeout back to 14 April 1865 and get into Ford's Theatre in time to intercept John Wilkes Booth and keep him from shooting Lincoln. Knock him in the head. Kidnap him. Something. And reveal the whole conspiracy—it's pretty well accepted that there was a conspiracy. We've even recovered some of the documents of Secretary of—"

"Okay," Melanie said, almost snapping at me. "Go on."

"All right. Lincoln doesn't die, goes on being President, cleans out the nest of vipers in Washington, sees to the Reconstruction of the South on terms that make it really a reconstruction and not a military occupation. He turns out to be the saviour of his country twice over. Still with me?"

She grunted in the darkness, but didn't speak this time.

"All history would change afterwards. No books would have ever been written about Lincoln's assassination, all the problems of Johnson's term as President, the brutalities of Reconstruction, and so on, because none of that ever happened. A different sequence of events followed that April night. So when I get back to the future—the Now—there would be no record of the assassination and all ever having happened. No one would know . . . except maybe me, and maybe not even I would know."

"Huh?"

"Well, one school of thought says that when I reincorporate myself with the continuum of time, I would once again be a part of the 'continuous flow' and thus would have no memory of this little 'bump' in time during which I'd gone back and altered the past. Nobody, then, not even I, would know that Lincoln *ever was* assassinated. For all practical purposes, for all purposes in the reorganized universe, he never was. It didn't just un-happen. It never happened in the first place. And to the reordered world I didn't go back. No data."

"I think I see."

"Of course, that isn't the only school of thought about altering the past. There are just about as many as there are people with opinions on chronal displacement, but some say that I, as an agent who put myself outside of the flow of time, would be independent of the 'historical data' of an altered world and would remember a history different from everyone else's—in which Lincoln had been killed and I'd gone back to undo it. And that's wild.

"And then," I went on after pausing for breath, talking as quickly as I could, maybe anticipating what Melanie was going to say and trying to keep her from saying it, "there're some who say that once I'd come back to the present and 'forgotten' that I'd saved Lincoln, I wouldn't have really done it, since in that framework I hadn't: I would never have known he'd been assassinated and thus not have had motivation to go back and save him. And then time would snap back into its original configuration: assassinated Lincoln, trip back to save him, undoing history, going uptime, then forgetting it, etc. An endless cycle of encapsulated time, a loop in time, so to speak, with a little pocket world a hundred and sixty or seventy years long with an un-assassinated Lincoln, while for the bigger, outside world of time *he had been killed* and I had never really been able to do anything about it, even though I'd traveled through time and stopped Booth. Still with me?"

"No, I don't think so."

"Well, let me put it this way—"

"Gene," Melanie said earnestly, rolling over so that I felt her soft breasts against my arm, "don't. Just answer me this, will you? Do *you* think that the past can be altered?"

"I just don't know, Melanie. Why is it so important?"

"A lot of people think it can be changed."

"I know," I said, "but 'a lot of people' have been known to be wrong pretty often. They just don't have the data. No one does. And maybe there's no way of ever getting it."

"I want the past changed, Gene . . ." Her voice was dead serious.

I tried to be light. "Don't we all. I wish I'd met you ten years ago."

"I'd have been too young for you then," she said, answering my lightness, but then becoming serious again. "I mean it, Gene. The historical past."

"What do you mean, Melanie?" I knew that I wasn't going to get her off the track now. I would have to hear her out.

"I don't want the Appointed One ever to have been born."

The thought of electronic bugs in the apartment flashed through my mind. The Church/State monitored everything, or just about everything. But the very first night there in Melanie's apartment, she had assured me that the place wasn't bugged—in fact, couldn't be bugged: she'd seen to that. But then that was her *business*, a part of it; she was one of the Project's top techs and if anyone could debug this place I guess she could do it.

But if she were wrong? I didn't like to think that a handful of Lay Brothers of St. Wilson might come charging into this room in a few minutes, ready to take us in on charges of heresy and treason. I didn't like to think of it, but . . .

Finally I spoke, keeping my voice even, trying to make a joke of it. "A lot of people wish he'd never been born."

"What do you think the world would be like now if he hadn't?"

I shrugged in the darkness, some of the sudden fear easing inside me. "I don't know. That would be some pretty useless speculation, wouldn't it?"

"No."

"No?"

"You're a historian, Gene. Think about how the world *could* have developed. What if the U.N. had been made stronger; what if it'd become a real 'parliament of man'? It could be a world of peace, maybe, with freedom and prosperity—a good, clean world where it isn't a sin to be a healthy and happy human being."

"That's just speculation, Melanie. It could have gone the other way. Things could be worse."

"Could they?" Anger and bitterness were in her voice. "Maybe if you'd lost your parents in the '09 earthquakes and had been taken in by W.E.C. missionaries and raised in one of their 'kennels' and had been drilled day and night with the garbage they call 'truth and light,' maybe if you'd seen what they do in the name of love, how they twist and distort little children and make them into monsters who hate their parents because they're not—or weren't—Doverites, maybe if you'd been forced to grow up as one of Father Allen's Angels and then a Victorious Virgin and—" Her voice cracked and gave way.

There was silence in the room for a few moments. Melanie sobbed, and I put my arms around her. Then she stifled her sobs and pulled away from me.

"I'm sorry, Gene. I didn't mean to do that."

"That's okay."

"No, it's not. And that doesn't change anything."

"Change what?"

"Gene, listen to me, will you?" Her voice was cold and earnest again. "You can do it."

"Do what?"

"See that *he* was never born."

"My God, Melanie, what're you saying?"

The fear of electronic eavesdroppers in the room surged through me again. I suppressed the desire to grab my clothes and run like hell from the apartment, to get as far away as I could from the things she was saying. The Lay Brothers and the Proctors would have a time with us both if they knew what was on our minds. Dammit, you just don't talk about things like that! but I stayed where I was and listened to her.

"You know exactly what I'm saying, Gene."

Now she was sitting up, her full breasts silhouetted against the window and the starry sky above the city lights below.

"You want me to make an unauthorized displacement downtime," I said, finding that the words came with great difficulty, "and—what?—smother Dover in his cradle or something?"

"Kill his mother," Melanie said slowly, coldly, a chill of arctic winter in her voice. She really meant it.

"Kill his mother?"

"Kill his mother. Shoot her down while she's pregnant with *him*. Make certain that he's never born. Gene, I can give you the exact time and place where you can do it and get away with it. The perfect situation. You can make sure that he never lives to do—to do *this* to the world." She made a gesture toward the window and the crowded city below.

"You're talking crazy, Melanie. It's treason just to suggest it."

"It's not just me, Gene. It's a lot of people asking it. The whole world."

"You mean 'the Cell'?"

"Yes, 'the Cell,' and a lot of other people, too."

"What other people, exactly?"

"Will you do it, Gene?"

"It's crazy."

"You can do it. Once you get downtime you've got complete control over the chronalcage. I know that. You can go just about anywhen and anywhere you want. 23 September 1971, Chicago."

"It's crazy, Melanie," I said again.

She pulled herself close to me, her arms wrapping around my bare shoulders, her face near mine. "Think about it, Gene. I don't have to have an answer right now."

Then she kissed me and I forgot all about the Appointed One and the Church/State and everything but Melanie and . . .

When dawn came and the curfew was lifted and the tan-uniformed force of conscripted poor came out to clean up yesterday's accumulation of litter, I made my way out of the apartment building and into the streets of the city I'd once loved, but could love no longer. The Chicago of my birth didn't exist. The city that had come up from names like "Slab Town" and the "Mudhole of the Prairies" to become one of the major trade centers of the world, a city not only of industry and commerce but one of the arts and sciences as well, the city of Sandburg's poems, the city where I'd been born and whose fascinating past had led me into my love affair with its history and that of the world—well, that city had been murdered and in its place stood another of the creations of the followers of Allen Howard Dover, called the Appointed One, but maybe the supreme Antichrist of all time. I hated this travesty of Chicago, and I realized, as never before, my hatred for the people who had made it this way.

From Melanie's apartment I made my way to the nearest UPT station and slipped my credit card into the slot and rode the monorail back toward the Project and the dorm I was supposed to have slept in, thinking that I would have to shave and shower and change clothes quickly if I were going to make First Service, and realizing that I was wide awake yet felt that I was in the middle of a nightmare and if I kept up this kind of thinking a Monitor was going to notice and there'd soon be a dark-vestmented Proctor coming to take me in for a spiritual checkup and . . .

Somehow I got through that day, and the next.

And I kept on seeing Melanie.

6

I watched for the bear, but he didn't return. I suppose he thought me very antisocial.

Three times a day, some days more often than that, I would climb to the top of the giant's staircase and crouch among the gnarled oaks, looking through the binoculars toward the chronalcage in the valley below. No one else was there yet, and at that distance I could see no sign of the earlier visitor's impressions. The snow had probably covered them by then, if they had ever been there at all. I began to feel that I'd just imagined them. Was that wishful thinking? Or fear?

For two days, a week or so after my arrival, it snowed too hard for me to reach the top of the stairs, and even if I had I couldn't have seen a dozen meters away, much less the distance to the cage. But I didn't much mind the snow then: I was too sick and feverish to go outside, anyway.

For those two days and most of the next I just lay in the cave, trying to keep my fire going, though I had a camp stove nearer to me that gave out a fair amount of heat and kept my section of the cave comfortably warm. The bowl of ice toward the cavern's center partly melted in the warmth, but the water was too dirty to drink. I melted snow for that, when I did drink.

During that time I didn't eat much, and what I did eat came back up again, usually within a few minutes, though water would sometimes stay on my stomach for an hour or more. I began to fear that if I didn't get better soon I wouldn't be able to do anything when—if?—they came.

The medicines in the kit I had didn't seem to be doing me a damned bit of good, despite the clinical claims made on some of the packages, and I wondered whether it was really the flu I had. Generic flu had been blamed for a number of similar diseases that had been sweeping Chicago during the few weeks prior to my departure. It occurred to me that the EcoEuropeans, just before I left, could have dusted North America—and Chicago, in particular—with some sort of germ. They'd tried it before, but they had never been successful. In my fever, that struck me as kind of funny. What if, I asked myself, they had hit us really bad just before I left and the Rector-for-Life had kept it a secret to avoid panic while he figured out how to get back at them; and now everyone uptime there, up in 2032 just beyond the day when I'd outtimed, was too sick to come back and get me? Maybe they'd made one trip downtime, overshot my position by a few days, and then had to go back uptime because they were too sick to complete their search. Oh, God, what a joke! I thought. Maybe I was delirious.

When I felt I had the strength, I would snap on one of the torches and read some of the books I'd brought back with me, or one of the standard chronalcage texts. *My* books were studies of Elizabethan and Jacobean England, around the turn of the sixteenth century and the first couple of decades thereafter; histories of Europe and England and the plagues; and biographies of Shakespeare and Ben Jonson and Francis Bacon and people like that. One of them was the book I'd published, based on my doctoral dissertation. Rereading it after all these years, I found that it wasn't as bad a book as I'd thought, though now with (hopefully) added maturity I saw things in it I didn't like. But then, I was supposed to rewrite it after visiting— "Hell, man," I told myself, realization coming back to me. "That was another world. You won't ever rewrite that book now. You'll probably never even get to Elizabethan England."

The others, the standard ones that were always in a cage, were, of course, *The Newest Testament, The Words of the Appointed One,* W.E.C. catechism, standard prayer books, and some cold, dry military-type survival texts: how to live off the land in various climates, and stuff like that. One book was about how to troubleshoot and make minor repairs on a chronalcage. That one was too elementary to begin to assess the damage done to my cage, and in the theory sections far too complex for me to really follow it. Technician I ain't. If only Melanie were with me . . . I tried not to think about her.

Finally the fever began to pass and I got to where I could keep fluids down and then solids. The afternoon of the day after the blizzard, I half dragged myself out of the cave and painfully climbed to the top of the stairs with my binoculars.

At first I couldn't even find the cage. Accumulation had drifted over it so that it was hardly more than another bump in the snow, like the boulders and the bushes but with sharp, angular, grayish metal sticking out of the drift instead of limbs bent beneath the load of fresh flakes. There wasn't another cage there. Maybe never would be.

As I went back to the cave I felt despondent, more so than I had during the worst of my illness. So maybe they weren't coming back after me at all, maybe I was stuck here for the rest of my life. Conditions being what they were, I didn't figure it would be a very long life. A city boy has no business in this kind of wilderness. The books couldn't give me practical experience in survival, and my supplies wouldn't last more than a few weeks. I seriously doubted that there were any *people* around to show me the ropes. No *people* people. Not in this part of the world. Not in this age.

During most of its history the climate of Earth had been far different from the way we humans know it. Mostly it had been a seasonless planet, a world of uninterrupted summer, with tropics climbing into what we know as the temperate zone, palm trees in the Dakotas, and lush savannahs in Canada.

But about a million and a half years before my time something happened, some disaster struck the world and its climate altered radically. What really happened no man knows. Cosmic dust clouds? A dramatic lowering of solar output? A reduction in the greenhouse effect? An unlocking of the polar sea that allowed winds to bring out moisture that came back south as snow? No one knows. We do know that it had happened before in Earth's long, long history, and it happened again then. The Pleistocene began, the Ice Ages came, four of them, the most recent a mere ten thousand years behind us, behind 2032 A.D. Uptime there, we're really just beginning to recover from the last glaciation. Maybe we're entering the Fourth Interglacial. Or maybe it's just a brief warm spell before the ice moves south again to sweep across our cities and fields. Again, no one really knows.

This we do know: a million and a half years ago the snow began to fall. Only a little at first, in the far north and the high places, but when that first cold winter was over and when the snow began to melt, not quite all of it melted. Some of it still stayed on the ground, there in the far north and the high places, more than had remained a year before. And winter came again and snow, and when the next summer came a little more snow was there for the sun to melt and it didn't melt quite all of it.

Years piled on years and centuries piled on centuries and the residual snow grew to be a little more with each year, snow that packed the accumulation beneath it into ice, ever growing ice in the far north and the high places, ice that weighed over twenty-seven kilograms per cubic foot, which, when it built up to a depth of ten meters, would exert a ground-level pressure of 41,166 kilograms —at thirty meters, some 123,166 kilograms. Under these conditions ice begins to flow like a very viscous liquid—a glacier.

Out of the far north and the high places, out of Labrador and out of the center of Canada and out of the

Canadian west coast, the ice began to flow southward, great, grinding, massive sheets of ice flowing down into a world they were making colder, into a world that had lost its endless summer and now knew chill, flowing outward and southward at an average speed of some thirty meters per year—sometimes faster, sometimes slower, but always flowing.

In Eurasia the ice came out of Scandinavia; from northern Germany to north-central Siberia; eastern Siberia, flowing down across the world's largest continent.

The ice flowed on, changing the course of rivers, rounding hills and mountains, scooping out the soft spots in the earth, grinding across the hard, smooth stone of the Canadian Shield, carrying with it boulders and pebbles and stone ground as fine as wheat in the mill.

The world was changed drastically. A disaster it might have seemed to an immortal observer who could have stood at a distance and watched the glacial movement over tens of thousands of years, watched the retreat of the animals and birds and fish before the ice. Many of the world's creatures fled southward toward warmer places. Those that stayed adapted, grew long fur to defend themselves from the cold, developed patterns of annual migrations. And somewhere along the line of years, one of the great apes who had lost his fur during the warmth of the Pliocene found out how to use fire to keep himself warm, began to make other adaptations to the cold, and learned to use the big brain that had already begun evolving.

You know who that hairless ape turned out to be: you; me.

During those million and a half years, the ice came and went four times, sometimes sweeping further south than others. During the Wisconsin Glaciation, the most recent one, the city of Chicago would have been under the ice; and at one time the ice so blocked the flow of rivers that a lake five times the size of Lake Superior formed over what we know as Minnesota and the Dakotas. The ice around Hudson Bay was so great, so massive, that it probably depressed the land there as much as three hundred meters below its present level. Maybe it's still rising now, recovering from the weight of ice that was in some places over twelve hundred meters thick, maybe as much as fifteen hundred meters.

So the ice came and it went, melting back when warmer weather came, leaving behind boulders worn smooth, pebbles, hills of debris called moraines, and plains formed when water from the melting ice flowed away and left behind its load of dust-like stone.

During the height of the glaciations the average world temperature was something like 4° C. and during the warm interglacial periods it rose as high as 22° C. Our average world temperature today is 14° C. You can make of that whatever you wish.

During those tens of thousands of years, the ape who walked erect did not grow back his hair. He learned to use somebody else's, as he had learned to use fire and to harden the ends of sticks in the fire to make weapons, and later learned to tip those weapons with stone. He went out singly and in groups and slaughtered the beasts who lived in the forest with him and learned to cook them over his fires, as he sometimes did his human brothers as well. But he also learned to look up at the stars at night, and he told stories about them, and stories about his gods, his demons, his afterlives.

As the Pleistocene was something different for this world, so was that ape. Viewed on the vast geological scale of Earth's long history, the Pleistocene is no more than a brief and minor disaster. Can the same be said of that ape?

I wonder. I wonder.

That night I slept poorly, disturbed by dreams of death from cold and hunger, my bones buried by snow and earth and rock and of them being discovered centuries in the future by some paleontologist who made the announcement that modern man was far older than anyone had ever believed—by a million years or more, perhaps. But even in my dream I knew that this damned place was no Olduvai Gorge and would call no Leakey to dig it, and probably nobody would ever find *my* bones nor the rust of the chronalcage.

My misery brought memories.

It was some three weeks after the night when Melanie had suggested that I could kill the Appointed One in the womb and forestall the coming of the Church/State, two nights before my scheduled trip downtime to 1602, when she asked me to come to her Oak Park apartment again. She wanted to show me something.

It was almost dark when I got there, only a few minutes before curfew, and I had been afraid that I'd be caught and have to explain what I was doing out. But the UPT was on schedule for once—maybe the engineer wanted to make curfew, too—and I got to Melanie's apartment building about the time the day's last stratoship lifted from the Chicago skyport and briefly lighted the heavens with its glare. A moment later, the sirens of curfew began to wail and it was no longer safe for private citizens to be on the streets unless they were nightouts. Oh, the cops would patrol the streets for an hour or so, while there was still some lingering twilight, but then they would withdraw, too, if they wanted to live to see the sun rise. After curfew the barbarians of the twenty-first century would roam at will. The night was their world. None of mine. Thus, the New Jerusalem!

The grubby old man who was landlord–desk clerk–superintendent gave me a leer as I entered the building using a duplicate key Melanie had given me, and said, "You just made it, feller. I was about to trigger the baffles. Your life wouldn't a been worth a prewar dollar if you'd come two minutes later."

"Yeah," I grunted and made my way across the decaying lobby as he hit a series of switches on the wall behind the desk and the great armored plates, in sections stacked three stories high and rumbling, grumblingly rolled into position across the face of the building. Doors and windows were sealed off from the outside world until dawn made it habitable again, if barely.

"Have yourself a good time," the filthy old man said as the elevator doors complainingly slid closed behind me, as unwilling as the baffles. I hadn't replied. He isn't worthy of a reply, the old pornophile, I said to myself, then regretted using the term. It was one the Doverites used, and I didn't like the meaning they put to it. Any man with a healthy sexual appetite was a "pornophile" to them.

The elevator took me up, slowly and with sounds that seemed to indicate that if this weren't its last trip, it was its next-to-last. Finally a flickering *18* lighted above the doors and they slid open.

Still feeling a guilt I despised in myself, and unable to keep from glancing around to see if anyone else saw me entering, I made my way down the worn carpeting to the door of Melanie's apartment. Even though I had a key, I didn't enter without announcing myself. Melanie had an illegal handgun and might use it if someone entered her apartment unannounced. That would have been the smart thing to do, anyway, and Melanie was anything but stupid.

She opened the door for me, dressed as she usually was in her own private place, in a short red skirt and a bright-yellow sleeveless blouse. On the streets of Chicago she'd have been arrested for indecent exposure—you could see her knees, among other things.

"I was getting worried," she said before I entered the living room.

"Had to stay a little late this evening," I told her. "I'm scheduled to go downtime day after tomorrow, and there's a lot of work to be done before then."

"I know," she said, and there was a special significance in her voice that I heard, felt, feared.

What had she wanted to show me? What persuasion was she going to use now?

I followed her into the living room. She wasn't alone. A man was there.

Melanie stopped and turned as I came to a halt, a look of concern on her face. Then she smiled and said, "Oh, Gene, don't worry. It's nothing like that."

The man, who had been sitting alone on the room's single, large, comfortable sofa, rose and extended his hand. He was middle-aged, balding with a fringe of graying hair around a shiny spot on the top of his head, well dressed like a professional man: a doctor without his caduceus; a lawyer without his scales of Blind Justice; a professor without his scroll. Yes, I decided, that's what he is, a professor of some type. I knew the type. I should have. I'd been one of them not so long before.

I took the man's fleshy yet firm hand as he said, "I can't tell you my name, Dr. Stillman. I hope you can forgive that."

I rather liked the feel of the man's hand, but I didn't like his keeping his name from me.

"I don't understand," I said.

" 'The Cell,' " Melanie explained. "This man's one of our leaders. You might recognize his name, and that wouldn't be good."

"Oh," I replied, feeling something like jealousy, feeling that I was being left out of some part of Melanie's world, something she didn't share with me. But then I had refused to join "the Cell," hadn't I? It was my own fault, wasn't it?

"Let's sit down, shall we. Anyone for coffee?" Melanie asked.

I nodded; the professor said, "I could stand a cup, if it isn't too much bother."

"No trouble at all," Melanie said. "It's already perked." None of this instant stuff for Melanie. "It'll just take a minute." And she swirled out of the room, the red skirt all but showing her thighs and panties. The professor followed her with his eyes, a lascivious look unknowingly on his face. I can't say that I blamed him: I probably had a similar expression on my own face. But I was jealous again. Dammit, Melanie was mine! Wasn't she . . . ?

The HV was playing, its cylindrical column now filled with the miniature head and shoulders of a man sitting before a desk, a newscaster whose face I recognized, but whose name I couldn't recall. I suppose that Melanie had had it on to fill in gaps in conversation while we waited to get down to whatever business she had called me here for.

The newscaster was saying something about the Euthagenics Lottery numbers for this week, and then his head and shoulders vanished and the HV tank showed something like the illuminated scoreboard used for athletic events and it was displaying a running series of eight-digit numbers that represented human lives, or, rather, the end of human lives. These were numbers that had been assigned to the old, the infirm, the diseased, the retarded, numbers such as those that would be assigned to me and to Melanie and to the professor when we each reached age sixty-two or in some other way lost our value to the Church/State.

Their "numbers had come up," those who were represented by that display, and they now had a week to conclude their affairs on this Earth and to report to a nearby Euthagenics Clinic, where they would be painlessly taken from this life and, hopefully, if they had found favor in the sight of God, go on to a better one. A land of abundance, of "milk and honey," perhaps awaited them —a land where they would forever bask in the radiance of the Lord God of Hosts and His Sons, in the glory of the Appointed One.

I turned my face away from the cylinder. The lottery always made me sick, but then . . . well, it was humane, and there were far too many people in this world. What else was there to do?

As I was about to say something to the professor, find some bit of small talk to take my mind off the lottery and the world it represented, the newscaster's face appeared again and I heard him say something about the current round of negotiations that was still going on in Geneva.

"There appears 'to be some progress on the British issue . . . " he was saying, "although full agreement to all terms of the Rector's demands has not yet been achieved. Ambassador Robinson has repeated the essence of the Rector's statements in saying, 'It is the duty of America to protect and aid our English-speaking cousins of the British Isles in this, their time of need.' Ambassador Robinson also stated that many of the surviving Britons have been converted to the W.E.C. and thus it is not only our historical duty but our religious

*duty to send additional missionaries and their support
units, composed mainly of nonmilitary units such as the
Lay Brothers of St. Wilson . . ."*

Non-military?

Another face flashed briefly into the cylinder, that of
the Secretary-General of the European commonwealth.

"In reply," the newscaster said, *"Secretary-General
Demarest states, as he has before, that he is in, quote,
philosophical agreement with the Rector, unquote,
although . . ."*

The professor was not looking at the HV now. He
was removing from his pocket a parcel wrapped in thin,
black plastic and then laying it on the coffee table,
chrome and glass like the ugly chair I'd decided to sit in.

"I hate this cloak-and-dagger business, Dr. Stillman,"
the professor said above the voice of the newscaster, "but
under the circumstances, it *is* necessary." He had a cul-
tured voice, this professor, maybe one with lingerings of a
rural Southern accent that he'd carefully wiped away, a
voice with great experience at speaking to large groups
of students, the voice of a man usually at ease with people—though I could sense that he was uneasy now. "I
believe that Melanie told you she wanted to show you
something."

"That's right."

"This is it." He unwrapped the parcel, carefully re-
folding the black plastic and laying it aside. It had contained a small, flat, unpretentious book with red buck-
ram binding.

"What is it?" I asked.

Before the professor could answer, Melanie came
back into the room with coffee, cream, and sugar on a
clear-plastic tray that she placed on the table near the
book, careful to avoid spilling coffee on it.

The professor's attention, momentarily distracted
from the book, switched for a few heartbeats to Melanie's bosom, unencumbered by a bra beneath the thin
fabric and low neckline of her blouse. I could almost see
the professor's pupils dilate.

"I'll turn that thing off," she said, gesturing toward
the HV and the newscaster, who was still speaking:

. . . *has confirmed reports that personnel of Station Beta have sighted what can be nothing other than major troop movements in the Schleswig–Holstein area of northern Germany. Several divisions seemed to be heading toward seaports where, recently, several large ships, capable of carrying troops and their equipment, have docked. Spokesmen for the White House have declared that if there are additional troop movements, and if these troops show indication of movement toward the British Isles, the United States will consider this sufficient provocation to terminate the meetings at Geneva and—"*

Melanie's hand touched a switch on a small plate on the table and the image within the HV cylinder collapsed into darkness and silence.

"Not another war!" she said, half to herself. Then she turned back toward the book on the table.

I did the same.

"This isn't the original," the professor said when he'd finally gotten his coffee, sweet and brown, and managed to switch his attention fully back to the book on the table. "It's a reproduction. But there are only six of them in the world, to the best of our knowledge. I can't reveal how we got this one. Too many lives are at stake there."

"What is it?" I asked as I sweetened and lightened my own coffee.

"Deborah Watstone's diary," Melanie said dramatically, her cup of black coffee halfway to her lips.

I stared into her dark eyes, questioning, and I must have looked startled, for the professor said, "You probably didn't even know she had kept one, did you?"

I shook my head. I may be—may have been—a historian, but the Appointed One had never been a specialty of mine. Still, if his mother had kept a diary, I should have known about it. Hell, the whole world should have known about it.

"She started it some ten months before Dover's birth," the professor said, "and continued it until he was about six years old. The Church/State considers it one of the most valuable relics concerning the Appointed One's early years."

"But there's a lot of it they'd never want revealed," Melanie said, then laughed. "They would never want the world to know that the great and holy Allen Howard Dover had toilet-training problems."

I smiled, nodded.

"Or that his father was a Jew," she added, her voice suddenly going cold.

"What?" I asked, startled again, almost spilling my coffee.

"Dover was a bastard in more ways than one," Melanie said, coldness still in her voice.

It was the professor's turn to look startled, then angry and embarrassed. His mouth opened, then snapped shut.

"Oh!" Melanie gasped, beginning to blush herself. I didn't mean it that way. I'm sorry, I truly am."

The professor gulped quickly, then raised his coffee cup to his mouth. He didn't yet speak.

"I didn't mean his being Jewish made him a bastard," Melanie interjected quickly, almost stumbling over her words. "I mean his being illegitimate."

"That's quite all right," the professor finally said, his voice firmly polite. "I suppose I'm overly sensitive about my ancestry."

"You have reason to be," Melanie said, then stammered. "I didn't say *that* right either, did I?"

The professor smiled. "I understand," he said, "and what you said is true." His eyes came back to me. "Robert Allen Dover was not the real father of the Appointed One. This is made clear in the diary. That's one of the reasons its very existence has been kept so secret."

"I can't believe it," I said, believing it.

"It's true," the professor repeated. "The man who fathered Deborah Watstone's baby was named Harry Greenbaum. He was a college student, a classmate of Deborah's. He was killed in a motorcycle accident shortly after the conception. I doubt that he ever knew he was to be a father."

"I'll be damned," I said.

"Probably," Melanie said, lightness in her voice now that her embarrassment was gone.

"I'd love to read that diary," I told the professor, giving Melanie a pseudocaustic glance.

"I wish I could allow that, Dr. Stillman; as an historian I'm sure you'd find much of interest in it. But I'm afraid that I can't let it out of my possession for even a few minutes. I'm sorry."

"I think I understand," I said. "If it has revelations like that in it."

"It does," the professor confirmed. "But we have more pressing business to attend to at the moment, don't we, Dr. Stillman?" A coldness shot through me. "Melanie has outlined what we'd like you to do for us." It wasn't a question.

I slowly nodded, grunted.

He opened the book to a place that had been marked with a purple ribbon, and began to read: " 'September 23, 1971. A.M. This morning I cut classes. I didn't feel too well. Upset stomach or something. What a bummer! Probably one of those virus-things that're going around.' Morning sickness," the professor interjected. "No doubt about it. She was already pregnant then. She was on contraceptive pills at the time, but this was one of those rare cases where they didn't work."

"Her pregnancy's one of the reasons we chose that date," Melanie added. "We have to be certain of getting *him*."

The professor read again: " 'Got to feeling better around nine, but didn't want to go to class. Remembered that I'd told Harry'—that's the child's father, Greenbaum—'that I'd meet him under Goethe's statue in Lincoln Park at 10 A.M. Better go now. I'll take my psych book and study for that exam tomorrow while I wait. Harry's a cool dude, but he's always late.

" 'Later. Harry didn't show up. Wonder what happened? Dammit! I just waited around there in that freaking park all morning for him. He'd better have a good excuse. Just sitting there all by my lonesome, not even anyone to rap with and—' "

He broke off his reading, turned to look at me.

"Ten-thirty A.M., Thursday, September 23, 1971,"

he said. "That's the perfect time; and Lincoln Park, under the statue of Goethe, is the perfect place."

"You can pull the cage in there," Melanie said, a fierceness to her voice, "kill her, and be gone before anyone even sees you."

"I will be just another unsolved murder," the professor said. "Chicago had a lot of them then, almost as many as today."

"But . . . I'm not a cold-blooded killer, and even if we knew it could be done, if the laws of chronal travel would permit it, I couldn't just—"

"Do you realize what this could mean, Stillman?" The professor was as fierce as Melanie, maybe more so, maybe a fanatic out to complete a holy quest through the agency of another person. "You have the power to rid the world of the Appointed One, to see that he was never born. Stillman, don't you see, don't you understand? You could be the *real* saviour of mankind."

It was crazy. He was crazy. Melanie was crazy. The whole damned world was crazy. Except me . . . ?

Yet, maybe there was some sanity there, maybe the idea wasn't as wild as it seemed at first. Nobody *knew* it couldn't be done.

"But . . ." I stammered, stalling, trying to think straight.

"But, hell, man! You've got to do it! It's got to be done!"

"Maybe it can't be done!" I said frantically, yet I was thinking: "Maybe it can . . ."

"Even if it can't, it must be attempted," the professor insisted, his eyes ablaze with mission.

"I—I don't know," I said. I had to have time to think, to consider, to try to think this thing out rationally.

"Well," he snapped, looking away from me in disgust, "that's the story." When he turned back toward me his eyes again looked like those of a sane man and the fury was gone from his voice. "It's up to you, Melanie. You convince him." He rose, carefully rewrapped the diary and put it back into his coat pocket. Looking at Melanie, he said, "I'll talk with you tomorrow." And then to me, "Think about it, Stillman." His voice was quiet, calm, but the wildness flickered back into his eyes again for a moment.

The man scared me. Maybe Melanie did too. Yet, perhaps there was more sanity than insanity behind the words they had spoken. Could I really . . .

Whether he spent the night somewhere in the apartment building, I don't know, or, if he left, how he managed to survive a passage through Chicago's dark streets, but he was gone and we were alone, Melanie and I. She got me a drink and then spent the rest of the night, in her own special ways, trying to convince me to kill the mother of the Appointed One before he was ever born.

The professor had said *I* could be the real saviour of mankind. It was crazy, yet . . .

7

The morning after my nightmares, weak, tired and depressed, I climbed to the top of the giant's stairs again to crouch among the oaks and the snow and the wind, chilled to my bones. Without the binoculars I saw no signs of animal life, save for a single bird flying high some great distance away. A big bird of prey, I thought, as it flew into the distant sky, swooping to become a speck above remote trees and then vanishing.

When I touched the twin barrels of the telescopic instrument, I could feel the cold metal even through the gloves I wore. Slowly, for some reason feeling a great reluctance to do so, I raised the glasses to my eyes, felt the cold bite of their metal and glass against the flesh of my cheeks, and then looked down into the shallow valley. I saw . . . a second chronalcage, untouched by the snow, sitting bright and shiny a dozen meters from mine, slightly to the north. Two men were standing outside it, both wrapped in heavy parkas. One of them was pointing in the direction of the stony hills where I was hidden. The other was loading a rifle.

I didn't know whether to feel elation or fear. Maybe I felt both. They *had* come back; they were here. But for me to get to their cage, to get to it and use it—though I wasn't certain what I'd do when I got there—I would have to fight, maybe kill. I didn't want to, but . . .

For an hour or more I sat on the ridge, huddled among the twisted trees, trying to make myself invisible, though I knew it would have been a difficult thing for them to see me even if they'd known where to look. I brooded over what I had thought I would do if they actually came after me, as they had now. The world around me was cold and quiet, terribly silent. The men in the valley were too far away for their sounds to reach me, and there appeared to be nothing nearer, save the sometime presence of the wind, and now even it had died. I longed to hear its whistle through the branches of the gnarled oak.

Oh, it wasn't as if I'd never fired a shot in anger or had never had one fired at me. I'd killed, and that more than once, back during the Sino-Indian War, *but that had been war*; and even though I hadn't all too well liked the government that sent me into that war—it was during Livingston's administration, before the establishment of the Rectorship—I had felt that the war was justified.

But then maybe this was war, too, I tried to tell myself. Of a different sort. Maybe I was going to be firing the first shots of a civil war that would one day set my country free from the theocratic tyranny that ruled it— but maybe I was still a little feverish then; some of my ideas were rather grandiose. Or maybe I'd be firing the last shots; some of my thoughts were less than grandiose.

The two men—I couldn't hope to recognize their faces at that distance, even if they hadn't been covered with scarves and snow goggles—moved about the damaged cage for a while, cleaning the snow off it, and noting not only the damage but, discovering that the supply and equipment lockers were almost empty, that everything a person might need in this climate had been taken. They then sat down on a tarp they had spread over a flat area of snow, set up a camp stove like the one I used, and prepared themselves coffee and a hot meal.

I could smell the aroma of that coffee! And I had the idea that they had come downtime with provisions other than the nearly unpalatable emergency rations that had barely kept me going. While they ate and drank their coffee, they kept looking in my general direction, toward the hills where they must have figured, as I had, that there would be caves and shelter.

When the cold finally got to be too much for me, I went back to the cave. My feeble fire had all but burned out in my absence, and suddenly I began to wonder if they had seen smoke from it. It hadn't been smoking much, but then it would not have taken much smoke to be visible a long way against a sky that was clear and clean, blue and cloudless, since the blizzard had blown itself out. I didn't dare pour water on the fire—that would make too much smoke—so I just kicked it apart and one by one carefully snuffed out the embers. That left me with only the smokeless camp stove for heat, but it was enough.

I warmed my hands over the stove and tried to think carefully. Okay, I told myself, they've come back, two of them, and they have a workable cage. Am I really going to do something about it?

I hadn't been a coward in India. My Bronze Star was proof of that, wasn't it? But, well, I was older now, not so far from forty that I couldn't anticipate how I would feel when that birthday came around. Also, I was more cautious and I didn't want to chance the kind of risks I'd taken as a fuzzy-faced kid when they'd awarded me that temporary commission. *Then,* all the regular officers of the company were lying dead somewhere behind us. But, on the other hand, my life was at stake here, too.

I had three choices, I told myself, ticking them off on my fingers in the cave's semidarkness. Maybe I could just hide here, stay out of their sight until they get tired of looking for me, and let them go back uptime empty-handed—which also meant that I would probably die here before winter was out. Or, I could let them find me, surrender to them, and let them take me back to stand trial before a Proctor's court—and that was just as certain death as freezing and starvation. Or—or I could fight them for the cage and then maybe go on and do what I'd finally promised Melanie I would do; at least I stood a chance of coming out of *that* alive. I kept telling myself I did.

I was scared; maybe I'd have been scared shitless if I still hadn't had diarrhea. I'll admit that. But I was even more scared of the alternatives I saw. I didn't have much choice but to go after that chrónalcage, and hope.

I wasn't a damned bit hungry, but I knew that I was still too weak; that I needed all the energy I could muster. I realized that putting things off wouldn't help either, so I forced myself to eat a packet of high-protein rations, washed it down with water, and wished, for the first time in days, that I had a cigarette or a drink of something a lot stronger than water. Preferably both. I thought of a little speakeasy in Cicero where I could have gotten both, but that was a hell of a long way off . . .

Then, shaking as much from nerves as from cold, I checked the Weatherby 8.5mm and the needle pistol. I paused to turn off the camp stove, thinking that I would probably never need it again, no matter what happened, and wondered whether the bear would finally come back to the cave when I was gone. He was welcome to it.

Pulling on my snow goggles, I stepped into my snowshoes, tested the straps, set out.

I climbed the stairs again and looked down into the valley through the binoculars: only one man was visible near the two cages. Whether the other man was inside one of the cages where I couldn't see him, or whether he'd left, I didn't know. I decided to wait a while to see if I could spot him.

A chill wind began to blow out of the north again, rising until it began to sing and moan in the oak branches above me—a song timeless and agonized, I thought. On the horizon to the north and east, above the distant, dark trees, clouds began to form and I wondered if another blizzard was coming. I didn't expect to be around long enough to find out.

After sitting in that wind on the ledge for something close to thirty minutes, I saw no sign of the second man. And if I still couldn't see him from where I was, that must mean he had left the cages, must be coming into the stones and the foothills below me, and was somewhere not too far away, maybe searching each limestone cave and cavity as he came to it. That could take a while, as I knew, but it probably wouldn't take him much longer to find my cave than it had taken me the first time. By now he might have been searching for—how long? An hour? An hour and a half? That gave me sixty, maybe ninety minutes, no more, before he found me, or at least found my cave, formerly Mr. Bear's.

Okay, I said to myself.

Swallowing a lump in my throat that tried to strangle me, I climbed down off the ledge and then struck out northeast in a line perpendicular to that which the Proctor or blueshirt or whatever he was must be taking. I figured I could go that way until I was in the hills north of the cages, then head straight south. I would come up on the blind side, if you could call it that, hidden and sheltered by the growth of trees closest to the clearing where the two time vehicles sat. Then . . .

Well, then, as soon as I was close enough, I would wound or kill the man who was still at the cages and try to get the hell out of there, uptime, before the second man came back.

Maybe that wasn't much of a plan, but then was there anything better?

An hour or better later, I was close enough to see the two cages clearly through the trees, the damaged one that had brought me here and the good one that had brought my two pursuers, and I spotted the man who knelt between them, warming himself before the camp stove, his goggles off, the scarf removed from his face and a big, ugly, military-looking rifle across his knees.

I pulled my binoculars out of their case, pressed them against the plastic lenses of my goggles, and recognized the man who knelt by the stove: Dr. Welles Kennedy, Jerry Maughton's chief assistant, and a man I could have called my friend.

"Dammit!" I muttered to myself. "Dammit! Dammit!" Why couldn't they have sent someone else? Why Welles of all people? Why not someone I didn't like, or at least didn't know?

But I knew why they had sent Welles. It was simple. Of all the chronalnauts, Welles Kennedy was the most experienced, and he was the one with the best technical background. Unlike most of us, he wasn't a professional historian. His degrees were in electrophysics. He had been working in chronal theory for better than a decade. History was just his hobby, or had been before he'd become Chief Chronalnaut.

Now what the hell was I going to do?

Shoot down Welles Kennedy in cold blood?

Maybe I didn't always agree with Welles in every respect. There were some quirks to his personality that sometimes rubbed me the wrong way, but isn't that so with most people, even the ones you like best? And he was a faithful church member and would never have considered heresy. He probably hated me now that he knew I was a certified heretic, had been associated with members of "the Cell." But, dammit! I had shared a few bottles of wine with Welles—when I could get it—and he wasn't *that* strong a Doverite, and I'd won a few poker pots from him. Hell, you don't just casually shoot down a man you know like that. *I* don't.

And even though Welles would dislike, despise my heresy, maybe he wouldn't shoot me down either . . . maybe. Perhaps I could talk to him. Maybe I could . . .

He wasn't like that damned blueshirt Carl Fulford, for example. Sometimes I believed that Fulford and his kind had been manufactured in a laboratory and programmed to search out and destroy all those without total allegiance to the World Ecumenical Church.

I got up off my knees and put my binoculars away and took off my goggles and scarf so he would be able to recognize me. I snapped the safety back on my rifle, but I didn't sling it over my shoulder by its strap; I kept it loose in my hand, like a casual hunter coming back to camp after a day of unsuccessful plodding through the woods after game that wasn't there.

Then I came out of the trees into the clearing and headed toward the two cages.

I was still a couple of dozen meters away when Welles saw me, came to his feet with a grunt I could hear that far away, and brought up his rifle.

"Welles," I called, "it's me, Gene Stillman."

"I know it," he called back. "Come on slow, Gene. And drop that rifle."

"Let me keep it, Welles. I'm not going to use it."

"Throw it away, Gene." Then, releasing his grip on the rifle's forearm, but not letting the barrel waver from me, he reached with his free hand to unclip a small, rectangular device from his parka's belt. Drawing it near his mouth and keying it with his thumb, I heard him say, "Brother Fulford, Gene Stillman's down here at the cages."

I couldn't hear "Brother" Fulford's reply, but I could hear Welles say back to him, "Yes, I understand. I'll do as you say." Then, after a pause, "Yes, Brother Fulford, I do understand the seriousness of Gene's crimes."

While he talked, and then while he clipped the little transceiver back on his belt, I continued to walk toward him, no faster than I had before, no slower, the 8.5mm Magnum still in my hand, heavy and cold.

But I wasn't as calm as I might have looked to Welles. I was beginning to get worried, seriously worried. It seemed Welles was more of a fanatic than I had thought. Or maybe he was scared, too, scared not to do what Fulford expected of him. I could understand that.

"Gene, you'd better put that rifle down," he said when I'd crossed half the distance to him. "Please, Gene, for God's sake, don't make me shoot you!"

"Then don't shoot, Welles. I don't want to fight you." Maybe my voice sounded calm. I hoped it did. But I didn't feel as if it did.

"I've got orders, Gene. You're a public enemy now. A heretic. You know that. And . . . Gene, the order is to shoot you on sight if you offer any resistance."

"Can't we talk, Welles?"

My mouth was dry and empty, no saliva at all, yet tasting of hot bronze as if the fillings of my teeth were being heated up by some kind of radio transmission. My knees felt as if they were made of ice that was melting under a warm summer sun, not the cold, distant orb that now hung heatlessly in the middle of the sky.

"There's nothing to talk about. Just drop that rifle and do as I say. Fulford's on his way back here."

"You know what they'll do to me if you take me back, don't you, Welles?"

"I know, Gene, better than you might think. But you brought all that on yourself. You should have known better."

"But I'm no criminal. I haven't really done anything wrong."

I was still walking toward him, wondering how long my legs would last, and if I could really walk as far as he was from me.

"They say you're a criminal."

"I'm not."

"Stop, Gene. Oh, for God's sake, stop!" He paused, then spoke quickly again. "You've been sick, haven't you, Gene?"

"What do you mean?" I broke stride for a moment.

"You've been sick, vomiting and diarrhea and all. I know. We've all been sick, all of us."

"So?"

"We've got something, *all* of us. We don't know exactly what is sweeping Chicago. The whole city's got it, maybe the whole nation."

"What're you getting at?"

"You're going to need a doctor, inoculation, treatment, or—"

"Or what?"

I began to walk again, moving slowly toward him.

"Just believe me, you need medical help, the same as all of us."

"Can't you tell me more?"

"No."

"Come on, Welles, I just want—"

Welles lowered the rifle barrel, now gripping the weapon with both hands, and fired. A 7mm slug dug into the snow, kicking up a small spray of loose whiteness a meter or so to my left. The report of the weapon was unnaturally loud in the still landscape, more like a cannon than a rifle. Birds fluttered into the air from the trees behind me, circling upward and then looking down at us to see what all the commotion was about. I doubt they understood.

"I mean it, Gene," Welles called to me over the narrowing distance.

Maybe he did, I thought. Maybe he really did mean it.

"So do I," I called back to him.

He fired again, close but still at a safe distance.

The wary birds continued to circle. Echos reverberated from distant hills.

"I'll put the next one in your leg, Gene."

I thought he meant it but found I couldn't believe it. Then it was happening.

The rifle in Welles' hands fired again and made a tremendous racket that seemed somehow far louder than the two shots before, and then someone I couldn't see hit my left shin with a baseball bat and my leg went out from under me, all shattered and squashy. I pitched headlong into the snow.

Instinct, conditioned reflex, something, took over and all of the sudden I wasn't in a Pleistocene forest any longer, but somewhere in India—Rajpur, was it?—and Welles Kennedy wasn't there at all, only a bunch of khaki-clad Imperial Chinese, and they were trying to overrun the position that had cost half my company and I was wounded, maybe bleeding to death. But, by damn, they weren't going to get this little piece of earth back again!

Somehow I got the rifle out from under me and clicked off the safety and was pulling the trigger before Welles realized what I was doing.

My first slug took him just above the belt of his parka, and as he was pitching backward from the shock of it, my second took him high in the chest, in the middle of his breastbone, I think. The next two shots missed him altogether, but that didn't matter. The second one had killed him if the first hadn't.

I tried to get up, forgetting that my left leg didn't have much bone left in it between the knee and the ankle, and fell down again. Then I started crawling, leaving a wide, red trail behind me in the white snow, and I started to cry because I realized that it was Welles Kennedy I had just shot, and not some Imperial gooker.

Even before I got to him I knew he was dead, and I was sorry as hell that I'd killed him. I should have just wounded him like he'd done to me. But there hadn't been time and I hadn't been thinking very well and—

And I remembered that he had radioed Fulford. The blue-shirted Deacon Carl Fulford was coming back to the cages and *he* damned sure wasn't likely to consider me his friend.

The undamaged chronalcage was about a thousand kilometers from me, though if you had measured it you might have thought it was only a couple of meters or so. It took me the better part of the next twenty years to get to it, bleeding all over everything I got near and dragging behind me a lump of red-colored ice that looked something like a human leg, but not much.

I'm not certain to this day how I ever got to the cage, nor how I got my snowshoes off and dragged myself up into the seat, nor how I managed to get the controls working. I had been weak enough before and was getting weaker and weaker by the second now, and my head did not seem to want to stay attached to my body, wanted to go floating off like a child's helium-filled balloon. Yet I managed to keep in mind that if Carl Fulford got me I was a dead man, and I'd better get into that cage and get it somewhere outtime from here in one damned big hurry.

As I slumped forward in the bucket seat, held in place by belts I didn't remember fastening, I tried to remember the date and the place Melanie had given me, assigned to me, the time/place of *his* proposed execution.

My head swam. I thought I was going to faint. Maybe I did, momentarily. What was the mission I was to accomplish? I found myself asking. What the hell was the destination? What was I supposed to do now?

The place—the place was Chicago. I was certain of that, but the date didn't come to me too well. Sometime in late summer or autumn, wasn't it? September? And the year? 1971? Or was it 1871? Couldn't have been 2071. Couldn't go uptime to then. Oh, dammit, I just couldn't remember! But I *had* to remember. I had to go there and do something. I'd known what it was just a moment ago. I had promised Melanie that I would go there and I wasn't about to break my promise to her.

Then I looked up and saw someone running awkwardly across the snow on snowshoes, and he had a rifle just like the one Welles had had and he was yelling something I couldn't understand, though I knew I wouldn't like it if I could make it out.

What year? Oh, dammit, what year was it supposed to be?

I started trying to set up some of the controls before me, and found that the chronalcage hadn't been totally shut down, just put into standby. It wouldn't take much to get it going, if I could just remember when/where I was supposed to go.

I could hear Carl Fulford's voice better now, and he was yelling something like, "Stop it right there, Stillman!" He was firing at me with his rifle, bullets whizzing between the bars of the cage, but not close enough to anything so valuable that he was likely to damage and make this cage as useless for him as the other one was.

"Go to hell, Fulford!" someone was saying, using my voice, and then that someone—who? I found myself wondering—was using my numb and clumsy fingers to flip the last switches of the controls that would throw the return systems of the cage uptime, homing like a mechanical pigeon toward her time of origin or whatever chronal destination he may have unknowingly keyed into it. The whine of chronal displacement surrounded me, rose to a scream, and then suddenly twinned itself and there were two sets of sounds where there should have only been one.

Carl Fulford stopped in the snow, still holding his rifle toward me, but there was a look of astonishment on his face and he suddenly began to turn. With my eyes, I followed him.

Hallucination, I thought: we're both having the same hallucination. For there, midway between the two cages, the one I was in now, which had been Welles' and Fulford's, and the one that had been mine, was a third chronalcage, materializing out of time with that crazy whine. And sitting inside the chronalcage, a gun in his hands, was a man in some fantastic garb that I couldn't quite place but figured must be out of the nineteenth century—frock coat, porkpie hat, and bearded face—all covered with soot, and seared as if he'd just been in some terrible fire. I thought I should be able to recognize the man, but I couldn't, and wondered who the hell he was and what the hell he was doing *here*.

Fulford had turned and was bringing his rifle to bear on him, but the bearded man in the crazy clothes fired his own carbine and missed Fulford, whose own rifle went BOOM! amid the snow and blood and—

I flipped some more switches. I didn't feel like staying around to find out what happened. Now I could . . .

Fulford had turned back to me again and was bringing up his smoking rifle.

Then something hit me and I didn't know whether it was a bullet from Fulford's rifle or the displacement effect, and didn't much care right then. I went down into a deep, dark pit that didn't seem at all unpleasant at the time.

8

I have no clear memories of the next twenty-four hours. I say it was twenty-four hours because my watch, when I was next able to look at it clearly, showed that more than a full day had elapsed by its reckoning—although many centuries had gone by if other means of measuring time are used. During that time, day or millennia, some portion of my mind must have been working: something below the level of consciousness had enabled me to do some of the things I did. How I was able to do that much, I wasn't sure.

And then, some of the things I did, I couldn't possibly have done or have known how to do . . .

I seemed to have a vague memory of the cage coming out of time for a moment, settling into the "real" world that exists and can be measured (recorded in terms of calendars and maps). A street, dark and empty, illuminated poorly by remote, flickering points of light, garish, dim lights that cast long shadows. A horse somewhere —I'm certain the sound was that of a horse, though I couldn't recall ever having seen a live one outside a zoo —whinnied, struck the earth with its hard hooves. Other sounds I still can't place. An odor in the air that suggested water, and something else—faint, from some remote place, vile and sickening, a smell of death and decay.

The memory is vague and brief, but at the end of it I seem to see a figure coming toward me, a man dressed in old-fashioned clothing, a man with a beard, a pronounced limp, a cane assisting him to walk, coming up to the cage without surprise. Then the memory fades.

Somehow, as I was bleeding in the cold Pleistocene, I had keyed chronal references into the cage's systems and then moved uptime as Carl Fulford fired his rifle at someone else and then me. And while in the stream of non-time, moving through time days-per-second, years-per-minute, I seemed to have keyed in geo references, perhaps two sets of geo references, for the city of Chicago, circa 1871 A.D.

Then the cage appeared to have done what it had been told to do without any more help from me.

During another stage of semiconsciousness I'd somehow moved to one of the cage's supply lockers, the one that held the medical supplies, and injected myself with drugs to fight the pain and the loss of blood and halt any incipient infection, and then splinted and bandaged my shattered leg. Later, I found one of the empty ampoules on the deck.

How I did this, I didn't know, but I thought that I must have done it. There hadn't been anyone else to help me. Had there?

A feverish dream, another memory, something came into my mind, something relating to a warm darkness, the smell of fresh air, and growing things, and gentle hands touching my shattered leg, administering to me. But it must have been a dream, I thought.

And again I lapsed into unconsciousness.

My first waking impression, if I can say I was truly awake, was a sense of damp and stale air, a musty odor, a feeling of spiderwebs and rats and rotting wood and paper, a darkness that was not entirely complete, for pale, washed-out yellow light crept into the great, empty hollowness of the building in places around closed doors and boarded up windows.

I didn't know it at the time, and only later discovered that I was in an abandoned warehouse off South Clark Street, Chicago, in a bustling section of the burgeoning city where the building had been constructed, used for a while, and then abandoned when its owner went bankrupt. Exactly why it wasn't being used, I never really learned, though I later suspected that its ownership was in some dispute and tied up in law courts—some question of property rights. But I really don't know. But it was there, empty and unused by anyone at that time and for some months later, right up until . . . Exactly how I'd gotten *there*, to such an ideal location, was another question altogether.

When I tried to move, I found my body was so weak that I doubted I would be able to stand on my one good leg. My hands would not cooperate with me when I tried to unfasten the catches of the belts that held me, but after long and clumsy effort I managed to get them loose.

I stood.

The warehouse moved around me, spinning and tilting at crazy angles, refusing to remain in place as any reasonable geo location should.

For a moment I wondered what had become of my rifle. I couldn't remember having it after I'd shot Welles. The memory of shooting down a man who had been my friend came back to me in a painful, sickening rush. I'd left the rifle somewhere back in the bloody snow, in another world. But I'd had a needle pistol in my parka, hadn't I? But I wasn't wearig the parka any longer. It was too hot for that, far too hot, and where I'd left it I didn't know; if there were another needler or rifle back in the supply lockers of this cage—well, that was just too damned much trouble. Too damned far.

I wasn't going in that direction, was I?

I stumbled, hobbled, hopped across the undulating deck to the cage's bars, away from the lockers. In a moment I was grasping the bars in my hands, hoping that the building would cease its spinning around me. It slowed some, but not enough, not nearly enough.

I had a great dryness in my throat and mouth, but water was a long, long way from me, back on the other side of the seat, back near the lockers and the weapons they must hold as well, and I still didn't want to go back that way.

Yet which way did I want to go?

I wasn't really certain. But like a moth I felt drawn toward the pale light that filtered through the chinks in the boards over the windows and doors. I had to go there, had to get out, out of the cage and out of the building, out into the world where there were things that were still alive, where it wasn't cold and where there were no snow and no cave bears and no blood-lusting Carl Fulford, Proctors, or blue-shirted Lay Brothers accusing me of heresy. I wanted to be out in a world where there were people, alive and free, in a world as it was before Dover had turned everything upside down. I had to get out, *out . . .* OUT!

I knew I needed medical attention, the services of a real doctor. Somehow I had done everything I could for myself, but the pain warned me that wasn't enough. I needed more help and rest and the skills of a physician to heal the throbbing, ugly, twisted thing that had once been my leg.

Sweat dripped from me, soaking my clothes. I had already realized that by some means I'd removed my cold-weather clothing, but I was still too hot. I think I realized that the stale air in the old, decaying building wasn't really that hot, that a lot of the heat was coming from inside me, but it made no difference. I was still too hot, but felt too weak to pull off my gray uniform jacket. I lowered myself between the cage's bars, my good right leg toward the littered floor in the dim light, my booted foot touching it.

Moving slowly, carefully, I found that I could hobble after a fashion, my right leg supporting most of my weight. The splints were sturdy enough for me to put a little weight on my left leg. It didn't hurt now, but there were sensations from it, dull and unrecognizable, and I thought I would have felt pain, maybe terrible pain, if I hadn't been so drugged.

I moved.

At a distance from me that I felt could be no less than a thousand kilometers there appeared to be a door, at least a rectangular framework of light. That was *out*. I moved toward it.

The first time I fell, I lost consciousness, then again alternated between vague awareness of what I was doing and complete ignorance. During those periods I crawled, hobbled, stumbled, dragged myself across the warehouse's dirty floor, the eight or nine meters from the cage to the door.

When I awoke again, I thought Melanie had been here with me, telling me what a coward I had been to run off like that, even though she'd screamed for me to flee. I should have stayed with her, she seemed to have said, defended her against the MinSec Proctors and their tortures for heresy. I asked her what I could have done to help her or myself, but she hadn't answered, save to look at me with an expression that filled me with shame and guilt.

Melanie wasn't here at all; she never had been. I was sitting alone on the floor, leaning against the door that had been my destination. My leg was throbbing, but in a way that brought me no pain and less concern than it probably should have.

Still, I'd gotten to the door, I told myself. The world was just outside it. And wasn't I supposed to go someplace? Meet someone? The vision of Melanie had reminded me of the promise I'd made to her, the destination that she and a man whom I'd called "the professor" had given me. Lincoln Park, wasn't it? And to meet . . . to see . . . a girl. Someone named Deborah Watstone. Debbie Watstone . . . Now, there was something very important in that name, but I didn't seem to know what it was.

I rose to my feet—my foot—and leaned against the door only to find that it was supposed to open inward, but was nailed shut, two boards crossing it, nailed to the doorframe.

The wood was dry-rotted and the nails rusty. Only a little effort would be required to pry them, one and then the other, away. Little effort, did I say? It took every ounce of strength I had to do, and when I'd completed the job and the two boards lay on the dusty floor, I collapsed in heaving dizziness and allowed my head to swim away as it would, a long way across a groggy lake of near-unconsciousness.

I was sick, far sicker than I'd been back there in the cave, sicker than I ever thought a man could be and still be able to function in any fashion at all. Was it just the wound in my leg and the loss of blood, I wondered during a period more lucid than most, or had the sickness that I'd had back in the cave come over me again as well? Did I have some terrible disease that was going to kill me even though Welles Kennedy and Carl Fulford hadn't been able to? Was that what Welles had been talking about back there, back then?

With weak fingers gripping the wooden framework of the door, I hauled myself up again and cast one glance back into the dark, shadowy interior of the great, empty building and at first I couldn't see the chronalcage. Had it gone off without me, leaping uptime, back into the time/world of Melanie and the Proctors? Then my eyes adjusted, focused enough that I could see it and knew that it was still there. It would be waiting for me when I came back to it. *If* I came back to it.

I fumbled the door open.

The light from the world outside nearly blinded me as I stumbled into it, breathing air that couldn't possibly have been as clean and fresh and pure as I thought it smelled. For a long while I stood just outside the doorway, my lungs heaving in air, gasping for breath that I hoped would clear my head but didn't as much as I wanted it to.

When my eyes had adjusted to the sunlight, I could see that I was at the end of an alley, on three sides of me wooden walls, faded, peeling of paint. The alley was littered with trash and debris. The ground under my feet was soft and muddy, as if there had been a recent rain. Maybe that's why the air had seemed so clean.

At the end of the alley, with eyes that didn't want to focus on anything any distance away, I could make out a street, unpaved and as muddy as the alley, plank boards for sidewalks, buildings mostly wooden, a tree or two, moving figures that must have been people.

People.

I stumbled forward again.

I fell.

I crawled.

I got to my feet again.

And I fell again, splashing mud and filth across clothing that was already soiled and torn.

After a geological eon I reached the end of the alley, wavered on my feet, tried to call out to someone, anyone, to help me, but the words wouldn't come into my mouth and I fell again, across muddy sidewalk planking and onto the edge of the street.

For a long time I lay there, unable to move, wondering why someone didn't come to help me.

I could hear, and now and again I could open my eyes, and through these senses, as unreliable as they seemed to be now, I perceived something of this world.

9

Someone—don't ask me who; I don't recall—once said that the past is a different place; they don't do things there the way we do.

Any historian should know this, and none better than one who is also a chronalnaut.

The city is a randomness, a mindless patchwork craziness of structures put together without apparent plan, a brick building here, a wooden one there, raw and unpainted, weathered by sun and rain and wind, tilting at an improbable angle. Here a horse comes down the muddy street, pulling an open carriage, pauses in its slow walk to drop dung into the mud. No one notices. No one cares. A man pauses, hacks and spits brown juices between the planking of the sidewalk, goes on as well.

Across the muddy street is a brick building with broad glass windows behind which are displayed items of antique, baroque furniture: chairs, sofas, beds, all old-fashioned-looking, quaint to my eyes, something out of a romantic novel or an HV costume epic. And beside the furniture store is a tumbledown thing hardly more than a shanty, which displays a faded, hand-lettered sign reading *Clark Street Social Club,* GENTS BARROOM *Ladies Welcome.* Before it stands a tattered, slovenly crew chewing something—tobacco?—and spitting a brown juice between their teeth, into the street. I think one of them might be looking in my direction, but I'm not certain. If he sees me, he doesn't care that I'm sick, weak, maybe dying. No one cares.

Along the planks, avoiding the men before the barroom, walks a group of men and women, their heads held high to avoid looking down at the filth through which they walk. The men are dressed in tall silk hats and long, double-breasted coats named, if I remember correctly, after Prince Albert. Their shoes are shiny where mud hasn't splattered them; but the tips of their elegant walking sticks are encrusted with it. They wear beards and waxed mustaches and billowing sideburns. I'm certain they're wealthy.

And the women, their garments are fantastic—even for someone who is supposed to be familiar with their era—or would seem fantastic if I were rational enough to think clearly. Behind, they are built-up with the great frameworks of bustles, and trail material after them like the cabooses of a railroad train, fifteen or eighteen inches of artificial rear end. In this they hardly look human, these women. And spilling down from these bustles, curled and bowed and folded and finally trailing in the mud on the planking sidewalk, are long skirts of silk and other fine fabrics, covered with embroidered flowery decorations. They carry parasols to shield their fine complexions from the sun and wear upon their heads ridiculous constructions that may be hats. Arm in arm they walk with their elegant men, and look away from both the barroom stalwarts and the sick man in the gutter, who is now too weak to call out to them for help.

Though the sun is shining out of a cloudless sky and I am still sweating as profusely as before, there is a cooling wind in the street, blowing from the east, from off the lake, I think, for I can remember where Lake Michigan is—or had been, back before it was filled. I chill and I shiver in the mud and try to put my arms under me so that I can rise, but I find that I no longer have the strength to do that.

I lie there, barely able to move.

I hear a voice, a woman's voice, I think, speaking English with what seems to me to be an accent, a remote strangeness to me that is somehow right and fitting in this time/place. "Isn't that disgraceful? Drunk in the streets at ten o'clock in the morning."

"Best to ignore such things, my dear," a man's voice says from the same general direction, behind and above. His voice too has that strange though proper accent. "Above all things, I detest a public drunk!"

"Those are Mr. Abernathy's—the temperance lecturer—those are his very words."

Planks clatter as feet tread them.

"The man should be arrested," the woman's voice says.

"If I set eyes on a policeman, I'll tell him, dear."

"I wish you would, George."

The clattering moves away from me, the people move on. They haven't even paused to look at me.

A small boy jeers.

A passerby accidentally splashes mud in my eyes. I can't wipe it away.

A carriage clatters by, drawn by two horses, one black, one white.

"Isaac, stop for a moment!"

The voice seems to come from the carriage, though I'm paying it no more attention than I am anything else. I can't get up. I can barely move. Probably I'm dying.

"Father!" a female voice says, a younger voice than the one before.

"Give me just a moment," the man's voice is saying.

"It's just another drunk," the young woman's voice says from the carriage.

"Are you certain?" The man's voice is coming nearer.

I try to move my head, to raise my hand to show them that there is some consciousness, some awareness within me, that I'm not dead, nor dead drunk.

Feet squelch in the mud near me. I can see boots or shoes, mud-covered now, gray trousers with a sharp crease. They pause.

The man's voice, deep and somehow very fatherly, speaks near me. "Are you ill, my man?" he asks.

I try to speak. I only grunt.

I feel a hand touching me, brushing the mud from my left leg, numb and throbbing, pulling away the loose fabric of my trousers where it is torn and cut.

"This man is injured," the voice says. "Isaac, come assist me."

"Father!"

"This man needs my help, Sharon."

Then hands are going under me, lifting me, cradling me, carrying me to the open carriage. For a few moments I'm able to get my eyes open and look up into the faces of the two men who have stopped to help me. One is young and black and almost beardless, an open face, a gentle one, I think. Yet I can't help but feel a tensing of fear: has he come to harm me? The other is older and white and he wears a beard that's more white than brown. A kindness and a sympathy shine in his eyes, and I think for a moment that maybe he's God, the way I imagined God when I was a small child.

Then I pass again into unconsciousness.

I'm lying in a bed and my torn and dirty clothing has been removed and I'm dressed in some loose-fitting garment of subdued colors. The room is large and high-ceilinged; flowery wallpaper covers the walls and curtains have been drawn across the windows. Jets of gas burn from fittings on the wall, giving the room a feeble illumination. That's all the light I need.

A woman as black as the young man who had assisted me stands near my bed looking down at me. There is no animosity in her face, no hatred of the whites who had enslaved her race; none that I can see, at least.

She is young, twenty or twenty-one; her hair is pulled back and piled on top of her head and is covered with a white net. She is quite pretty. She wears a dark dress and a white apron. In her hands she carries a small tray on which sit two glasses and a vial of some yellow liquid. There's a spoon, too, I think.

When she sees that I've come to, her eyes widen and she calls out, "Docta English. He awake."

The gray-haired, bearded man comes in and stands

on one side of the bed, dressed in a white smock that re-
minds me of those worn at the Project, except that his
does not carry the sundial of the Chronal Corps. He is
wearing rimless glasses and there's a pipe in his mouth,
charged with tobacco heavy with aroma. He puffs on
the pipe and smoke billows from its bowl, his mouth, his
nostrils. I suspect that tobacco isn't illegal here-and-
now.

To the other side of the bed comes a young white
woman, a little older than the black girl, but maybe not
yet Melanie's age. She has auburn hair and blue eyes
and dimples in her cheeks and full breasts and a narrow
waist and is dressed in a colorful dress that reaches the
floor. She's fairer than Melanie, more plump, but she *is*
very pretty and I feel a pang of guilt in thinking of her
that way. I owe Melanie something, don't I?

"That leg needs to come off," the bearded man is
saying in a voice that's cold, clinical, almost like that of
a cynical surgeon who has seen too much of human misery to allow himself to feel anything toward a patient.
His voice sounds *almost* that way . . .

"Father," the young woman says, suddenly but sadly,
"that would be a terrible thing to do to him."

"The tibia is shattered," he states factually.

Neither of them seems to be aware that I'm awake,
that I'm looking up at them through half-open eyelids.

"There be hardly a piece of bone more than an inch
long here," he says, sketching with his fingers the part of
my leg he's talking about.

"But to take off his leg . . ." the young woman says.

"It will never heal properly, Sharon, even if I am able
to keep infection out. It's a medical fact."

"I shan't let you do it." There's a strength in her
voice.

I try to speak, to let them know that I'm listening and
that I agree with her, but I can do little more than manage to keep my eyelids partly open to see them.

"Rest now," the man says, bending toward me as if
now aware that I'm at least partly awake. "Your body
has had a terrible shock. And we don't have to decide

just yet what to do." As they leave the room, the man says, "And you were the one who wanted to leave him a-lying there in the street."

"I was wrong," she admits.

The door closes behind them.

"You're a very sick man," she says, trying to feed me a thin soup with a spoon. "You must try to swallow this."

I grunt.

"Don't talk. Just swallow this."

I grunt again.

"My name is Sharon English," she says.

The spoon is in my mouth, the warm soup passing over a thick tongue into my throat. I swallow. The soup is good. It's very welcome. Though there is about its taste a strangeness. I vaguely realize that for the first time in years I am eating naturally grown organic foods, not synthetics grown in vast, artificial cultures. I'm probably eating meat that was once part of a live animal. I'm not sure what I think of that

"My father is Dr. Houston English. He's a very fine surgeon." She has a sadness to her voice and to her eyes as she says these last words. "He'll see that you get well." She pauses, then adds, "And I won't let him take your leg off."

I want to say, "Thank you," but the arrival of a fresh spoonful of soup prevents me from even grunting.

The doctor sits on the edge of my bed, looking grave and gentle, very much as a doctor should look. He has just examined and rebandaged my leg. The young black woman has just carried away the old bandages and the implements of the doctor's trade. He has told her to burn the old bandages at once.

"Yours is a strange case," the surgeon says. "I don't believe I've ever yet seen anything quite like it."

I'm strong enough to speak now, though my voice is thin and I can hardly raise it above a whisper. I am afraid to ask him why he thinks my case so strange, fearful that he will tell me that he knows that I'm not of this world, that I'm from another time, another place, yet I ask anyway.

He shakes his head, draws a tobacco pouch and a pipe from somewhere beneath his smock. He begins to fill the pipe.

"I can't say that I'm really certain . . ." he says. "The wound in your leg is, in itself, not all that uncommon. I saw hundreds just like it during the War, and the fact that you've got a fever isn't surprising either. Secondary infections are common with gunshot wounds. But, well, there be something about your *fever*."

"What . . . about it, doctor?" my weak voice asks.

He shakes his head again. "I don't really know. Something unusual. Not quite like anything I've ever seen before." He pauses, then asks, a kind of tension in his voice, "You've always healed normally before, have you not?"

I nod.

"The scar on your thigh there"—he points to my thigh under the bedclothes—"seems like a normal enough scar."

"What're you getting at?" I ask.

"I'm not certain about that either," he says slowly, then rises and fishes a match from some hidden pocket, lighting his pipe. "Oh, you seem to be healing rather quickly, all things considered, and I don't see any traces of gangrene, but . . ."

I don't speak. I wait.

Once again he shakes his head. "There be something unusual about the way the *leg's* scar tissue is forming. Can't say exactly what." He puffs on his pipe, blows smoke from his nostrils.

"What about . . . amputation?" I ask at last.

"I'm putting that off," he answers, turning to look out the window. The curtains are parted slightly and the sky is visible to me from the bed. "Maybe I should have done it at once, but Sharon insisted that I wait. Mayhap we can avoid it."

"How soon will you know?" I ask.

"A few more days. If you continue to mend, and if no

more infection sets in, no gangrene, then mayhap we won't have to take it off."

"I want to keep my leg, doctor."

"I know," he says, then mixes something for me to drink in a small glass and holds it to my mouth.

"Try to rest now, then," he tells me and leaves the room, softly closing the door behind him.

I don't want to sleep, but neither do I want to stay awake. I drift into something midway between the two. I dream.

Sharon feeds me more often than does the black girl, whose name is Amanda, and sometimes she comes to me at other times. She brings tea and helps me sit up so that I can drink it, and I find that I'm developing a taste for tea.

Strangely, she asks me no questions about myself, about who I am, where I come from, how I got the wound. I expect her to, but she never does. I wonder why.

She asks me if I would like for her to read to me, and I say, "Yes, if you don't mind. I get awfully bored just lying here."

"I trust it must be that way," she says.

She asks me if I like poetry and I tell her that, "Yes, I do, or did when I was younger, though I haven't read much poetry since I got out of school."

So the next time she comes to bring me tea, she carries under her arm a book.

Now she is sitting in the chair beside my bed. It's almost dark outside and the room is lighted. Soon it will be dark and Amanda will ring her dinner bell below and Sharon will go down to the dining room; later, she will bring me a tray and help me to eat, or perhaps Amanda will bring me the tray this evening and Sharon will spend some time with her father.

Now we've finished our tea and she's opening the book.

"Do you like Mr. Browning?" she asks.

"Robert Browning?"

She nods and says, "Yes, Robert Browning," as if it's strange that I should have to ask his first name.

"Yes, I like Browning," I say, and wish that my voice were stronger.

"Here's one I like," she tells me and leafs through a few pages, then finds what she's looking for, begins to read:

"That's my last Duchess painted on the wall,
Looking as if she were alive. I call
That piece a wonder, now: Frà Pandolf's hands
Worked busily a day, and there she stands."

And as she reads, Browning's poem comes back to me, its irony which I once enjoyed so much, and I remember that once I did like Browning very much. Maybe I'm learning to again . . .

Though also while she reads, I'm watching her face, her eyes, this girl Sharon English. I find I like *her,* too.

Dr. English does not amputate, even though he says it's against his better judgment. My leg will never be the same, he says. At the very least I'll have to use a cane the rest of my life, maybe a crutch; my left leg will be shorter than my right, but . . .

I'm able to speak now. I thank him.

At night there are always dreams. When I have to take one of Dr. English's potions to sleep, the dreams seem to be worse. I wonder why.

Sometimes I dream I'm back in the Pleistocene, back in the cave, and the bear's coming in and this time my gun won't stop him, no matter how many times I shoot him, no matter how much blood he spills, staining the snow and rock crimson. And then it isn't a bear's blood at all, but mine, and the blood of Welles Kennedy, whom I've just shot, who's slowly dying with great bloody holes in his body; and his eyes gaze at me, flare at me, scream at me, saying, "You're guilty, Gene. You've killed me. You're everything the blueshirts say you are, and more. You're a murderer. You murder your friends."

In other dreams I'm uptime, at home in 2032, occasionally in the displacement chamber, or in a park, or in my cubicle in the dorm, but most often in Melanie's apartment, and she's dressed in that red skirt and sleeveless blouse, but there's no loving in her eyes now—only hatred, anger.

"What kind of a man are you, Gene Stillman?" she demands of me in my dreams. "You kill your friends, but you can't bring yourself to really love a woman or to carry out a duty. You're a coward, Gene, a spineless coward who can only kill his friends and betray women he says he loves."

And then I see her hands or her breasts or her thighs or her feet and I see what they've done to her, the Lay Brothers of St. Wilson—how they've tortured her—and I wonder how it is that she's still alive after that. I scream and tell her that I'm sorry, that I only did . . .

When I wake up it's dark in the house of Dr. English in Chicago in 1871, and I lie awake until dawn comes and wonder if there is any such person as Melanie Proctor and any such world as that I remember from 2032, uptime where I was born and lived.

Sometimes I wonder if there's even any such person as Eugene David Stillman.

Then morning comes and Sharon or Amanda or the doctor arrives to visit me, and I feel better and I forget the dreams . . . until the night.

10

Along with the soup and tea and, later, more substantial foods, my eyes and thoughts more on the attractive Miss English than on the bowls and cups and plates that were served to me first in my bed and then in a chair near it, I listened as she told me the story of the man who had saved my life.

Her father, Dr. Houston English, a physician and surgeon, had come west only a few years before.

He'd had a fine practice in his hometown in upstate New York before the Civil War and had early established a reputation as one of the best surgeons in that part of the country. He had planned after medical service among the northern forces to return to his home after the cessation of hostilities between the Union and the Confederacy, but no sooner had he done so than his wife suffered a stroke and went into a deep coma from which she never recovered. His own medical skills and those of his colleagues were to no avail. Her loss left him with a hollowness he'd never felt before, and doubts about his gifts as a healer—doubts that he'd never felt even during the darkest days of the War, when a surgeon could do little more for his soldier-patients than hack off injured limbs.

Once Elizabeth English had been buried in the family plot, the physician found that he could no longer bear to live in the town where they had both been born, where they had met, married, and built a new home from the earnings of his profession. The memories of those happy days before the war were too painful for him. He decided once more to leave New York State, but to go west to places he considered raw frontier and try to make a new life for himself and his daughter.

With Sharon and his servants, Isaac and Amanda—they had never been slaves—he moved west, having sold his home and property and turned his practice over to his brother's youngest son, a doctor who had gained some limited skill during the last bloody days of the War Between the States, a brash and arrogant young man who might, someday, Houston English hoped, develop into a competent practitioner. To Chicago, the young giant of the Midwest, Dr. English brought his family in the fall of 1867. They quickly established themselves, Dr. English building his new practice by treating the illnesses of the newly rich (of which the city had many). The doctor soon purchased a home on fashionable Willow Street, and Sharon moved, if briefly, into the city's social life.

Although the memory of his wife's death was still painful to him, English seemed to find a degree of happiness and satisfaction in his new home, and he enjoyed the respect and admiration of his new colleagues and patients—for a while at least.

Then, in late 1870, while treating the young son of one of the city's more prominent bankers, disaster struck. The boy was found to have a tumor, a serious one that required immediate removal. Once he had obtained the approval of the boy's father, English operated, successfully removing the tumor—and, medical arts being what they were then, this was no mean trick. But pneumonia struck, and within a week of the operation the boy was dead.

English was blamed. The grief-stricken banker, an elderly widower with no hope of having another child and heir, was vindictive. He demanded an investigation into the circumstances of the boy's death and was even suspected of bribing a coroner's jury to find English guilty of malpractice.

The doctor's new world dissolved around him. His friends temporarily deserted him; Sharon's social life dried up and she found herself cut off from the world as well. English began to drink heavily; for weeks he remained in an angry, bitter, drunken stupor. Finally, with Sharon's help, he was able to overcome the desire to drown his pain, and soon reduced his drinking to socially acceptable levels once more. Then he sought to rebuild his life anew, though he decided not to leave Chicago: he would face the city and perhaps one day prove that no negligence of his had brought about the death of the banker's son.

Well off, with inherited wealth augmented by wise investments in the city's expansion, English did not have to work for a living. Imbued with the Work Ethic as he was, however, he felt it criminal for a healthy man not to be striving for something. He opened a pharmacy that catered to those who'd once been his patients—not everyone believed him guilty of carelessness with the boy's life—and, with the passage of time, many of those who had doubted him began to forget and forgive.

Nevertheless, in late summer of 1871, he and his daughter and their two servants lived a quiet, almost secluded life in the Willow Street home.

Why he'd stopped that day to drag me out of the mud, I never really knew, except that, perhaps, he could never really give up the practice of medicine, and I was a chance to work at it again, in some small way.

I was thankful to him, more than I could express.

During the weeks I spent in the English home, from early July to early October, 1871, first as a bedridden patient and then as an invalid whom Isaac carried downstairs once in a while, I grew to like the feel of the house, the quaintness of it, the antiquity, the feeling of being and living in another world, another time. In my trips downtime before, I'd been no more than a casual observer, a detached reporter, an objective photographer; I had never fully participated in a segment of the past, never become immersed in it, had never been *fully aware* of the life and breath of a world before my own.

The people, the events, the house and everything in it, were from an earlier era, a slice out of the history tapes or an episode from an educational program, though no history tapes had ever been so vivid in imagery, so filled with things that touched the senses. It was a different world—a wilder one than my own, perhaps, beyond the genteel façades erected by the upper classes—a strange world to me, but a freer one than mine had been, a more active world, less structured and restricted.

At first, it didn't particularly bother me that in my delirium I'd gotten wrong the date Melanie had given me. I was a hundred years too early to do what I had promised her I would do. But that didn't seem to matter. The chronalcage was doubtless still there, sitting in that warehouse unnoticed, and when I was ready, when I was strong enough, I would go back to it and do what I had promised I would do—and perhaps the world to which I returned, uptime, would have more in common with this one.

But I was in no hurry. I had a machine that could command time. I had all the time in the world.

And in the meantime, I savored the world of 1871.

Books and magazines and newspapers were given to me to read. It took me a little time to master the somewhat undisciplined spelling and old-fashioned words of the English language of that period. After a while I could read with ease—I had often read old-style writing before, but it had not been for some time.

As well as subscribing to the local papers, the Chicago *Daily News* and the Chicago *Tribune,* Dr. English had mailed to him newspapers from out of town, the New York *Times* and *World* and *Tribune* ("The Cheapest Paper In The Union—Dear At Any Price"). Sharon would bring me *Harper's* and *Leslie's* magazines. In *Leslie's* I recall seeing photographs credited to Matthew Brady. *Scribner's Monthly* was also subscribed to, as well as several others, including a magazine called *Hearth & Home,* which I enjoyed reading for its ads: "The Continental Washing Machine" and the "Reliance Wringer," the "Woven Wire Mattress" and something called "The Wakefield Earth Closet." From these newspapers and magazines I began to get a picture of the world as it had been, as it was then, in greater depth and detail than I could have ever gained from a lifetime of historical study.

The Civil War had been over for only six years; many of its heroes and villains were still alive, active public figures in many cases, those of them who hadn't died during its bloody days, as had so many of the leaders of the defeated South. Although Robert E. Lee had survived the war, he had by 1871 joined Stonewall Jackson and so many others in the "cool tombs." Chicago had, it seemed, many veterans of the War, not a few of them lacking a limb or an eye to testify to their service to the Union. And one of the neighbors of the English household had a son who had been captured by the Confederates and had survived the horrors of Andersonville. I met him once, briefly, a haunted-looking man, old before his time, who would probably never be free of the memories of that prison and its terror. I was thus forcibly reminded that this world was not as pure and innocent as I might like to think it was.

This was reinforced when I read in the newspapers of the activities of the Ku Klux Klan in the Southern states, night riders in white sheets, lynching people and burning crosses, many of them men of social prominence and responsibility, supported by even more secret organizations such as the Knights of the White Camelia and the Order of the White Rose.

Ulysses S. Grant was President of the United States and as yet the graft and corruption of his administration was not public knowledge.

On a broader social scene, the America of 1871 appeared to be in a state of turmoil, compounded of growth and change. Immigrants were swarming to the United States from Europe and from Asia. The campaign for women's suffrage had begun in earnest; the suffragettes were even planning on running a woman for President! In the Wyoming Territory, women had already obtained the vote in 1869, and I learned that Wyoming would refuse to join the Union without suffrage. Workers across the land were learning of labor unions, of organizing to present their demands from a position of collective strength—coal miners were striking in Scranton in 1871. Many of them were called anarchists and socialists; some of them were.

I was reminded of the future of the labor movement one afternoon in late September, when riding with Dr. English and Sharon in their carriage through the streets of Chicago. We rode past Haymarket Square. I didn't comment on it, though I remembered that fifteen years away, fifteen years in the future, the Haymarket bombing, or "Massacre" would occur there. A labor meeting, a dispute, and for the first time in American history a dynamite bomb would be thrown, killing eight policemen; in the ensuing riot the police would more than avenge their number, killing a number of the "foreign-inspired socialists and anarchists." Four men would be hanged, later, for the bombing—men whom history later proved innocent of killing, if not of harboring "un-American" social ideas. The pall of the "socialist" bombing of Haymarket Square was to hang over the labor movement for decades.

I read in one of the newspapers, I don't recall which, that Congress was passing an act to end the practice of making treaties with the American Indians. Henceforth, such documents were to be called "agreements" and were to be subject to the approval of both houses of Congress. I recalled that George Armstrong Custer was to meet the Sioux at Little Big Horn in only five years.

I read, too, about the "Barons of Wall Street," Jay Gould and Jim Fisk (who was to be killed next year, 1872), and their brazen thefts and conniving confidence games—how they bilked men like Cornelius Vanderbilt out of millions of dollars. Boss William Marcy Tweed was riding high in New York, though his downfall was already in sight. Thomas Nast's cartoons, and the revelations of former sheriff James O'Brien in the July issues of the New York *Times,* were exposing Tweed and Tammany Hall, laying bare the corruption that festered in the city.

One of the magazines I saw showed drawings of the disaster that struck the Staten Island ferryboat *Westfield* in New York harbor and took a hundred lives, and another showed a scene near Revere, Massachusetts, where a Portland Express train rammed a stalled train and killed twenty-nine people, injuring countless more.

I read about the formation of the National Rifle Association and of the National Association of Professional Baseball Players. I learned about new rules in the game of baseball and about Harry Bassett's winning of the 5th annual Belmont Stakes, about Henry James' trip from Niagara Falls to Lake Ontario and the book he was basing on it. I read about the Irish riots in New York and about Grant's establishment of a Civil Service Commission. I read about the people and places, the times and the events, and I found that I was beginning to like 1871 very much . . .

11

The home of Dr. Houston English and his daughter was rather modest by the North Side's contemporary standards. Palatial dwellings two or three times its size were more common on Willow Street, but it was adequate for the four people who lived there and their occasional guests. It was not without its comforts.

The house consisted of two stories and a high, gabled attic, and was constructed of reddish brick, as were most of those in the neighborhood. On one side was the driveway that led from the yet-unpaved street up a porte cochère, beyond which was a fair-sized stable for English's two horses and carriage. The outbuilding beside the stable was a small cottage designed as servants' quarters, although Isaac and Amanda lived in the main house with the Englishes, and this cottage was now used only for storage. At the front of the house, bordered on one side by the driveway, was a broad, well-kept lawn and flower garden, both fenced with hedges. In the garden were hydrangeas and begonias, roses and marigolds, and a marble dryad, all but nude, almost shocking by Victorian standards, I thought, who held aloft a water-filled bowl in which birds wet their feet, splashed, and drank.

To one with any sense of the aesthetic, the house itself was a horror: bay windows and random projections, turrets and awkward gimcracks, all the rococo gingerbread the Victorian period had been able to dream up to ornament the artificial caves of its people, topped by a noisy, rusty weather vane that was supposed to look like a goose in flight, but didn't. Yet it had a charm despite its very ugliness, perhaps like a homely girl whom everyone says has "a great personality."

A hallway ran from the stained-glass door at the front of the house to the rear porch beside the kitchen; a passageway, in other words, from the domain of Dr. English (the sitting room and his "study") to Amanda's realm (the kitchen). The hallway was somber with brown wallpaper sprinkled with phantoms of dull flowers, and on the floor, running the hall's full length, was a carpet of deep maroon, almost black, that drank light like a thirsty demon. It was as if the hallway had been specifically decorated to remain in perpetual twilight, a quiet, almost secret meeting place for wives and lovers, daughters and suitors.

Midway between the front and rear doors, situated like a vertical channel running from a horizontal coal mine, stood a staircase that led up to the second floor and to the bedrooms. Halfway up, a stopping place for the lame and the aged, was a landing where a sharp turn left you face to face with a towering grandfather clock that loudly ticked the minutes and grumblingly tolled the hours with the voice of a Black Forest gnome. How Isaac navigated that turn and avoided collision with the clock when carrying my dead weight up and down the stairs, I'll never know. When I was able to walk I could barely manage it myself, and came to the conclusion that the house's architect had been a sadist with a particular dislike for the old and the infirm.

Not a single wall of the interior was without ornamentation, and, beneath that ornamentation, florid wallpaper, although I think that most of the concepts of the house's interior decoration were those of Sharon's late mother as interpreted by Amanda, rather than those of Sharon herself. The walls of hall and sitting room, kitchen and dining room, were spotted with photographs and lithographic prints, and with mottoes and clichés of yarn and cloth: *God Bless Our Home* and *Early to Bed, Early to Rise* . . . and the like.

The sitting room was one of the two social centers of the house, the more masculine; the other, the kitchen, was the more feminine. It was the sitting room to which Isaac most often took me, carrying me down the stairs when I was yet unable to walk them. There I would sit with Dr. English and/or Sharon, waiting while Amanda prepared dinner or nursing a cigar and a nightcap after dinner.

That room has left me with vivid memories.

In the middle of the room was an ugly and ornate table, large and black, on which sat a dish of wax fruit, brightly colored peaches and plums, grapes and apples, which Amanda dusted at least twice a day, never failing to say, "Ain't they purty 'nough ter eat?" Beside the bowl sat a highly polished music box, which Sharon frequently opened but which she usually closed before it had completed playing even one of its several tunes. It had been a gift to Sharon's mother, brought back by Houston English from a desolated Virginia after Appomattox, and I think that the music brought Sharon painful memories. Also usually on the table were several books and magazines: a medical journal, for Dr. English maintained his interest in his former profession, perhaps hoping to return to it one day; a copy of, maybe, Edward Eggleston's *The Hoosier Schoolmaster,* or John Burroughs' *Wake-Robin,* or *Their Wedding Journey,* Vol. I, by William Dean Howells; some romantic novels of Sharon's; perhaps a dime novel about the exploits of the latest Western hero or villain, though no one in the household would admit to reading such a thing; a copy of *Harper's* or *Leslie's* or one of the other monthly magazines; and the day's edition of one of the city's newspapers, carefully folded back into its original shape by Amanda after having gone through the doctor's hands, Sharon's, and mine.

At one end of the room, in a setting of white marble, stood the fireplace, an exquisite thing, perhaps the most attractive object in the house, excepting, of course, Miss English herself. Above it ranged a long marble mantelpiece, partly covered by a multicolored silk valance of Oriental design. A yellow cuckoo clock, made in Chicago by a family of German origin, sat in the middle, and on either side were photographs of the English clan—

brothers and sisters, aunts and uncles, the late Mrs. English, all of them dating to that happier period before Houston English and his daughter left New York State.

In one corner of the room was a "whatnot," a vertical construction of polished black wood with half a dozen shelves designed to fit into the angle of the room; on the uppermost shelf of it was a little marble group, better executed than such things usually are: a small boy holding up a fish he had caught to the admiration of an equally small, pigtailed girl. On the shelves below were a half-dozen watch-chain charms given to English over the years; a number of seashells of various colors and shapes, which Sharon had collected on a trip to Long Branch, New Jersey, more than a decade before; a miniature Bible, which probably hadn't been touched since the death of Mrs. English; and a gaggle of china chickens enclosed in a matchstick fence.

In another corner was a smaller, less ugly table; it held, on a white, silken cloth, an enormous family Bible that listed the births and deaths of the Englishes for generations back. I don't believe the Bible was ever opened except following a momentous occasion that must be recorded on its pages.

Between the two windows of the room that faced the street was a dark, massive organ with an open book of music on it. Sharon was a more than accomplished organist and had much better taste in music than one might have expected of a young lady in her social position. Melanie would have approved of the music she played.

Upon the walls hung framed prints: *Lincoln in a Shawl; Juliet on the Balcony Tossing Romeo a Rose; The Three Wise Men; Fulton's Steamboat;* Winslow Homer's *Bell-Time; The Driving of the Golden Spike;* and the like.

On the floor lay a brightly colored Persian carpet that must have cost a princely sum by the day's standards, and at the windows hung lace curtains with heavy green over-curtains of some damask-like material. Before the fireplace stood a dark-green, heavily padded settee that looked immovable, a permanent fixture of the earth around which the house might have been built. Against the walls and before the more massive of the two tables were chairs of plush and velvet, fringes and tassles, and on the back of each chair was an antimacassar of linen or lace.

The room was seldom opened to the outside; windows remained shut summer and winter. And about it was an odor that might have seemed stale had there not also been about it a pleasantness, a closeness that was comfortable, that bespoke of quiet and solitude, of a tranquil privacy shut off from the world outside and into which nothing unpleasant could intrude.

It was in this room, lighted by gas jets, that I sat one evening with Dr. English. I think it was mid-August, maybe six weeks after my arrival there. By then I was well enough to be brought downstairs and have my evening meal with English and Sharon in the dining room, sitting before a great table that Amanda always heaped to nearly overflowing.

On this August evening, dinner was over and Sharon had left the house to visit a nearby friend. She had gone off in the carriage, driven by Isaac; he would wait outside for her until she was ready to return home. She wasn't expected to be late.

In the sitting room Dr. English, with a full stomach and much contented, put aside the pipe which he smoked during the day and opened a box of Havana cigars. After taking one for himself and offering one to me, which I accepted, he poured us each a small glass of sherry, saying, "I fail to see how this can harm you, Eugene."

"Then I'll consider it my physician's advice that I have a little sherry," I said.

"Bully!" he said with a smile, sitting down in the room's second-most-comfortable chair. Like the good host he was, English had told Isaac to place me in the most comfortable.

"I trust that your leg hasn't bothered you greatly today," he said, not actually making a question of it.

"No, not too much," I answered.

"Well, it probably will give you pain when you begin to walk on it," he told me, after puffing the tip of his cigar to a bright glow and blowing a cloud of smoke toward the dark fireplace. "And I believe that mayhap in a week or so you should begin trying."

"I'm anxious to, just as soon as you think it's wise."

In my own world, I knew, I would have been up and walking long before this, but then in my own world the medical sciences were far advanced over those available to Houston English. There, uptime, my shattered bone would have been stimulated to regrow itself into its original shape, and other techniques as mysterious to me as they would have been to English would have accelerated healing. By this time, six weeks or more after the incident, you would hardly know I'd nearly lost my leg. Yet, I reminded myself, the advantages of 2032 America can't compensate for the disadvantages. I wasn't considering using the chronalcage to go uptime for medical services, not until I could expect to find a better world up there, at least.

"We needn't rush things," English was saying. "We must give Nature the time she needs to mend you. You should consider yourself very lucky to have kept your leg."

"I do, Doctor. *I do.*"

English opened his mouth as if to say something more, but closed it when we heard a knocking at the front door. "I wonder who that could be," he muttered to himself.

Amanda, in a dark dress and a white apron, hurried down the dark hallway. Then we could hear the door opening.

"Oh, good evenin', Mista Conwell," Amanda's voice said from a distance.

"Evening, Amanda," replied a man's voice. "Is the good doctor in?"

"Yessir, he is."

English was rising from his chair, putting down his sherry and cigar. "I won't be a moment, Eugene." He went toward the entranceway.

"Raymond, how are you?" English was saying.

"Fine and dandy, Houston. Fit as a fiddle. And yourself?"

"Fine, fine. What brings you out this evening? Not that I'm not always glad to see you!"

"I have something I want to talk over with you, if you're not busy."

"No, not at all. Come inside, my friend."

English returned to the sitting room accompanied by a tall, slender man, beardless but with a huge mustache and great bushy sideburns popularized in the previous decade by the Union officer from whom they'd gotten their name, if twisted about a bit: Ambrose Burnside. I'd have guessed the man to be in his early forties and, from the cut of his clothing, to be as well-to-do as English, upper middle class or higher. He was introduced to me as Raymond Conwell.

I, in turn, was introduced by my right name, but as a distant relative of the English family who was recuperating in the doctor's home after a railroad accident. I hadn't known up until then exactly what English had been telling friends and neighbors about me, but I hadn't been too concerned—though I had wondered about his failure to question me about my past. Of this I would learn later.

Conwell removed his overcoat, an unnecessary garment on this warm evening, and took a seat, refusing English's offer of a cigar but accepting a glass of sherry.

"I detest bothering you with business in this manner, Houston," Conwell said, sipping at his sherry and apparently finding it as excellent as I had, "but I have gotten a tip that I think perchance you would like to hear about."

"I don't mind your coming at all, Raymond," English replied. "I see far too little of you these days, as it is."

"We can talk business, can't we?" Conwell asked, his eyes flickering toward me.

"Certainly," English replied, perhaps a trifle irritated at Conwell for thinking that a guest in the English home was not someone to be trusted.

"Well," Conwell began, taking another sip of sherry,

"I dined with Harvey Goldstone this evening; he's a junior vice-president at Columbia Packing, you know."

"Yes, I know Harvey."

"Harvey and I have been chums for a long while . . ." Conwell went on. "We messed together during the War—tenting on the Old Camp Ground and all that. Well, you know that things haven't been going too well for Columbia for the past year or so. The big meatpackers are becoming rather rough in their purchasing tactics and the little fellows like Columbia just cannot keep up with them. They're having the deuce's own time to find meat fit to sell."

"Yes, I knew that Columbia was having some financial troubles," English said, "but I didn't think they were terribly serious."

Conwell shook his head. "Oh, and they're not so terribly serious—Columbia could probably weather the storm and even turn a profit for the year. But something has come up."

"Oh?"

"Here's what it is, and why I thought belike you'd want to know about my chat with Harvey. The trump is that Libby has made an offer to buy them out!"

"Oh?" English exclaimed again, seeming to wonder why that was important to him. I did, too.

Conwell nodded sagely. "Yes, and they are going to redeem Columbia Packing stock at *nearly double* its present value in Libby stock. Anyone holding Columbia stock stands to make something close to a hundred percent profit on his investment overnight."

"I see . . ." English said, the realization coming to him. "And you know where there be Columbia stock available?"

Conwell nodded. "And we can get it for a song, ten percent down from what it was a few weeks ago. Are you interested, Houston?"

English pondered for a moment, then asked, "Harvey's certain about this?"

"Absolutely. The papers have already been drawn up in complete privacy, but the announcement of it won't be made until some time next week, when they are signed."

"You're buying some yourself?" English queried.

"Absolutely. I'm putting as much money as I can raise into Columbia stock tomorrow, but I'm going about it quietly. How 'bout it?"

"If Harvey is right . . ." English pondered. "Let me sleep on it, will you not, Raymond?"

"Of course."

"Look," English said suddenly, "why don't we meet for lunch tomorrow at the Tremont?"

"Dandy!"

"And I do appreciate your telling me about this, Raymond."

"You've given me some good tips in the past, Houston, and I only thought it fair of me to return the favor, but I do wish you would keep it under your hat. If word gets out—"

"Of course. Mum's the word. Another glass of sherry?"

Conwell dragged a gold watch from the pocket of his vest and snapped open its case. It chimed. "It's early yet," he said. "Yes, I'll have another."

As English rose to get the sherry bottle from the black center table, he asked: "Eugene?"

I nodded. "Yes, please."

"Mighty sorry to hear about your accident, Stillman," Conwell said to me. "I hope you'll be recovering quickly. In Houston's house, I'm certain you will."

One glass of sherry led to another, until English sent Amanda to the cellar to fetch another bottle. The conversation wandered from local business gossip to national politics to the problems in Western Europe, where France was still recovering from the recent Franco-Prussian War.

"I read that the French President . . . what's-his-name?" Conwell was saying.

"Thiers," English replied.

"That's right, Thiers. I read that he's still having trouble with those 'Red Republicans' in Paris. Seems that they might be trying to take over the city again."

"Yes, I saw something about that in the New York *Times*—yesterday, was it not?"

"Or the day before."

"I thought they had settled the Communard problem back in May—'Bloody Week,' they called it," English added, "when the Army went in and gave them precisely what they had coming."

"Well, apparently the Army didn't give them enough," Conwell said. "They should have taken every last one of them and shot them, while they had the chance."

"I suppose so," English mused, "but I suspect that the newspapers have probably blown this new thing all out of proportion. Sensationalism sells newspapers, you know."

"Don't dismiss those Reds too lightly, Houston." Conwell was in earnest. "Since that Marx fellow wrote that book—*Das Kapital,* was that not the name of it?— since that blasted book, their type are springing up all over the place."

I wanted to say something about Karl Marx and Marxism and its future place in the world: about the changes that would take place in socialism, about the advances it would make all over the world, about the rise of labor unions and the welfare philosophy in America in the years to come, about things like Social Security and Medicare. But I knew it would be best for me to keep my mouth shut. I could very easily say too much in a very few words, accidentally reveal my knowledge of the future; and I certainly didn't want to do that. At the very least, I would probably give them both the idea that I was in favor of "socialism and anarchy."

I kept my mouth shut and listened to them.

"Do you know what really worries me, Houston?" Conwell asked.

"What's that?"

"It's the danger of those socialists and anarchists and free-lovers and labor unionists coming over here," Conwell said.

"To the United States?"

Conwell nodded gravely. "With so many danged foreigners coming into this country every day, I wouldn't be at all surprised if there weren't a lot of Reds among them."

"Oh, there may well be," English said, "but I would not get too stirred up over it if I were you, Raymond. People of that kind certainly don't stand a chance here. Labor unionism and socialism will never get even a good foothold in America. Hang it all, this is a capitalistic country and always will be! That's what has made it great: hard work, thrift, and a fear of God."

"I know all that, Houston," Conwell admitted, "but—"

"Those so-called socialists are mayhap gaining some followers in some countries in Europe, Raymond, but we don't have the kinds of problems in this country which they have over there. No real American would ever subscribe to their odd ideas."

"I hope you're right," Conwell said.

"I'm certain of it," English replied flatly, lighting a fresh cigar and pouring a fresh glass of sherry.

A few moments of silence followed, before Conwell asked, "Would you like to hear a strange story, Houston?"

English shrugged, lifted his glass to his mouth, downed half its contents in a single gulp. I was beginning to wonder whether he had regained the control over his drinking that Sharon believed he had, although this was a social occasion among men where a bit of excessive drinking wasn't all that unacceptable.

"Well, you know that I own some farmland across the river from Willow Springs."

English nodded, then seemed to discover that his cigar had gone out, and relit it.

"Well, I rent it out to a man named McBride—sharecrop it, I suppose you could say. McBride's got him a wife and three daughters. You ought to see the oldest. She's a real lallapalooza. Just seventeen and about the best looker I've ever set eyes on. With her looks, she could go a long way." His eyes closed for a moment and seemed to be visualizing the girl.

"But, anyway's, I was down there over the weekend,

to see how old McBride was doing—and he's doing very well. If he keeps going the way he has been, in a couple of years he's going to be able to buy the land from me, free and clear, and I expect to make a danged good profit off it, too. Anyways, while I was down there he told me a story that I don't quite believe, but he swears that it's God's own truth. Darnedest thing I ever heard a man tell, cold sober."

"Okay," English said, puffing on his relighted cigar, "tell us about it."

"Seems that McBride went to a card game—Tuesday night, I believe it was, Tuesday night a week ago—and he didn't head back home until past midnight. He'd been drinking a little, he says, 'shine from some farmer's still, but he wasn't drunk. I believe him. He's a sober, God-fearing man."

As if to prove that he wasn't exactly the same, Conwell emptied the second sherry bottle and English called Amanda for another. I sipped at what I had left in my own glass, but didn't want more. In my weakened condition, what little I'd drunk was already getting to me.

"Well," Conwell went on, "seems that McBride was walking back home about one o'clock of the morning, when he saw this contraption sitting smack in the middle of his fields."

"Contraption?" English asked.

"Yep," Conwell said, "that's what he called it, 'contraption.' He said that it was a big, boxy sort of a thing, maybe four yards square, made out of metal. Half of it looked like it was surrounded by sheets of metal like an ironclad's bulkheads or something, and the other half looked like it was made out of bars from a jail cell. It didn't have a top or a roof, and it was just sitting there on things that looked like short legs and sled runners."

"Is that a fact?" English asked.

"True as a trivet," Conwell replied.

I didn't say a word. I would not have been able to speak if I'd wanted to. I was too shocked. There could have been only one thing in this world or in any other that fitted the description that Conwell had just given. A chronalcage!

A chronalcage . . . somewhere near Chicago, in August, 1871 . . .

I was too numbed, too stunned to think of all the implications. But I was scared and I'm certain that the blood must have drained from my face. I nearly fell out of my chair, but caught myself and took a quick drink of sherry, my hands shaking. Neither Conwell nor English seemed to notice.

"McBride says there were a man standing there, right beside it, and he had a gun in his hand, a rifle or something. It was pretty dark, and McBride couldn't see him any too well. Anyway, McBride, he stopped and hunkered down and waited to see what the man was going to do. He didn't know what was a-going on, of course, and he didn't like the idea of some stranger coming in and setting up some sort of a contraption in his fields, but he certainly wasn't going to go up against an armed man. Not unless he went home and got his shotgun.

"So he just waited there awhiles, and pretty soon—you're not going to believe this, Houston, but McBride swears it's true—pretty soon there is this whining noise in the air, and pop! there's *another* contraption sitting there, just like the first one."

English shook his head in disbelief.

I believed, though I didn't want to.

"Well, Mac says he was scared. I don't guess he's really a very religious fellow, though he's an honest man and says grace at the table and reads his daughters a chapter from the Bible every night before they go to bed. But he says he swore to Almighty God that from then on he'd go to church twice on Sundays and to prayer meetings on Wednesdays if the Devil didn't get him right then and drag him off into Hell. That was about the only thing he could figure right then, that it was the work of the Devil himself."

"The work of a deluded mind," English said. "The man must have been as drunk as a fiddler."

"He swears on a stack of Bibles he wasn't," Conwell said.

"Go on," English said, refilling his empty glass from the now opened third bottle of sherry.

"Like I said, there wasn't much McBride could do, so he just waited," Conwell said. "Seems like there was another man in this second contraption, but he didn't get out. The first man, the one with the rifle, just stood there awhiles like he didn't know what to do either. Then he went over to this second contraption and climbed into it."

"Well, then what happened?" English asked when Conwell paused to empty his own glass.

"Nothing, for a long spell. The fellow kept fooling around inside the contraption, but he didn't say anything. It seemed like the man seated in that one was badly hurt or something, and the man with the rifle was trying to help him. McBride couldn't see well enough to tell what was really going on.

"Well, he waited there, McBride did, an hour or better, and then decided that the man with the rifle wouldn't see him if he was mighty careful about heading toward his house. It was root, hog! or die, McBride said. He was going to get his shotgun and a lantern and find out just what the heck was going on out there, the work of the Devil or no.

"So McBride, he went on home and got his shotgun. He was mighty quiet, he said, so that he wouldn't wake up his wife or his daughters. He didn't want to frighten them until he knew what it was all about. But as he was coming back from the house with his shotgun and the lantern, and had gotten about halfway to where those contraptions were, there was this awful sound again and then one of the contraptions just vanished, *pop!* like it had come."

"Impossible!" English said loudly.

"I know. Anyways, McBride says that the man with the rifle got back into the first contraption, and before McBride could get another fifty feet, it did the same thing, made this weird sound and then disappeared into thin air. When he got to the spot where they'd been, wasn't a danged thing there, excepting for the marks in the ground where the two things had been sitting."

"Do you believe a word of it?" English asked.

Conwell seemed to ponder for a moment. "Well, I

probably wouldn't have if McBride hadn't taken me out into the field and showed me the marks where the things had been. They messed up a nice piece of good potato patch."

By this time I was in a cold sweat, chills racing through my body as they had during the worst of my sickness after being shot; that is, while English was nursing me back to health and Sharon was fighting to save my leg. I was grateful when the physician, now more nearly drunk than sober, offered to refill my glass. Again he didn't seem to notice my shaking hand.

"Weirdest darned thing I ever heard of . . ." Conwell was saying, "but McBride says he'd swear on a stack of Bibles a yard high that every word of it was Gospel truth."

Two chronalcages in a potato patch not far from Chicago on an August night in 1871 . . .

I believed it was true—neither Conwell nor the farmer named McBride could have fabricated such a story out of nothing. But who had been in those cages? What had they been doing? And why had they been *here?* In this when-and-where?

It was possible, of course, that it had nothing at all to do with me. It could have been some research team coming back to 1871 for reasons in no way connected with a heretic named Gene Stillman. But I knew of only half a dozen chronal/geo locations that had even been visited more than once, or by more than one chronalcage simultaneously, and they were things like the Crucifixion or the Council of Nicaea or the Trenton Accord of 2011. Nothing had happened in 1871 to call that much attention from the chronal researchers of *my* world.

They could have been from further uptime, I told myself. In fact, it suddenly seemed to me, they had to have been from further uptime than 4 March 2032 A.D. Which meant . . . ?

How far uptime? "Aye, there's the rub . . ."

They could have been Proctors or Lay Brothers. They could have been men coming back to search for me. Hadn't I already added murder to my other crimes against the Church/State?

But how could they have known when/where to find me? They couldn't have come that close in time/space by accident.

Coincidence stretched the limits of reason.

My mind slipped gears and started running wild.

What imprint had I/would I have left on the pages of history by which they could trace me?

Raymond Conwell was rising, starting to leave, when we heard horses clomping into the driveway and Isaac's deep voice calling, "Whoa!"

English came to his feet slowly, awkwardly, unsteadily, seeming suddenly to remember that Sharon had been out of the house and would be returning—and certainly would not approve of his having drunk this much sherry.

"I had better be parting," Conwell said.

"If you must." Although English's face was flushed with wine, his voice was the model of sobriety.

"Noon tomorrow at the Tremont?" Conwell asked.

"I'll be there," English promised.

The front door opened. Sharon, apparently seeing the lights and hearing the voices from the sitting room, came in our direction.

"Oh, good evening, Mr. Conwell," she said, then glanced at her father, saw his flushed complexion, the half-empty wineglass, and give him a stern look.

"Good evening, Miss English," Conwell said awkwardly. "I was just leaving."

"Don't rush off on—" Sharon began, but looked at me and must have instantly realized that all was not well with me either. "Gene, what's wrong?"

As she crossed the room to where I was sitting, her father mumbled something to Conwell, who quickly made his departure.

"Gene, you're not well at all," she said as she reached my chair, touched my forehead, felt the cold perspiration there.

"I'm . . . okay," I mumbled.

"No, you're not!" She turned toward English angrily. "Father, what has been going on here? While you've been drinking your senses away, Gene has been getting sicker and sicker. What kind of a doctor are you?"

Not giving him a chance to answer, she stormed from the room, toward the rear of the house, and called for Isaac, who was unhitching the horses.

Within minutes I was lying in my bed, assisted into my pajamas by Isaac. He had quickly, gently, and seemingly effortlessly carried me from the sitting room up to my bedroom.

Sharon spent some minutes with her father. I could hear her angry voice from below, although I couldn't distinguish the words. When she had given him a sufficient tongue-lashing for his misdeed, she came upstairs with a glass of warm milk and comforting words for me.

I told her that I wasn't as badly off as I looked. I was just tired and a good night's sleep would put me back on top of the world. She smiled, waiting until I had finished the milk, told me good night and softly closed the door behind her as she left.

For a long while I lay in the darkness, unable to sleep but unwilling to call for anything to aid me in sleeping. I didn't want to think about Conwell's story, but I did, long and hard, and in the end I finally half convinced myself that it *was* coincidence. That's all it could have been. How could anyone from uptime possibly have known where I was?

At last, far past midnight, slumber did come to me, and surprisingly enough it was without unpleasant dreams. I don't know why.

The next day I felt as good as I could have expected to feel, though I'm afraid that I can't say the same for Dr. English. Hung-over and miserable, he left the house in the morning and didn't return until quite late in the day.

He did, I learned, keep his luncheon appointment with Raymond Conwell, did make an investment in Columbia Packing, and later did nearly double his three thousand dollars when Libby, McNeil, and Libby bought out Columbia "lock, stock, and barrel," as the saying goes.

The night had not been a total loss for the good doctor.

I wondered about myself.

12

About four weeks after hearing Raymond Conwell's tale of Farmer McBride and the strange "contraptions" in his potato patch, by the light of gas jets and a fire in the fireplace that wasn't really needed I sat late one night in the sitting room with Dr. Houston English. By this time I was able to navigate the stairs alone, if I were very careful and took my time in doing it, unaided except by an ornate cane the doctor had lent me. I had not yet been outside the house, but had been promised a trip downtown within the next few days. I was anxious to see downtown Chicago, 1871 A.D.

Sharon and the servants had gone to bed and English had laid aside the stereoscope through which we had been viewing scenes of foreign countries: the Tower of London and London Bridge, the fountains of Rome, the Pyramids, things like that. The stereoscope had been something of a surprise to me. I'd almost forgotten that even the nineteenth century had made its ventures into three-dimensional images, although holograms were still a long, long way off.

Although he had seriously restricted his intake of alcohol since Sharon's upbraiding a month before, English had opened a bottle of very expensive imported liqueur —something made by monks in a little-known monastery somewhere—and we were sipping it from tiny glasses while smoking Cuban cigars from a huge wooden box that sat on his desk in the room he sometimes called his "office" and sometimes his "study."

The room had been silent for some time. English was

gazing thoughtfully into the fire that Isaac kindled in the fireplace before joining Amanda in their rooms.

I watched the doctor as he sat before the fire, almost unmoving, and wondered what was going on in his mind, what deep, dark thoughts he was considering, what it was he had to say to me, what questions he had to ask of me, for I felt certain that he had planned this evening—the approaching moment—and would lay some of his cards on the table and demand that I do the same. I was more than a bit nervous, but I don't think I showed it.

I sipped at the rose-scented liqueur.

English turned the cigar between his lips, continuing to gaze into the fire.

I realized now that he was not as big a man as my first impressions had led me to believe—physically, at least—not really god-like. He was, however, a tall man, over six feet (to use the measures of the time), and must have weighed in excess of two hundred and twenty pounds. Most of that weight was muscle; English was not given to fat, and, as a physician, even in that period, he knew the desirability of regular exercise. On weekends he would often have Isaac drive him out of Chicago to a spot where he took long hikes in the woods southwest of the city, an area that had long since been incorporated into the metropolis at the time of my birth in 1995—a hundred and twenty-four years hence. Or he would go with Sharon to a riding club where were kept the two fine geldings he had bought for her shortly after their arrival in Chicago. Sharon was an excellent horsewoman—"a natural," her father had once said—and she had a great love of equestrian sports. I regret that I was never able to go riding with her, that she was never given the opportunity to teach me to ride, even though I suspect that I wouldn't have done well at it, even had my leg not been as it was, shortened and deformed.

English was a handsome man by the standards of his day, and must have been a dashing young doctor in his youth, when he courted Elizabeth, Sharon's mother. Now he was—well, dignified. His hair, beard, and sideburns were shot with white; they had once been a dark

brown, almost black, Sharon had told me, and showing
me black-and-white photographs of him in his younger
years. Of his features, the most striking were his eyes.
They contained a depth and intensity to them that could
show great gentleness and consideration; yet, I suspected, they could also show great anger. From experience I
knew that he had an excellent bedside manner, something which, during the days of his active practice in
Chicago, must have made him very popular with
wealthy ladies approaching menopause.

Sharon had inherited those eyes, carrying in hers
much of the same strength and gentleness that showed in
her father's. I think that is one of the things that made
her so attractive a woman—*one,* but then she had many
other qualities, too, many other aspects of feminine
beauty . . .

English was, I suppose, a rather typical man of his
time and place, of his station and education, although he
took a bit of getting used to, for there were few people
like him in my own world. He did remind me, however,
of some men I'd known in my youth, old men from the
Southern states—Virginia, the Carolinas, Georgia, perhaps—when, even after the final turn of the twentieth
century, some of the old Southern concepts of gentility
still remained, though they quickly passed into cultural
history, and anthropology.

Houston English was certainly not a "Southern gentleman" of his time. He had been born and had spent
most of his life in New York State. Yet during the middle decades of the nineteenth century, America was still
a largely rural nation; although industrialization was a
physical reality in America even then, the fullness of its
philosophies had not really sunk into the minds of the
middle and upper classes. It was a country of gentlemen
farmers and shopkeepers, still only giving way to indus-
trialists and financiers. Even New York State had more
in common with the South of its own time than it would
have had with itself a century later.

Houston English, M.D., had accepted most of the notions of his time without greatly questioning them—
which is not to say that he wasn't an intelligent and

imaginative man, but rather that he was very remote from
that later period of cynicism and skepticism. English
firmly believed that the universe was ruled by an Episcopalian God whose main concern was the prosperity of
the American nation, and though I'm certain he would
never have been so irreverent as to say so, I suspect that
he thought God would vote Republican if God were to
vote.

That the United States of America was the finest and
most righteous nation on Earth was not a matter of
doubt to him. Nor could he have doubted that the Almighty had a plan for America and her people that
would involve her spreading across all of the North
American continent and setting an example of capitalistic prosperity for the world to emulate—if never to
equal. "Manifest Destiny" was not a term that English
used—it was perhaps passé by then—but the ideas behind the term were entrenched in his vision of the world
and the place of America and her people in it.

Yet Houston English wasn't a narrow-minded, over-
bearing man. He considered himself broad-minded, and,
considering *his* world, I think he was probably correct,
if you are to judge a man by the standards of his time.
And what else is there to do?

He had been an abolitionist before the Civil War,
though not fanatical about it, and he had seen the War
as an example of God's divine will for human freedom
being worked out by clumsy but well-meaning humans.
He had voted for Abraham Lincoln both times, but had
had certain reservations about the man. Lincoln hadn't
exactly been his idea of the kind of gentleman who
should reside in the White House; he'd seen Lincoln as
something less than the polished aristocrats of the East,
who were English's models for public behavior. Yet Lincoln's death at Booth's hands had saddened and angered
him, though he couldn't see the dead President as the almost divine, martyred saint he had already become in
the eyes of some people.

English believed in the tenets of the Episcopal
Church, but was tolerant of both Catholics and Baptists,
and even a Jew had occasionally been a dinner guest in

his home. He attended church somewhat irregularly, though he insisted that Sharon only fail service on Sunday, morning and sometimes at night, for the most serious reasons.

He had little love for "socialism" and the forces at work to bring the concept of labor unionism into America; nevertheless, he had great sympathy for the problems of the working man. He would admit that at times business and industry took advantage of the persons they employed, but he felt that such problems could be worked out in time by men of goodwill without resorting to "the atheistic ideas of anarchists from Europe, this Karl Marx fellow and his ilk."

By the same token he felt sympathy for the women across the nation, who had begun to demand equal rights, or at the very least the voting franchise, although he felt that many of those heading the suffragette movement were not the sort of people he would invite into his home or wish his daughter to be associated with: "Free-lovers and socialistic anarchists," he once referred to them, "she-demons who think they're better than men."

All in all, I found that I rather liked Dr. Houston English, though I had some fundamental differences with him that I would never feel myself at liberty to express while living under his roof, accepting his food and shelter, and having no way to repay him. I hoped that I would never be forced into a position where I would have to disagree with him, or to lie to him about either my own past or my opinions of his world. However, I told myself, I would lie rather than tell him the truth about my origins.

And now, as we sat in the sitting room, smoking our cigars and sipping the imported liqueur, I felt as if I might be forced to begin that lying . . .

At length, after a long and now almost painful silence, English knocked a piece of white cigar ash into the fireplace and turned to me. "Eugene," he began slowly, the words seeming to come from his mouth very reluctantly, "I have asked you no questions about your-

self, as I'm certain you've observed, and I've requested
that Sharon ask you none as well."

"Dr. English, I'm very grateful for—"

He waved me to silence with a gesture of the hand
that held the cigar. "Please let me finish, Eugene."

"Certainly," I said, sipping again at my liqueur.

"I've asked you no questions, and I will not begin
asking them now," he said. "I rather have the feeling
that I'd prefer not to know very much about you."

I wanted to speak, to say something that might reas-
sure him, but I didn't know what words to say. There
seemed to be none adequate.

"I don't mean that I dislike you, Eugene," he continued. "Quite the contrary. I find you a very likable man,
and I have no doubt as to your breeding and education.
You strike me as a remarkably intelligent and literate
person." He paused for a moment before going on, gazing at the fireplace as if in it he saw omens, dark por-
tents. "Nor do I believe for a moment that you were
drunken that day we found you in the street."

He paused again to puff on his cigar and to look
thoughtfully once more into the fire.

"And," he said, searching for words as he spoke,
"you do not seem to be the sort of man who would be a
fugitive from justice, although I have the distinct feeling
that you have perchance fled from *something*."

"Dr. English—" I began to speak again, uncertain of
what words would follow.

"No." He waved with the cigar again to silence me.
"Hear me out."

Once more he gazed into the fire for a moment before
speaking. I wondered what it was that he saw there; was
it something perhaps akin to the dreams he still had of
the evening of 2 May 1863, of the crossroads at Chan-
cellorsville and Stonewall Jackson's strike against the
Union armies there?

"Your accent is strange," he said at last, "though I
would hardly call it foreign. And you have odd turns of
speech that I've never encountered before—and I've
been acquainted with men from all over the thirty-seven

states. You're not a foreigner, Eugene, but you're not any kind of American I've ever met heretofore."

The words that followed came even more slowly, more reluctantly.

"When we found you—I won't ask you to explain it —but when we found you that day in the street, your wound had already been given kinds of first aid that I've never seen or heard of before. There was some kind of gelatinous material over the wound that had prevented you from losing all your blood—though how you chanced to live through the loss of blood you *did* sustain, I'll never know."

The pause was heavy, filled with a terrible silence.

"Your leg was splinted," he finally continued just as slowly, "with a kind of metal that is as strange to me as the first-aid techniques used. A friend of mine in the steel business looked at one of those splints . . . and remarked it to be a kind of metal he'd never seen either, or heard of. Something like aluminum, mayhap, but far stronger. He wanted to know the secret behind your metal as much as I should like to know the secret behind whatever kept you alive until I found you." Another long, heavy pause. "But I don't dare ask. Nor do I want you to volunteer me information.

"Your clothing," he said, his words now coming in short, staccato bursts, "I have it stored away, should you want it. I've never seen garments like those before. With magnetic fasteners—That must be what they are. And the fabrics . . . I can't guess what they be. Furthermore, the cut of them is strange . . . strange. And I don't know what to make of the emblem on the breast of the jacket you wore. A sundial? What does that mean?"

He wasn't really looking at me as he spoke, and I knew that he expected and wanted no answers.

"And what sickness was it that you had—have? Something . . . I don't believe you'll ever be a fully well man again, Eugene. Never. There is something in you . . ."

Suddenly I wanted to tell him that I'd been born right here in the city of Chicago, but I knew better than to do that—and I really didn't think he would believe me if I said it.

"You're a strange man, Eugene," he murmured, turning away from the fire and looking directly into my eyes with as penetrating a look as I've ever gotten from another human being, "a haunted, hunted man; and there be something about you that suggests you have a mission, a goal, some quest which must be fulfilled, and which you don't really desire to fulfill—though what it be and how it might relate to *my* world I would not even want to guess, much less know." His voice paused now, but not his gaze: his eyes continued to bore into me. And there was a strangeness to his own voice when he spoke the next words. "I'm afraid of you, Eugene."

I had no words to say as he refilled our diminutive glasses.

He was looking into the flames when he spoke once more, perhaps seeing visions in them. "Life has been good to me in many ways, but I've also had my share of misfortunes, as I'm certain you are aware."

I nodded, sipping my liqueur.

"I've had my sorrows and I have no wish to inflict them upon you. And I've had my joys, particularly in my daughter. She is my life, Eugene. She's my family, my posterity, and my future. I want her life to be happier than mine has been, though I cannot say that I've ever felt that God has done me an injustice. I'm no Job." He turned to face me now. "As I said, Eugene, I don't desire to know your story. Something tells me that I should not be happy knowing it. And that same thing tells me that if *she* were to know who and what you are —whatever that might be—if she were to know and somehow become *involved with* whatever it is that you flee from and search for—well, I'm afraid that neither would Sharon be happy." He puffed on his cigar. His next words were blunt, almost brutal: "You hadn't planned on staying in Chicago long, had you?"

I shook my head, searching for the right words. "I have— Yes, you're partly right, Doctor. I do have someplace to go."

He nodded. "So I believed. Someplace very far from here?"

I thought: Somewhere farther from here than you might imagine—yet nearer . . . I said only: "Yes."

"And I don't suppose you shall ever be returning?"

I had found pleasure and satisfaction and, well, security in the world of 1871. Despite many things I might have disliked about it, I'd thought more than once of staying here, of living out my life in this isolated fragment of time and space. Yet the chronalcage was waiting for me in that warehouse off Clark Street and I knew that someday, sooner or later, when I had the strength and the will, I would have to go back to it. I'd promised Melanie, and something in that promise bound me as no other promise ever had, a feeling which, despite my desire to stay, grew stronger with each passing day.

"I doubt that I'll ever be coming back—here," I finally answered.

"When you depart," Dr. English said, speaking very slowly again, yet with a quietness and a sincerity and a gentleness I found almost touching, "I want you to leave with Sharon only the most casual of memories, Eugene. You're a stranger whom we have met and befriended as Christians, and whom we shall never, belike, see again. Sharon is engaged to be married to a very fine young man who can provide her with the kind of home and life she deserves. I don't want you to do anything—anything at all—that might jeopardize their marriage."

"I understand you, Dr. English."

"I hope you do."

"I would certainly never do anything to hurt you or your daughter."

"I had hoped—and believed—that you would feel that way." After a brief, awkward pause: "I don't wish to seem inhospitable, Eugene, but I do wish that you would be on your way as . . . as soon as you are well enough to go."

"That is my intention, Doctor. Honestly."

"I'm glad to hear that."

"I owe you far too much to ever—" I found myself at a loss for words again.

"Don't speak of it. Let us say that what I did for you was no more than my Christian duty to my fellow man."

I tried to smile but found it impossible.

"Good night, Eugene," he said, throwing the remainder of his cigar into the fire. "Do you need assistance?"

"No, thank you, Doctor. I can make it up the stairs on my own."

Houston English remained behind me in the sitting room while I made my slow and still painful way up to the room he'd given me. Though when I'd climbed that long flight of stairs and crawled into bed, I found sleep a difficult state to achieve.

13

Sharon English was born in 1848, which made her my senior by one hundred forty-seven years; but in 1871 that didn't seem very relevant. She was twenty-three then; I was thirty-seven. By those standards, and those were the only ones that seemed sensible under the circumstances, I was fourteen years older than she. I was—had been—would be—twelve years older than Melanie, but I tried to avoid thinking of Melanie. It tended to be painful.

I tried to avoid thinking of Sharon, too.

It wasn't painful, but I feared that it could be.

During the period that I stayed in the English household, beginning in July, 1871, I was in daily contact with the attractive young woman who was my benefactor's daughter. Initially, she and Amanda had shared the duties of nursing me, and I must admit that when my strength was sufficiently returned I felt a stirring of interest in both of them. I was a normal, and had been a reasonably healthy, adult male, and I'd not lacked an at-least-normal sexual drive. On more than one occasion Johanna had called me a "sex maniac," which was her term for anyone who thought a man and woman ought to have sex more than two or three times a month—but then that was toward the end of our short marriage. My sexual drive was now returning, or at least coming to the surface, and in this world of 1871 no government-administered antisex drugs existed to curtail such cravings in single men, though in my world most men knew how to avoid ingesting most such supposedly secretly administered drugs.

Two young women in the house . . .

Something in Amanda's attitude squelched an incipient desires I might have felt toward her, young and physically attractive as she was.

Although Amanda was a free woman, she was also black, and thought of herself in the terms of her period. She wasn't a slave and never had been, born and raised in the Northern free states, the daughter of freeborn black parents. Yet she was a servant, a *black* servant—a lower order than her white master and mistress—who knew her place in the universe, a definitely inferior one, and kept that place. These feelings, these attitudes and ideas, she somehow radiated to me, and they evoked something in me that I didn't quite like.

I had been raised in a home where racial distinctions were ignored, as far as the reality of the times would allow. By the turn of the twentieth century the black people of the United States had long since polarized into two groups: that portion who still embraced the idea and the ideal of "integration," of brotherhood between and mixture of the races, who denied the concept that any real human racial groupings existed outside the prejudiced minds of little men—a position strongly supported by whites of my father's ideological persuasion —and that portion of blacks who had totally rejected racial integration and had set out to establish a strong black culture within—or outside of!—the political framework of the U.S.: black segregationists; black nationalists.

It wasn't always a pleasant situation, the Integrationists vs. the Black Isolationists, but it was one that had finally been worked out with a minimum of violence and which allowed a certain measure of individual freedom for the members of both parties.

This not-too-happy polarization ended even before the Doverites got fully into power, however. The increase of world tensions and the beginnings of the collapse of the world economy in the first decades of the twenty-first century brought about such further polarization between the races *and* the black factions that, finally, in the late 2010's, the racial skirmishes, if not all-out civil war, that had been avoided for so long exploded across America.

Blood flowed in the streets.

Guerrilla warfare was staged in the cities.

Blacks retreated into the ghettos, not yet defeated.

Chaos.

Finally, armistice: a beginning of coming to terms, the possibility, though slim, of peace again.

Then . . .

When Archibald Victor Larch, "Archy the Terrible," came to power, and eventually threw out the Constitution and formed what came to be called the Church/State, the vast majority of American blacks found themselves disenfranchised. Many were "relocated" into camps that were nothing more or less than political prisons.

Oh, there were a few blacks who had joined the W.E.C., perhaps two to five percent of the total U.S. black population, and they were still accepted by the Church/State, held up as models to the world that this was not *really* a racist government: "No, not at all; look what we've done for our black brothers." But it *was* racist and those duped blacks were hardly more than Larch's puppets; they fooled no one but themselves.

Whatever I might have felt about black people, I don't believe that it was ingrained racial prejudice. I hadn't been brought up that way. But . . . but I did feel an alienation from them, even a fear of them—though I suspect that more of this fear had been instilled by Doverite propaganda than from any real sense of menace by blacks I'd actually met.

In Amanda was none of that hostility toward whites that might have been common in my world. In its place was something quite the opposite of hostility (I think), a fawning submissiveness that made me realize why many of her descendants a century and a half from now might hate the men and women—the *race*—who had made their ancestors feel like lesser beings, animals who looked something like men and had a not fully developed power of speech.

And there were within the United States at this very moment, the year 1871, thousands upon thousands of blacks who had been but newly granted their "freedom" —on paper at least. Slavery had been outlawed in these thirty-seven states. But an uncounted number of those who had been "emancipated" would never have any idea of what freedom really meant; they and their children and their grandchildren would live under conditions little better—and in some cases actually worse— than slavery. And many of them would consider themselves their masters' slaves until their dying days.

I could have felt very little toward Amanda, had there even been any chance of communication between us. And she *was*, legally, a married woman.

Sharon English was another matter. I didn't want to consider her romantically. I knew better. I had sensed the things that her father wished to say to me long before he had spoken them aloud.

But spending day after day in the presence of a young, attractive, intelligent woman of my own race and social standing—though separated culturally by a hundred and fifty years of time—I could not help but feel an attraction toward her.

I didn't want to, but at my age I should have realized that most of a person's experiences are things he wouldn't have wanted to happen if he'd thought about them in advance.

Sharon's hair was auburn and her eyes were blue. She was short, even for her time—about 5'2", English measure—and wore on her body a little more flesh than might have been fashionable in mine. That isn't to say that she was fat—"plump," perhaps, though maybe even that suggests a person more fleshed out than she was.

She was quite pretty, remarkably so even when dressed in the outrageous street clothes of the period. And she was equally pretty, perhaps more so, in the simpler, more realistic clothing she normally wore when within her home, clothing which, unfortunately, was still extravagantly puritanical, but which, fortunately, did not wholly deny that a very attractive young woman-body was beneath the fabric and metal and whalebone.

For her time, Sharon English was an educated and literate young lady. She had been sent to some of the better girls' schools in the Northeast and had a good grasp of general knowledge—perhaps even more than was seemly for a young woman of the gentility—though she had spent only a year in newly opened Vassar College after the Civil War, before moving west with her father. Her main interests in life were music, horses, and poetry. She was both an excellent organist and a fine equestrienne; although I was never privileged to witness her riding skills I heard her father speak much of them. As unfamiliar with horses as I am—was then and am now—I might not have been able to appreciate her abilities anyway. I *could* appreciate her ability at the organ. Between my earlier introduction to music by Melanie and my further education by Sharon, I could, perhaps, have come to develop good taste in music.

She was moderately active in some of the social and charitable works performed by the ladies of the upper levels of society in the Chicago of 1871, as befitted the position her father had—or, rather, had had before the unfortunate aftermath of his operation on the banker's son. Her activity in such "good works" took her out of the house more often than anything else, except her shopping trips with Amanda and Isaac. Under other circumstances, Sharon might have been something of a social butterfly, a bright and cheerful girl swept up in the activities of the young men and women of her class. That she wasn't I attributed mostly to circumstances that, for a time at least, had made her and her father semi-outcasts.

And there was to Sharon's mind a serious turn.

By this I don't mean to suggest that she was moody —"melancholy," to use the contemporary term. She wasn't, at all: for the most part, she was a cheerful and seemingly happy person. But there was a sadness to her thoughtful eyes that was never totally erased by the smile that drew little lines around them, radiating from their outer corners. She had read enough and seen enough to have some awareness of the world outside her own circle, to have some appreciation of the problems and complexities of society, and she had not found as much security in the old ways of thought as had her father. She'd read Thomas Henry Huxley, if not Darwin himself, and had found in herself a distrust of the monolithic pseudotruths of the Episcopal Church that her father had never had.

Sharon was also, if in a mild and gentle way, a supporter of the movement to grant the vote to women. She had worked with some of the less active, more aristocratic groups, though I don't believe she had ever marched in any parades or taken part in demonstrations. She wasn't really a rebel, but she could have developed into one had some of her dissatisfactions been nurtured. Perhaps, with the passage of time, her feelings would become more intense, not less so as happens to many people; I suspected that I could see a spark of zeal in her eyes, still confined, but ready to burst out at the proper moment. Under similar circumstances, Melanie might have been like her, and she could have been like Melanie.

Sharon liked to read, but outside of the magazines directed toward women, she generally confined herself to romantic novels, gothic things of love and terror. She had a great love for Sir Walter Scott and found a morbid fascination in the fiction of Poe. She also read popular histories and, of course, poetry.

As we sat alone, she would often tell me about the books she had recently read, mentioning, among others that I recall, Lewis Carroll's *Alice's Adventures in Wonderland*, which she considered to be more than just a children's book. I generally tried to keep my own comments brief, as too much ignorance or too much knowledge on a specific subject could have been embarrassing to me.

And she had read poetry to me: Matthew Arnold, Alfred Lord Tennyson, Robert and Elizabeth Barrett Browning, Fitzgerald's *Rubáiyát*—of which her father disapproved—and Poe. More than once she read to me

Arnold's "Dover Beach." In it I found a chill, and an understanding of Sharon and her view of the world that I might never have had otherwise.

The sea is calm tonight,
The tide is full, the moon lies fair
Upon the straits;—on the French coast the light
Gleams and is gone; the cliffs of England stand,
Glimmering and vast, out in the tranquil bay.
Come to the window, sweet is the night air!
Only, from the long line of spray
Where the sea meets the moon-blanched land,
Listen! you hear the grating roar
Of pebbles which the waves draw back, and fling,
At their return, up the high strand,
Begin, and cease, and then again begin,
With tremulous cadence slow, and bring
The eternal note of sadness in.
Sophocles long ago
Heard it on the Aegean, and it brought
Into his mind the turbid ebb and flow
Of human misery; we
Find also in the sound a thought,
Hearing it by this distant northern sea.

The Sea of Faith
Was once, too, at the full, and round earth's shore
Lay like the folds of a bright girdle furled.
But now I only hear
Its melancholy, long, withdrawing roar,
Retreating, to the breath
Of the night-wind, down the vast edges drear
And naked shingles of the world.

Ah, love, let us be true
To one another! for the world, which seems
To lie before us like a land of dreams,
So various, so beautiful, so new,
Hath really neither joy, nor love, nor light,
Nor certitude, nor peace, nor help for pain;

And we are here as on a darkling plain
Swept with confused alarms of struggle and flight,
Where ignorant armies clash by night.

Over the passage of days and weeks, I found myself more and more drawn to her, a feeling which I knew I had to fight. This time was not for me: I had no place in it. Perhaps I had set out to alter history, but not in this fashion, not by plugging myself into a world where I really had no business being. I had a duty, I told myself, and I loved Melanie, not Sharon, even though Melanie didn't exist yet in this world and might not ever, if . . .

I thought about another poet, one of a later time than this, and of an arrival at a crossroads and the decision to take one path rather than another, and how such a decision "made all the difference," now and forever more . . .

There were so damned many things it was better to avoid thinking about.

I tried, gradually, to draw myself away from Sharon, tried to remember what the doctor had told me and what I had told him, and what I had told myself.

I tried.

14

On Sunday evening, the first day of October, 1871, close to two weeks after my talk with Dr. English, Sharon and I were sitting on the front porch, rocking slowly in separate chairs, as red dusk fell along Willow Street. The evening was still warm, almost hot, and terribly dry from the winds that had blown for several weeks from the southwest plains, bringing a drought to the city and the farmlands outside it, dust into the streets, and dryness to the pine buildings of the city.

Even though it was Sunday, Isaac had driven Dr. English to a meeting of investors who were considering the backing of a new Chicago newspaper and was not expected to return until quite late. In his absence, Sharon had elected not to attend evening church services, although Amanda had gone to her own church with a friend, a church whose long and loud services, filled with threats of fire and brimstone and promises of a better world in the hands of God, were not expected to be over until equally late.

We were alone, the two of us.

I should have known better.

Sharon had gotten me one of her father's cigars, for which I'd developed a great liking, and had just prepared us tea. We sat and rocked and sipped tea and watched the redness spread across the sky and then turn purple and edge toward blackness, fanning ourselves with paper fans lithographed with religious pictures—something Amanda had brought home from a church social. A few stars were already visible between the teasing streaks of cloud that seemed to promise rain they would withhold from the parched city. A lamplighter had come down the street, bringing flame to the gas lamps, spreading a feeble illumination across the lawns and the fronts of the houses.

For a while we had been talking of one thing and another, Sharon telling me about some of their neighbors; and then our conversation wandered from the probable downfall of Boss William Marcy Tweed and Tammany Hall (the *Times* had published certain secret Tweed accounts) to the future of the Western Territories now that the transcontinental railroad had been completed. Sharon read the newspapers almost as thoroughly as did her father.

Then we were silent for a time, listening to the sounds of nighttime insects in the garden, hoping that a cool breeze might come in off the lake to kill the unseasonable warmth that lay over Chicago.

How many more years of life does that lake have? I asked myself when Sharon spoke of it. How long before it's too filthy to be allowed to exist and takes up too much space that could be used for human habitation? When does the draining and filling begin? I didn't do the figures in my head; it didn't seem important then. That was a *long* way off.

"Father said that you may perchance be leaving us soon," Sharon finally said, the words almost hesitant.

"Yes," I answered as casually as I could, "just as soon as he·pronounces me well enough to travel."

"Must you go?"

I nodded, grunted.

"There's no way I could implore you to stay?" she asked, carefully avoiding my eyes in the dusk. "There's a good future for an alert, intelligent man in Chicago. Everybody says it's going to be a great city someday, mayhap second only to New York. We already have three-hundred thousand people and more arrive daily."

"I know . . ." I said, hoping that the significance I felt as I spoke the words didn't sound in them.

"Father says that there's something you must, belike,

do elsewhere and that you probably won't ever come back to Chicago."

"Your father's a very perceptive man."

"Gene . . ." As she said my name there was an earnestness in her voice, an almost painful quality. She turned in her chair to face me now. "I won't ask you anything about yourself. You don't have to tell me anything you don't desire to. But . . . but you're not a criminal or anything like that, are you?"

"I've broken no laws of these United States," I said, unable to lie to her and equally unable to tell her the truth. I hoped that my words weren't too enigmatic.

"I knew you were not a criminal."

Again there was a silence, but she didn't turn away. Her eyes stayed on me now.

"There's something about you that's very strange," she said. "And perchance I'm a little frightened of you. I didn't want Father to pick you up that day when we saw you in the gutter."

"I know that, Sharon."

"I thought, well, that you were just a common drunk, some ruffian injured in a barroom fight or something. But then, when we'd gotten you home and I saw your face, I knew that you weren't anything like that. I didn't know—I still don't know—what you actually are or where you're from or where you're going, but . . ." Her words trailed off to a momentary silence. Then she said: "I don't want you to leave, Gene."

"Sharon, I'll have to go someday. Soon."

"But I don't want you to go."

"Don't think about me, Sharon. I'm nothing in your life. Nothing."

Suddenly I had a feeling of constriction, of tightness around my heart, and of something bordering on fear. She was, well, so young, so innocent; she knew nothing about me and my world, or the madness and hell up there! I'd never thought anything like this would actually happen. I'd had no idea . . .

"I want you to stay here in Chicago, Gene. You can—"

I forced myself to interrupt her. "Your father said

that you're engaged to be married, that you have a fiancé."

She nodded, then shrugged, sipped her tea, tried to retreat behind her cup, to regroup her forces, perhaps, to return with a more determined attack.

"Yes," she said at last. "I am—I was—engaged."

"You've broken the engagement?" I asked, fearful of her answer.

"Well . . ." she said hesitantly. "No, not exactly."

"What do you mean?"

"Howard doesn't know—he doesn't know anything about you," she said. "You see, he's an architect, and he's been back East gaining experience by working in a big firm there, and, well, I haven't seen him for a spell —over two months. We write, of course, but I don't tell him about you or hint at anything . . . in my letters."

"There's really nothing for you to tell him about me, is there?" I asked, wishing there were some way I could break this off, now and cleanly, but suddenly not certain that I would, even if I knew how.

I was held in a kind of terrified fascination by the young woman seated in the rocking chair, by what she was intimating, by the possibilities she was suggesting . . .

"No, I judge not," she was answering.

"And you do love him, don't you?"

"I—I'm not sure." She held the china cup before her like a shield. "I mean, I believed I truly loved him and wanted to marry him, but that was before . . ."

"Before?"

"Before you."

I couldn't be certain in the dusk and by the feeble illumination from the gas lamps near the street, but I thought she blushed and lowered her eyelids.

"Sharon," I forced myself to say as coldly as I possibly could, "I'm nothing in your life. Nothing. You know that."

"You could be, Gene."

"No . . . I can't be."

"Why not? I . . ."

"You know that I must go away, Sharon. I've got to leave Chicago and everything in it and I know that I'll never be back. Not back here. I won't be able to return afterward . . ."

"Afterward?" she asked when I failed to continue.

"After I do what I have to do."

"And what is that, Gene?"

"I can't tell you."

"And it's as important a thing as that?"

I nodded, said, "It's as important a thing as that," and quickly drank the last of my tea, now cold.

Full darkness had now descended on the city, and the thin clouds had vanished, taking their promises with them; the sky was full of stars, bright, brilliant, hardly twinkling, hardly dimmed by the lights of the city. The stars and the pale light of the gas lamps gave the only illumination now. In the darkness of the porch I could but barely see Sharon's face.

In the distance a horse neighed; the dull thud of its shod hooves against the packed, dry dirt of the city's streets, and the curse of a drayman as he urged the horse on, could be heard clearly. Perhaps he was carrying produce into Chicago from one of the outlying farming communities. From somewhere nearby a baby cried in the early night, and from the direction of the lake, farther away, a voice sang a song that I couldn't quite distinguish, accompanied by the tinny sounds of an old piano. Then a gust of wind brought words that might have been from "Old Black Joe."

This is Chicago, the irrelevant thought crossed my mind, distracting me for a moment from Sharon and what she was trying to tell me. This *was* Chicago, but it was no Chicago I'd ever known. This wasn't the New Jerusalem of Allen Howard Dover and his followers, the city that was the seat of power of the World Ecumenical Church, which ruled the theocracy called the Church/State. The sky, the air were clear here, clean; and the lights of the nighttime city were yellowish and few compared to the perpetual glare of the city I'd been born in. Here were no mass pollutants in the air, heightening the greenhouse effect that was increasing the world's annual temperature at an alarming rate.

Here, in this Chicago, the Kansas Pacific Railroad is just beginning to use refrigerated cars, while farther west mass buffalo hunting is still going on. Here, Loyola University has existed for only a year, and they are just beginning to use cement to pave the streets. Here, most of the city is made of wood—resinous pine—and the single pumping station has a wooden roof. Here, many veterans of the Civil War mingle in the streets with newly freed slaves and recently arrived immigrants who can hardly speak English. The immigrants are establishing miniature communities of their own ethnic groups—here, in this Chicago.

Here there are no UPT monorails, no layered streets packed with motorized traffic and MassTrans buses. Under them are no crowded subway tubes filled with perpetual movement. Here are no highrise apartments towering from the land-built-from-garbage where Lake Michigan had once been, housing thousands of the city's millions in pinnacles that reach arthritically into a hazy sky. Here are no "Indexes of Forbidden Knowledge" and no government listening devices in public places and private homes. Here, wild life is abundant; while *up there* are few species of wild animals left, few cats and dogs, too damned many people. Here is no world of anxiety and fear and whispered secrets to be kept from the ever-present Monitors of the all-seeing Church/State. Here are no blue-clad Lay Brothers of St. Wilson, no dark-vestmented Proctors. Here . . .

The New Jerusalem is yet to come to *this* world.

Sharon's voice brought me back, forced me to return to face the problem. I couldn't hide from her in dreaming.

"I don't know what to say now, Gene," she said slowly, quietly. "I judge that I've made something of a fool of myself. I'm sorry. I—"

Then her words were broken by a sob, and even in the poor light I could see that tears were in her eyes, running down her cheeks. God, I hadn't wanted to hurt her!

I shouldn't have done what I did next. I should have realized the full and dangerous potentials of the situation. I was old enough to guess at what would happen, what was bound to happen, what was inevitable when I made that move. But I simply didn't think that far ahead. Dammit, maybe I didn't want to.

Awkwardly, with my one good leg and my cane, I rose from the rocking chair. I stood over her for a moment, looking down at her face, dark in the shadows, her eyes glistening in the light of the distant lamps, and the tears she had shed. I touched her cheek with my hand, brushing away the tears.

"I'm sorry, Sharon."

She looked up at me for a long, lingering moment. "Kiss me, Gene," she said. "Please, will you kiss me?"

And I did.

And as I did, she rose from the chair and, half-supporting me, continued our kiss, brought her body tightly against mine, put her arms around me.

"I love *you*, Gene," she said when at last we broke from the kiss. "I love you and I want you to stay. I want to convince you to stay here with me."

"Sharon, no . . ." I found myself saying.

"Let me convince you to stay, Gene," she whispered.

"Sharon . . ."

I tried to speak again, but her mouth was against mine and her body was against mine and I felt the will to resist slowly ebb. She was offering me a bribe, and I thought I knew something of the importance she attached to it, the importance attached to it by this world, this society, this culture. She was offering me herself, her body—virgin and untouched—if I would stay. I knew that I should refuse, tell her "No!" loudly and resoundingly, but I knew now that I couldn't. I could only accept what she offered.

Later, in the bed that her father had lent me—I tried not to think of the trust I was breaking—Sharon slowly, shyly, even fearfully, removed her clothing and let me look at her beautiful young body in the light of an oil lantern that sat on a table on the other side of the room, let me place my hands on her, my lips on her, feel the warmth and pleasure of her.

Then she just as fearfully helped me to remove my own clothing and drew me to her, into her, uncertain of what she should do or how she should do it.

Sharon was giving me what she considered to be the most precious thing she had in the world.

No man had seen her naked before.

She had been a virgin until that night.

Her eyes, her mouth, her hands, her breasts, her navel, her vagina, her thighs, her legs . . . I was enfolded in her, immersed in her, swallowed up and consumed by her. I was infatuated, enraptured. I was lost and I was found.

I was separated from time and space and existed in a universe that consisted of only the two of us and the coupling of our bodies.

For a while I forgot . . .

I had made her no promises, not in words, though she thought I'd merely left them unspoken.

Perhaps I had.

I know I had.

I lay in my bed alone, turmoil in my mind. Sharon had gone to her own room, happy and more than happy, the brief pain of her first penetration forgotten, washed away in what had followed, and had fallen to a sleep which, I suspected, was filled with dreams of our eventual marriage. We hadn't discussed it, but I believe she expected it to come to pass in the winter, perhaps near the Christmas holidays.

I heard sounds now from below as Amanda returned from her late church service; and later I heard horses clop into the driveway and stop, heard Houston English speak to Isaac before he led the horses back to the stable behind the house. I heard the doctor enter and prepare for bed, and still later Isaac joined his wife in the room they shared downstairs, in the rear, near the kitchen. Silence again reigned over the house on Willow Street.

And still sleep would not come to me.

I hadn't *really* promised Sharon that I would stay,

but . . . But maybe I did love her—and there were things I liked about this world, a simplicity within its brash arrogance and raw vigor, a youthfulness about Chicago and the country that was still almost three decades from the twentieth century and all the horrors that it would bring to the planet, over a century and a half from the day when a dark-vestmented Proctor would come bursting into the displacement chamber to drag Melanie away to—

And I could avoid that world, the twentieth century and the twenty-first, which would follow. All I had to do was—nothing! I would be an old man, sixty-one, by the time H. G. Wells wrote his fantasy about the possibility of a "time machine," and I might even be dead before the Wright brothers made their first flight; in this world, sixty-nine is old. Surely I'd never live to see the beginning of "the War to End all Wars."

All I had to do was nothing. And all my life I'd been very good at doing nothing, at avoiding.

I could do as Sharon wanted. I could marry her, make a home for us, and I felt certain that with my knowledge of future events I could easily make myself a far more wealthy man than her father had ever been.

It wouldn't be such a bad life. I'd already adjusted to the lack of many things I had once considered necessities, and I would never again have to fear the Proctors and their cries of heresy. I would never have to risk my life trying to complete a promise that I might not be able to fulfill, anyway—I didn't *know* that Time would not cut me off in a closed loop when I tried to alter history, and there was no certainty that I or anyone else could do *anything* to prevent the creation of the world from which I'd fled.

It could be a good life here. All I had to do was stay.

The grandfather clock on the landing above the hall-way boomed out two o'clock in the morning as I drifted off into a haziness that preceded sleep.

15

The next morning, Monday, the second of October, I was late in rising and when I did, after washing and dressing, I was reluctant to go downstairs.

Yet when I finally did, nothing seemed amiss. I really shouldn't have expected there to be. Dr. English had already gone to the pharmacy to open it and help his clerks and his pharmacist prepare for the workday; then he had returned home. Sharon had gone with him and had been shopping while he attended to business; she'd bought another new hat, one of her weaknesses, another dreadful, gaudy, ridiculous thing that somehow looked good when she wore it. I was already acquiring the tastes it would take for me to accommodate myself to this time and place, I told myself.

When I had completed my painful limp down the long, awkward staircase, both Sharon and her father greeted me in the normal fashion, though English showed concern on his face.

"Did you not sleep well?" he asked as I followed him toward the sitting room, Sharon at my side, though not terribly close.

"No, I'm afraid that I didn't, Doctor," I said; it wasn't totally a lie. "That's why I'm so late in rising. I didn't get to sleep until far after midnight."

"I hope your leg wasn't bothering you," Sharon said, and gave me a look with her eyes and lips, soft and subtle, that would probably not have been noticed by anyone who wasn't looking for it.

I was. And it was the look I'd expected, had hoped to

receive from her. She had no guilt in her, only happiness. We were going to be married, weren't we? Then it was okay, wasn't it?

"If you continue to have that sort of trouble, Eugene," Dr. English said as we entered the sitting room, "—trouble in sleeping, that is—I can have something prepared that will aid."

"Thank you, Doctor," I replied. "If I have many sleepless nights, I'll ask for something."

"Please do."

In the sitting room Amanda had placed a tea service on the large oak table, and with it a steaming pot of tea and some sugar cookies sprinkled with confectioner's sugar. Dr. English asked me to join them, himself and Sharon, at tea in lieu of breakfast. Sharon insisted that I should have something more substantial, but I begged off, saying that tea and cookies would be fine. I wasn't all that hungry.

As I accepted I felt awkwardness and discomfort, half believing that I would stay in this world, as Sharon had requested. Somehow I could find a way to make it right with her father . . .

That feeling of discomfort didn't pass quickly, nor could I find the right words for small talk as we sipped our tea and ate our cookies. But I think Sharon understood.

The day itself was uneventful enough. Sharon and I had little real time alone together before night, though when darkness and quiet came over the house, she crept into my room and again we made love and there was still no guilt in it. Not on Sharon's part. And very little on mine now. I'd committed myself to her, hadn't I? I was going to stay, wasn't I?

The next day was only a little unlike many days that had gone before it: in the morning Dr. English went to open his pharmacy; Sharon went to a hospital with a group of young society belles to entertain children and pass out cookies and hot drinks. In the afternoon English persuaded me to go with him to a cobbler he knew, in order to have a special shoe fitted for my left foot. As he had predicted, the healing of the shattered bone had left my left leg shorter than the right, and if I were ever to hope to walk without a terribly pronounced limp, my left shoe would have to be specially elevated.

During the ride in the open carriage, Isaac driving the horses as they *clop-clop-clopped* along the hard-packed road, English and I sitting behind like gentlemen of leisure, I thought I felt a chill in the air, perhaps the beginnings of autumn. That winter was not far away was signaled by the trees along the sides of the streets, turning from the green of summer to the reds and yellows and golds of fall. Grass in the yards of many of the houses along the streets was yellowed, but I suspected that that had been caused more from the long dry spell than from the season. There was yet to be a frost, I believe.

Summer was gone now, a memory, and it was during the summer that I had come into this world. In July, I had plunged out of Time into 1871. Now it was autumn, October. I supposed, then, that I would see winter come and snow fall across the streets and buildings of Chicago, and eventually a spring would come to thaw it out and another summer would follow. Before that came, that next spring and summer, if Sharon had her way, we would be married. It was not a prospect I looked forward to with dread. Not at all.

Sharon English would make me a fine wife, a beautiful wife, and with only a little more delightful practice she would make me an excellent bed partner as well, not that I'd found any dissatisfaction with her performance to date.

No, I wasn't unhappy at the thought of spending the rest of my nights sharing a bed with her.

As we rode through the city streets, Dr. English pointed out the sights to me as if I *were* the stranger to the city I actually was.

He showed me the stockyards, the packing houses, the railroad yards, the huge warehouses of wholesale companies who had shifted their headquarters west to Chicago, the grain elevators that were making the city the center of the Midwest—the heart of the "Breadbasket of America."

"That's the Briggs House," he said, pointing to one imposing edifice. "It's said to be the largest hotel this side of the Alleghenies."

He went on to tell me that some fifteen years before, prior to his coming to Chicago, over two square miles of the downtown section of the city had been raised a height of twelve feet to alleviate the marshy conditions that had given the city the name "Mud Hole of the Prairies."

"They sucked mud up from the river," he said, "and spread it over the streets, and then they raised the buildings to match the new street level. Business as usual, right through it all. In fact, the Tremont Hotel—that big brick building over there; they've a fine menu in their dining hall; you should try their food. Anyway, the Tremont was raised up by jackscrews. George Pullman was in charge of the operation. They say that no one spilled a single drop of coffee while they were jacking it up!"

"That must have been jim-dandy," I said. By then I was picking up Old Chicago speech patterns.

"Some rascal that George Pullman is! Take my word, he's going to be a 'king' just like Marshall Field or Bill Ogden one of these days. I have, my own self, a few shares in his railroad-car company. They'll be worth their weight in gold in a few years."

As interesting to me as was anything he pointed out, however, were the handcrafted wooden Indians, stern and noble, who stood before the tobacco shops and advertised their goods.

Then, at last, the tour was over and we arrived at our destination.

While measurements were being made by the cobbler —an unpleasant little man named Henry Appleyard— the doctor left me for a while to attend to some business of his own, although he promised that he and Isaac would return later in the carriage to take me back to the house on Willow Street.

"It not be war wound, I reckon?" cobbler Appleyard asked as he carefully measured the depth of my instep.

"No, it's not," I told him, fumbling in my vest's

watchpocket for a match to light one of the cigars the doctor had left with me.

"Thought not," Appleyard said. "Seems too recent fer that."

"An accident," I said. "Happened a couple of months ago."

"Yep," he muttered, meaninglessly I supposed, beginning to gauge the width of my heel. "Got a wound in the War meself, y'know."

"Is that so?"

"Yep. You in the War?"

"No, I'm afraid not."

"Oh? Why not?" he asked, looking up from my heel to my face as if I were some sort of untouchable.

"It's none of your damned business!" I felt like saying, but I actually replied: "I was out of the country."

"That so?" He was looking at my heel again.

"South Africa," I said on the spur of the moment, to forestall further questions, though without success. "Kimberley, South Africa."

"Down in the diamond mines, was ye?" he asked, seeming at last to be satisfied with my heel. "Made yerself a pot, did ye?"

"I'm afraid not. Just a lot of wasted time."

"And I reckon that's why you talks kind 'er funny," the cobbler said.

"How's that?" I asked, rather startled.

"Don't mean no offense, Mr. Stillman, but there's somethin' kind 'er strange about the way ye talk, like mayhap you be some kind of a fureigner, but then I don't reckon ye're that."

"Oh," I said. "I suppose you're right. There's a lot of Englishmen and Dutchmen down there," I said, hoping there were and that I wasn't confusing times and places, "and I guess I could have picked up some of their speech habits."

"I were at Antietam, y'know," he said, after asking me to rise so that he could begin measuring the difference between my right and left legs, his curiosity now satisfied, perhaps. "Served under McClellan there. A dandy man, Gen'ral McClellan was. A real trump, no matter what they be sayin' 'bout 'im now."

"I'm sure."

"Don't like McClellan?" he asked.

"I've really got no feelings one way or the other, Mr. Appleyard," I answered as pleasantly as I could.

He snorted through his nose and continued to measure. "Fine gen'leman, 'e was. Best gen'ral we ever had. Men loved him," he muttered after a while. Then he said aloud: "Got shot 'n the chest."

"General McClellan?" I asked, wishing I hadn't, even as the words came out of my mouth.

"No," he snapped, looking up sharply as if doubting my sanity. "Hang it, *I* did! Right yere." He pointed toward his right breast, but higher, more nearly his shoulder. "Took a Reb minié ball. Damnedest thing ever happened t' me. Y'see, there was five of us, B Comp'ny, Fifth . . ."

And he proceeded to tell me, in minute and eventually gory detail, about how he and four others had stumbled into a Confederate ambush in the early-morning light. The way *he* told it, he was the hero of the day—and had he not fought his way out of the ambush and rushed back to warn his company, bleeding copiously from a minié ball wound just below his right shoulder, firing his Henry repeater as he backed away, his company would have been overrun and with it the whole regiment. And from that would have come the undoing of McClellan's master plan for the battle—that, and total defeat.

Which might have been just as well, from what I recalled of the battle, bits of Civil War history coming back to me now. Nobody had really won it. McClellan hadn't had the strength of character or the courage to really put the pressure on Lee despite the fact that the Union general had the advantage; although during Antietam's twelve long and bloody hours of battle, Lee's Army of Northern Virginia did come to know, maybe for the first time, that it could actually be hurt by the Yankees.

As Appleyard continued to measure and tell me about his exploits as a war hero, I thought that perhaps I was doing him an injustice in disbelieving his story. Maybe on the battlefield he was a more courageous man than he appeared to be, kneeling now before me. Stranger things have happened.

Appleyard paused in his labors to fill a dark, heavy pipe that looked too large for his face, and then said, as he rummaged through a drawer for matches, "We was talkin' 'bout yer accent a little whiles ago."

"Yes," I said, sitting back down in the chair he had offered me.

"You got 'ny friends in Chicago who was down there in South Africa with yer?"

He succeeded in finding a match and in lighting the pipe. The aroma of the tobacco was an atrocity—if it were tobacco at all, and not floor sweepings.

"No, not that I know of."

"Funny," he said, retrieving his tape measure. "I was over at Clancy's th'other night—that's a tavern a couple of blocks from 'ere, an' Clancy ain't really 'is name. Jew-boy, 'e is, name of Baddenstein or somethin'. Dandy feller when ye get t' know him, though."

I nodded, wondering what he was getting at.

"Anywho," he went on, drawing up another chair and reaching for a pad and a pencil that lay on his cobbler's bench, "there be these two fellers in there, havin' a beer or two, sittin' up at the bar, and when they were talkin' I heard that they talked kind'er funny, y'know? Didn't think much of it at the time. So danged many fureigners in town these days, it's hard t' find a real 'Merican."

"They talked funny?" I asked, now beginning to feel a curiosity within myself, and an anxiety.

"Yep," Appleyard said, beginning to jot figures on his pad. "Talked a lot like you do. Hadn't thought about 'em 'til jest now."

"What were they saying?"

The cobbler shrugged. "Don't reckon I was really payin' 'em any mind."

"It's possible," I said suddenly, wondering whether I

should try to improvise another story, "that there are some others in town who were in South Africa. What did they look like?"

"Didn't pay much 'tention. Big fellers, both of 'em. Oh, there was somethin' odd about 'em, I reckon. Both of 'em had real short hair and didn't have no beards ner mustaches. Strange-lookin', I tell you. And they was packin' guns, too, but that ain't too strange 'round here. Ain't like back East. An', well, ye might say they was well-dressed, like mayhap they'd picked up a few of them diamonds down there, but they wasn't spendin' heavy."

"And you don't remember what they were talking about?"

I was afraid to admit to myself what was running through the back of my mind, and if I'd admitted it to myself would probably have dismissed it as wild conjecture. But then there was Conwell's story about the "contraptions" in Farmer McBride's potato patch . . .

"Nah," Appleyard said, shaking his head, still jotting figures and then making a rough sketch, "not really. They might have said they were strangers in town and they was lookin' fer a friend of theirs, somethin' like that." He looked up. "Think they was lookin' fer you?"

"I don't know," I answered, feeling a tingling of fear along my spine. "I wasn't expecting anyone."

"Ye might want to drop in over at Clancy's one o' these nights," the cobbler said, returning his attention to the pad of paper. "He's got good vittles there, if ye're in a mind fer a bite to eat. And them fellers might be hangin' out there."

"I may do that," I said, wondering whether I would have the courage.

I was prevented from asking him any more questions by the return of Dr. English, who insisted that Appleyard complete his measurements as quickly as possible; we were going to be late for dinner if we didn't start home at once, and he was in no mood for another of Amanda's tantrums. (Nothing upset Houston English's cook any more than his being late for a meal.)

Appleyard finished his measurements, promised that the shoes would be ready in two days—after English promised a ten percent bonus for prompt delivery—and we made our escape from the cobbler.

Appleyard yelled after me, "If ye drop by Clancy's I'll buy you a beer."

Outside, Dr. English asked, "What was that about Clancy's?"

"Oh, nothing," I said, and hoped it were true.

At dinner that evening English made a seemingly casual announcement the full significance of which I didn't realize until much later. This was on the evening of Tuesday, 3 October 1871.

"Oh, by the way, Sharon," he said between mouthfuls of roast beef and potatoes, "I chanced to run into Howard's father downtown today."

"Oh, did you?" she said, glancing up from her plate and giving me only the briefest of looks.

English nodded, lifted a china coffee cup halfway to his lips. "And he told me that he expects Howard to be back from New York on Sunday."

"Oh?" Sharon asked, sipping milk and glancing at me again over the rim of her glass. She put the glass down, delicately wiped the white mustache of milk from her upper lip with a linen napkin. "He is certainly due back, isn't he? He's been gone a very long while."

English nodded, chewing until his mouth was empty. Then he spoke: "The architectural plans took longer to complete than they had expected. Something about the use of some new type of steel structural supports, I recall Richard said. Something revolutionary, I understand, opening up all kinds of new avenues for architects."

"Is that so?" Sharon said, her voice devoid of interest in the subject, though I believe it was the tone she affected, not what came naturally to her at the moment.

"Anyway," the physician went on, somehow subtly adding a weight of significance to his words, "he's due in on the noon train from the East and I took the liberty of inviting him and his parents over to take dinner with us Sunday night. You may miss church for an occasion like this."

Sharon hadn't mentioned to him that she had missed evening church service the Sunday before, as well.

"We do owe them a dinner, I trust?" she replied.

English shot his daughter a quick, almost angry glance. His eyes began to turn toward me, but he seemed to catch himself and returned his gaze to his half-empty plate. "It would be an opportunity for you and Howard to see one another again. I should think you'd be anxious to see him after so long an absence."

"Oh, I am, of course," Sharon said suddenly, brightly, but with less feeling than she probably meant to convey.

We had decided to wait a few more days to announce her decision to break off her engagement with Howard. And this did not seem like a good time to say anything to the doctor about it.

"And I should like for Richard to meet Eugene before he leaves us," English said, the same deep significance in his words, especially the last four.

"Howard's father?" I asked, feeling that I should try to contribute something to the conversation, even if it were no more than a question that showed my ignorance of the full import of what was passing back and forth across the table.

"Richard? Yes," English said, giving me a worried look even as he said it. How much did he suspect, I wondered. "He's an architect, you know, a darned good one, and I believe Howard is going to be an even better one when he really hits his stride."

During this exchange Sharon gave me a short, intense look which I don't think her father caught, and which I *hoped* he hadn't caught.

"Tomorrow I'll tell Amanda to begin preparing for the dinner," Sharon said. Then she asked her father, "How was business doing at the pharmacy today?"

English was reaching for the potatoes, a china bowl of whitish spheroids sprinkled with green flecks of parsley. He didn't reply at once. His mind seemed to be on other matters.

Later that evening, when the rest of the household was asleep and Sharon had again come to my room—against my advice and better judgment, for I now suspected that, for all his gentleness, her father could be a violent and vindictive man were he to catch us together—we made love again and it was even more satisfying than either time before.

Awhile after, Sharon lay at my side, slightly uncomfortable in her unaccustomed nudity but willing to suffer it for my sake. She whispered to me: "Gene, when Howard and his parents are here Sunday night, will you tell them—and Father?"

"About us?" I asked.

She nodded in the room's dim light.

"Yes," I said simply, though the emotions I felt were anything but simple. But I *had* decided, hadn't I? "I'll tell them," I said softly to her, my voice sounding very loud in the room.

"I love you, Gene," she whispered to me, and then rose to dress and return to her own room.

The next three days passed in a fashion little less than idyllic—or would have, had I not felt the shadow of English's impending wrath hanging over me, over us both. I feared how the man might react when we told him what we had decided to do. Still, I thought—hoped—that when he saw that Sharon had made up her mind to marry me and not Howard, he would accept it.

There was no doubt in me now that I had firmly decided to stay here in Chicago, 1871. If I had any reservations now, I didn't admit them even to myself. I chose to ignore the world of the future, the future beyond the lifespan I expected to spend with Sharon—for I refused to consider the world beyond the opening of the twentieth century. That was another place, where things were done differently and would no longer be any concern of mine. Perhaps, without radically altering the flow of history, perhaps our children and grandchildren would help to make a better world than the one I'd known *up there*.

Yet . . . though I *knew* that I loved Sharon, knew it in the depths of myself as I'd never known any emotion before, I couldn't help but feel some doubts about that love. I wondered whether it was really love, as the word had been defined to me in my childhood, or whether it was something else, infatuation or simple sexual attraction, a trick I was playing on myself to relieve myself from the loneliness I felt, I'd always felt all my life, and felt now more than ever in a world where, despite what I might have known about it in an intellectual, historian's manner, I was really a stranger.

And why should I love this girl? I asked myself, except for her obvious physical attractiveness, the feminine sexuality that I hadn't really perceived before that Sunday night there on the porch, and later in my bedroom. Why? Most of her feelings and attitudes were alien to me. Hers was a rather primitive world by the standards of mine—not so alien to the world I had left in desperate haste, but to the world as I'd perceived it in my father's home as a child, before the coming of the Church/State. That was the world in which Sharon would have been an anachronism, a person with old-fashioned thoughts, reactionary ideals.

And what of Melanie? In some segment of time, even in that last segment of time on 4 March 2032, she was alive, and she might still be alive. To say that Melanie had not yet been born made her no less alive during those weeks of our affair in the early months of 2032. And I had said that I loved her. Had I? Did I? Would I, if . . . ? How could I so easily fall in love with Sharon if I really loved Melanie? Could I love them both in different worlds of time?

Melanie. Melanie. I *did* love you. I did!

And if I were to compare them—a thing I knew I shouldn't do, but couldn't help—when I compared them I knew that Melanie had qualities that Sharon didn't possess, or if she did possess them, they had never fully developed. There was a strength in Melanie, a dedication in her that I admired, respected, envied. Sharon did not have Melanie's strength of will. Nor did I.

Nor, I suspected, did Sharon have Melanie's intellect.

I never knew what Melanie's I.Q. was, but I believe it was probably greater than mine. What Sharon's might have been with a proper education, I couldn't guess. But I didn't think she would ever be Melanie's equal, under any circumstances.

And, despite Sharon's obvious beauty, there was a dark slenderness, a softly carried voluptuousness, a full realization of her own beauty and sexuality in Melanie that Sharon had never dreamed of. Sharon carried herself like a gentlewoman of the 1800's, as was fitting. Melanie carried herself like— Well, I can't think of the right term. Neither like a Babylonian whore nor a Hollywood starlet, but like someone who commanded the better qualities of each, and more. A Greek hetaera, perhaps. Melanie's sensuality was in a league far beyond Sharon's simplicity.

Despite all this, however, I knew that what I felt for Sharon English was an order of magnitude beyond anything I'd ever dreamed of feeling for Melanie Proctor or Johanna or anyone else.

It was Sharon I loved.

Not Melanie.

I was certain of that.

But what of my *duty* to Melanie? My duty to the future? I had promised, hadn't I? Was I still bound to that promise? What bound me to it? Melanie had been taken by the Proctors, had sacrificed herself so that I might go back and—

It was madness! I'd known that all along, this scheme to kill the Appointed One unborn in his mother's womb. A scheme devised by desperate madmen to rid their world of what they considered to be a festering evil, a cancer that was consuming what was left of the planet.

A mad scheme! One I should reject out-of-hand, as I should have months before, a century and a half ahead of this here-and-now.

Yet I found that I couldn't reject it. It was there in my brain, like still another wound that wouldn't heal properly, and I could not rid myself of it.

Somehow I managed to push most of this into the back of my mind and concern myself with the more im-

mediate problems, those at hand, those that now seemed
more real than any world of the twenty-first century.

As I've said, we had decided not to tell Sharon's father that I wasn't going to leave as I'd promised him I
would. We would wait until Sunday for that. We would
let him find out, come Sunday evening and the dinner
with Howard's family, when Sharon would publicly
break her engagement with the young man and I would
ask Dr. English for permission to marry his daughter.
We'd talked it over and decided that would be the best
way to do it.

During that time, those last few days before Sunday, I
strongly considered telling Sharon the truth about myself, but I could find neither the proper time nor the
proper words to do so, nor did I then consider it really
important. What *was* important was that we loved each
other. Strange, I kept telling myself, to have a feeling of
such intensity at my age; wasn't a love like I felt reserved for people much younger than I? And, well, I
would have the rest of my life to tell her that my father
would not yet be born when we were both long dead.

As for my physical condition, it was now about as
good as I could expect it to be, though I still had brief,
uneasy bouts with chills and nausea, fever and sweating
—symptoms not unlike those of malaria, though I knew
it wasn't that—and believed that English rather antici-
pated my leaving shortly after the Sunday dinner party.
I was still somewhat weak, and my left leg was very
painful if I exercised it too much, but I was growing
used to the fact that it would never be what it had been
before—though at night, with Sharon, I never felt pain
as we made love, only later when she was gone and I
was alone in the bed. In my own world, of course, my
leg could have been wholly restored, shattered bone replaced by synthetics, or a whole new limb regenerated if
necessary. A trip uptime to get that done was, of course,
something beyond consideration: it would be worth my
life. A game leg I could live with, if Sharon were my re-
ward for suffering it. I thought it more than a fair exchange.

At times I thought about the chronalcage and wondered what I should do about it, sitting in that lonely warehouse, gathering dust. Eventually it would be discovered, I knew: that warehouse couldn't sit idle for long, not with Chicago growing the way it was. And I didn't want to consider what kind of impact it would have on this world, the discovery of a device of highly advanced technology capable of moving about in Time itself. *That* would turn all of history upside down. Eventually I would have to do something about it—send it, unmanned, backward in time to get lost in some prehistoric limbo—but for now the warehouse seemed safe enough and I didn't need to get overly concerned about it.

So the days passed quickly and during them I further acclimated myself to the world of 1871. The nights I spent with Sharon.

And then Sunday, 8 October 1871, came and with it the dinner party.

16

On Sunday morning I went with the Englishes to church for the first time, a handsome Episcopal church near the heart of the burgeoning city. Dr. English and Sharon were dressed in their finest and I wore a new suit that the doctor's daughter had had tailored for me without my knowledge (I would hate for the physician to have known how she got my measurements) and had presented to me as a gift only that morning. Even the horses seemed to be at their finest for this occasion; Isaac must have spent hours grooming them. Though exactly what the occasion was, I wasn't certain.

The sabbath ritual within the church was long and boring, especially the rather dry sermon delivered by an educated and articulate, but humorless, man of the cloth; it lacked something of the pomp I'd expected, but then perhaps this wasn't the kind of Episcopalian service that my father had often talked about. Some elements of the service did remind me of the rites of the World Ecumenical Church, but not really enough to give me the sense of discomfort I'd halfway expected. It was low key, you might say, restrained, very civilized, and despite the minor grandeur of it, there was not about this service the awesome sensation of lying beneath a towering monolithic structure that might as easily and casually crush you as bless you—a sensation I'd often felt in the compulsory W.E.C. services . . . back home.

We returned to Willow Street in the carriage, after chatting briefly on the church lawn with some friends and acquaintances of the Englishes. Howard's father and mother, whatever their last name might be, were apparently not Episcopalian; but I got the impression that both God and English had forgiven them that transgression some time ago. We found that Amanda had laid out for us a sparse meal of tea and cold cuts. It was something, Sharon told us, merely to take the edge off our appetites. The real meal of the day, Amanda's masterpiece, would be served that evening, when Howard and his family came.

Despite her seeming reluctance to see Howard again and then be forced to break off the long-standing engagement, Sharon had gotten caught up in Amanda's excitement over the meal and was willing to devote the rest of the day to helping her in the kitchen. Only once, while the others of the household were occupied elsewhere, did Sharon take the time to be alone with me for a few seconds in the dark, illicit hallway, give me a brief kiss, and say that she was glad that the waiting was nearly over and that we could tell everyone how we felt about each other.

As I held her in my arms, pressing her soiled apron against my starched white shirt, I smelled on her the odor of her own sweat (for it was very hot in the kitchen with both wood-burning ovens going), as well as the aromas of hot fat and garlic and spices; and I found in the odors a pleasure and delight, a wild sensual arousal. The smell of Sharon's body and the scents of naturally grown organic foods were ones I now expected to smell the rest of my life, and I was looking forward to it.

"You'd better let me go," she said at last, "or somebody mayhap will catch us."

"I don't care," I whispered.

"You should. What would people think?"

"Let them think what they like," I told her.

"If you can't wait until we're married," she whispered back, "at least wait until we've announced our engagement."

"I can't wait."

"You can. Until tonight, at least."

Then she broke away from me and dashed back into the steam and heat of the kitchen and I hobbled back to find a place to sit down and something to read to pass the time.

Sharon was still in the kitchen with Amanda, amid the pots and pans and roaring oven fires; Dr. Houston English and I were in the sitting room smoking cigars and trying to carry on a halting conversation; and Isaac was tending to last-minute details and then running an emergency errand for his wife, to fetch some condiment she had forgotten during her earlier trips to the markets, as dusk fell over the house on Willow Street, filled to the eaves with the good odors of food in the oven and on the stove, on the evening of 8 October 1871.

At half past seven in the evening, after dressing in still another suit of new clothing fresh from the tailor— this, I supposed, a "going away" gift from the good doctor—and in the specially constructed shoes from H. Appleyard, Esq., Cobbler, I stood for a moment before the mirror Isaac had brought into my room prior to helping me dress.

"Well, how do I look?" I asked him.

"Jus' fine, Mista Gene," Isaac said, his voice polite, almost reverential.

I had the suspicion that Isaac and Amanda had some pretty wild notions about me, romantic ones, as if I were some pirate finding seclusion in the doctor's house, or more likely some Western outlaw come east to escape the fury of Wild Bill Hickok.

"Do I really, Isaac?" I asked.

"Yessir, you look jus' fine t' me."

I realize that I've said very little about Isaac, less than I have about any other member of the English household. It hasn't been my intention to slight him, nor to present him as a cardboard cutout, or even less to give you the idea that he was the sort of blackface atrocity already being presented on the American stage in 1871. He wasn't that.

Oh, I knew a little about his background: born in New York State some twenty-three years before my arrival in Chicago, the son of an escaped-slave couple who had fled North on the Underground Railroad shortly be-

fore the birth of their first son. They had paused to rest
on their flight to Canada in English's hometown and had
been taken in by the young doctor and his bride. Isaac
had been born under English's roof. His mother had died
in childbirth and his father had taken to drinking (as
the doctor himself was to do when his own wife died),
had later killed a man in a drunken fight, and had died
in prison when his son was ten or eleven. The baby
Isaac was raised by an elderly black woman called Aunt
Sarah, who was then Houston English's housekeeper.
When of age, Isaac had joined the household as a servant and had remained so, except for a brief stint in the
black Union forces near the end of the Civil War. He
never saw action. Upon his return home, he'd married
Amanda, and they, still childless, had followed English
west.

So much for history.

What of the man?

I wish I could say. Isaac spoke very little to me, very
little to anyone save his wife. He was a good servant,
deferential and courteous, always ready to do what was
asked of him. He did just about all of the odd jobs
around the house, and seemed to take great pleasure in
tending to the pair of horses that pulled English's carriage. Both he and Amanda could read and write,
though I'm certain their education had been very limited.

I was afraid of him.

Perhaps I shouldn't say that, and I hope that I never
showed it to him. But . . . well, I've mentioned how
things were, uptime. Nevertheless, if there were hostility
toward me seething below the surface of Isaac's calm,
patient face, he never showed it to me, nor anyone else
that I know of. He may have been, probably was, exactly what he seemed to be, and maybe he was content with
his place in the scheme of things. A man could have
been worse off than he.

Yet I sometimes wonder if perhaps there wasn't at
times a flash in his eyes, a hotness in his chest, a desire
to see things other than they were.

He was a very private man, toward me at least, and

I'll never know. Is there a debt of guilt I feel I owe him . . . ?

He'd said that I looked "jus' fine" and would say nothing more, so, hobbling on my cane, I went downstairs to join the physician who was my host, my benefactor, and so much more—and a man whose trust I had broken and to whom I would, in an hour or two, announce in public the fact that I had broken those promises made to him, lied to him—perhaps tell him I'd even seduced his daughter under his very roof. People of that time and place would see things in those terms; I suppose that, at the time, I did as well.

Sharon was waiting for me at the bottom of the stairs.

"I think they're arriving now, Gene," she said, her nervousness not showing in her voice, but in her eyes and by the moisture on her upper lip.

I followed her out onto the porch to see a carriage much like English's pull into the driveway, driven by an elderly black man with a great shock of white hair. From the carriage dismounted a handsome woman of about English's age, a somewhat portly man three or four years her senior, and a rather handsome young man who could have been no more than two or three years older than Sharon: Howard.

Dr. English, leaving his cigar behind in the sitting room, came out onto the porch to welcome them, stepping ahead of Sharon and myself.

"Richard, Deborah," English said warmly, extending his hands to them as they came from the walk and up the stairs to the porch. "It's so good of you to come, and on Howard's first night home."

"It's always a pleasure, Houston," said the man he had addressed as Richard.

Until this moment it had not really struck me as strange that I had never heard their family name mentioned, and perhaps it shouldn't have then. Even *now,* it shouldn't seem odd to me: there couldn't possibly have been a conspiracy to keep their family name from me. There is no way that English could have known who they were—that is, who in a historical perspective that could have been seen only from a hundred years and more away. Yet, *I hadn't heard their last name!* A coincidence? It could have been nothing more. Yet it haunts me still, and will to my death.

"And it's nice to have you back with us again, Howard," English was saying to the younger man, a fellow who, to me at least, seemed to carry his handsomeness and youth and aristocracy like a medallion to ward off lesser beings. I was only imagining that, wasn't I?

Sharon, too, had extended her hands to them and was greeting them as Mr. and Mrs. Watstone . . .

Watstone.

I stumbled forward and somehow managed to steady myself with my right hand by grasping the back of a rocking chair and by planting my cane firmly on the porch's floor, and listened as Houston English told them how I was their houseguest while I recovered from injuries I had received shortly after my return to America from some years spent in South Africa—a story that he and Sharon, and I, had been giving out to explain me away, a distant relative, to the neighbors and to friends. It explained away perhaps even to English himself what I'd never told him about myself, my past, and their future—the future of their world.

Sharon led us all into the house, for it was evening and it was October and a dry chill was in the air outside.

Inside, in the sitting room, before the fireplace that now roared and crackled with an enormous fire that seemed likely to burst out into the room and set it aflame, while waiting for Amanda to complete the final preparations for the meal I tried to find words to say, meaningless small talk to keep away from true conversation. I also tried to avoid looking into the eyes of Deborah Watstone and her son, Howard.

Watstone, I said over and over to myself. Well, maybe that's not an uncommon name here in Chicago in this day and time. There might be lots of people named Watstone here in Chicago right now, and more of them coming during the next century . . . Surely it's a more common name than I think. And, of course, Deborah is certainly not an uncommon name, not here and now, and won't be a century hence. Really, I said to myself, there's absolutely no reason, *no reason,* to believe that this Deborah Watstone is an ancestor of *that* Deborah Watstone. *No reason at all!*

I kept telling myself that it was just too damned much for coincidence. It was too big a world for that . . . for me to have come back, downtime, and accidentally met the woman who was to be the great-great-great-grandmother of the Appointed One's mother. Dammit, man, things like that just don't ever happen. They don't!

Reason told me that—calm, cool reason that I found it very hard to hang on to—but something inside me told me differently, something I didn't want to believe, but couldn't ignore. Hadn't the Appointed One's, hadn't Allen Howard Dover's, ancestors lived in Chicago for a long time? Wasn't that what the official biographies all said?

I sat there in the sitting room, waiting for the dinner bell, and tried to seem as if I were alive, but I don't think I was too successful. As we rose to go to the dinner table when Amanda's dinner bell finally did ring, Dr. English asked me if I were feeling well.

"No," I stammered out as the Watstones preceded us out of the room, "I don't, Doctor. I've got a dizziness, a faint spell, something. I'm not sure."

"You don't look at all well," English said, sounding now very much the physician he was.

"I'll be fine in a minute," I said. "Just let me sit down for a while."

Sharon, who had come back into the room, squeezed my hand while no one was looking, and then went back to make excuses. I heard her, from the other room, telling them that I would join them at the table once they had begun their appetizers.

I was grateful to be left alone before the fireplace, if only for a few moments, to try to gather whatever wits were left to me.

If this Deborah Watstone, I thought, were an ancestor of *the* Deborah Watstone of Chicago, 1971, one hundred years hence, and if Howard Watstone were her son—oh, how well I remembered the name of the Appointed One: Allen *Howard* Dover—then *who* was to be the mother of Howard's children, of the child from whose line would one day come the religious leader who had set the stage for the theocratic dictatorship of 2032? Sharon?

For the first time in my life, I wished that I'd studied the history of the World Ecumenical Church and its founder more closely.

Howard Watstone was a young man, a handsome man, what I supposed the people of here-and-now would call "dashing." He was only a few years Sharon's senior, twenty-six, perhaps twenty-seven. Somewhere along the line, before I had learned the family name, I'd gathered from Sharon or from English the impression that Howard was the only heir of Richard and Deborah Watstone, their only son. Deborah Watstone was, quite probably, from my observations, beyond childbearing age. The descent was certain to be through him, and as a young man he would have before him many years during which he could procreate. I felt it likely that he would have no great trouble finding a young woman willing to marry him, carry his name and his children. Sharon wasn't the only possibility.

Yet . . . and the thought agonized me, had Sharon been?—was Sharon to be?—in the line that led to Allen Howard Dover, born 2 June 1972? Was she to be *his* great-great-great-grandmother?

If so, what could—what might—my presence here in Chicago during 1871, my being here with those who may be his ancestors, do to alter that? Was history mutable after all? What's more, had I *already* done something to change the world I had known? If I had, how should I feel about it? Should I be glad? Or should I . . .

Sharon came to me again and urged me to the table with them, if I felt up to it.

"I suppose I do," I replied, trying to put strength into my voice. "I don't know what's come over me."

"Too much excitement today, darling," Sharon said. "You've done too much and I imagine you're nervous, mayhap. That's all it is."

"I suppose."

"Gene, you're not as well as you want to think you are," she said soothingly in a voice that reminded me of her father's best bedside manner. "You'll have to take life quite easy for a time."

"You're right," I said, slowly rising from the chair.

"Gene," she said suddenly when I'd gotten the cane under me and was standing as nearly erect as I could, "I was going to give Howard the mitten tonight. Do you think, now, that we should postpone it?"

"No," I said just as suddenly, without thinking. "We'll go on with the announcement just as we'd planned."

"I'd hoped you would say that," she murmured, taking my arm and leading me from the sitting to the dining room, and to the table upon which Amanda had spread her feast. I hobbled on a leg that seemed to have lost all the strength it had regained, assisted by the cane on one side, by Sharon on the other.

I hardly recall the meal. I must have eaten something, but I don't remember what. Nor do I remember anything of what was said during that dinner, except a passing remark of this earlier-day Deborah Watstone, who said something like: "We'd just about decided that Howard was going to remain a bachelor all his life." She was speaking to Houston English while Amanda, in stiff, starched white, delivered a fresh plate of rolls to the table, hot and steaming from the kitchen.

Deborah Watstone, Mrs. Richard Watstone, was in her mid-fifties, I would have guessed, hair that had once been dark now shot with gray. She was an attractive woman, who had not lost her figure to fat—an athletic woman, I suspected, perhaps an equestrienne like Sharon, though I'd heard no mention of it. Her face no doubt had been pretty, if not beautiful, in her youth, and now there was a handsome dignity to it, a handsomeness much like that of her son, though it was not marked by the youthful arrogance I thought I'd seen in his. If she looked at all like the man whom I believed to be her descendant, the Appointed One, it was in her eyes: deep, intelligent, a strange bluish-green color not unlike those of Dover in the official portraits that hang in every church sanctuary, in every official building in the United States from which I'd come. Yet maybe I was reading a resemblance into her face that wasn't there; even if she were the great-great-great-great-grandmother of the Appointed One, the genes would have been so mixed over the decades to come that any resemblance would be very unlikely.

"I doubt that he would have ever considered getting married," Mrs. Watstone was going on to say, "if he hadn't met Sharon."

And I also remember that while these words were being said, the younger Watstone was studiously looking at the mashed potatoes and gravy on his plate, pretending that his mother wasn't saying them, embarrassed, now looking more like a small boy than like the brash, arrogant young man who had come up the steps like a conqueror to take Sharon's hand and kiss it out there on the porch.

And at the same time Sharon was looking at me, saying with her eyes that she hated to hurt Howard, but . . .

Finally, after what seemed like an interminable period, the meal was over and we rose, congratulating Amanda on the excellence of her cooking, Richard Watstone saying that he'd never had a finer meal even in the best restaurants in New Orleans or New York. We returned to the sitting room once more, where Dr. English broke open a fresh box of Havana cigars and asked Isaac, once more dressed in his rarely used butler's livery, to pour us brandy.

I heard the grandfather clock at the landing on the stairs toll nine o'clock and then nine-thirty, and felt all the while a strange, unholy apprehension. Somehow, some way, I knew—yes, sensed within the very depths of myself—that significant things were unfolding this night, had already begun to unfold. And I was certain that it was even more than the nervousness I felt at the forthcoming announcement of the breaking of Sharon's engagement with Howard and her plans to marry me, more than the shock of realization that I was, most likely, in the presence of ancestors of the Appointed One, whom I had promised to seek through time and murder in his mother's womb. Something more than these, something more frightening, more momentous, perhaps, but what it was to be I couldn't have said. My leg pained me and I sweated and chilled as if I were again in the depths of fever. The cigar and the brandy snifter in my hands shook as if I were a palsied old man.

English and Richard Watstone and his son spoke of business conditions in Chicago and how the city was growing rapidly and how, in the future, it would be unnecessary for an architect to go outside his hometown to find gainful employment and challenge worthy of his talents. Buildings as grand as any of those in the Eastern cities were beginning to grace the shores of Lake Michigan, and more were certain to come. Big money was coming to Chicago, bigger money than it had ever seen before. It was a wonderful place, this Chicago, now the fifth-largest city in these United States, and it offered the chance of a great future for an enterprising young man . . .

They spoke of the drought that had left the city so dry and of the fact that Chicago needed a better, more fully equipped fire department than it presently had; that the city was actually a tinderbox and that the sooner the old, wooden buildings were replaced with skyscrapers of brick and concrete and steel, the better. They spoke of President Grant's proposal to annex the island nation of "San Domingo." They spoke of the formation of America's first professional baseball association, the National Association of Professional Baseball Players, which replaced the amateur association, and of the new rule in baseball which allowed the batter to call for a high- or low-pitched ball, as he desired. They spoke of horse racing and of other sports, athletic events with which I was not familiar, and I felt an alienness in myself, the truth again that I was an outsider here.

Sharon and Mrs. Watstone talked of whatever it was that women talked of: of horses and flower gardening, of women's clubs and the work they were doing to help the sick and the poor, of cooking and of the newest clothing fashions from New York and Paris. When I could, I would again cast glances at the older woman and try to read into the lines of her face some further resemblance between her and the portraits of the Appointed One, and the more I looked at her the more I thought I saw that resemblance, both in her face and in that of her son. I kept telling myself that it was probably mostly my imagination.

Howard Watstone inquired about my health and my "railway accident" and my distant kinship to the English family and about my past, and I told him the truth about my present health and lied about my kinship to Sharon and her father and about my past, told him stories of South Africa as I remembered its history during this time, hoping that I was dropping in no anachronisms that would give me away; and he seemed to accept my words. He was friendly but reserved, and seemed to feel a slight resentment at my having spent so much time with Sharon during the past weeks.

As we talked, though, Howard Watstone and I, I began to revise my opinion of him, my unjustified snap judgment. He didn't seem to be as bad a sort as I had thought at first, perhaps as I'd wanted to believe. Maybe I had wanted to find traits in him that were unpleasant so that I would feel no guilt about taking Sharon from him.

The grandfather clock chimed again, ten loud, brazen times, and then ticked on from the landing above the hall, now in shadow. The gas lamps on the second floor had not been lit.

I felt my body demand that I go to the toilet and relieve myself, but I didn't dare leave them for a moment. Why, I wasn't sure; but something told me not to go out of the room alone. Foolish fears, I suppose, but of what . . . ?

Then Sharon said to me, bending to my ear while the others seemed to be occupied with a story Howard was telling of New York, whispering just loudly enough for me to hear, "Should I say something now, Gene?"

I swallowed heavily and nodded and was about to speak again, when Isaac came into the room, still dressed as a butler, and announced, "Docta English, I think there's somethin' you betta see."

"Oh?" English asked. "What is it, Isaac? Is it really urgent?"

"Yessir," the chauffeur-*cum*-butler said, concern written across his dark features, "you an' th' otha gent'emen."

"Very well," English said, rising and putting down his brandy snifter. "Deborah, please excuse us for a moment. Richard, Howard, Eugene, would you care to come with me?"

We rose and followed, me and my thumping cane bringing up the rear.

Isaac led us outside the house, out onto the porch and then into the yard, into the flower garden amid the brown, flowerless perennials and the dryad and the birdbath. Other people outside, not in the garden but in the street, pointing southward, gesticulating, speaking loudly.

"Dat way," Isaac said simply, and pointed as the others were doing.

It was like the rising of a dozen suns: southward the sky was aglow with a brilliant reddish-yellow light, a ghastly gaudiness that rose from the horizon, climbed upward, silhouetting houses and trees, coloring the sky all the way to the northern horizon. It was bright enough to cast shadows, this light, bright enough to read a newspaper by, and the gas lamps along the street looked dim by comparison.

"Dat's one dam' big fire," Isaac was saying to Dr. English.

"That it is," English agreed quietly.

"Where do you think it is?" Howard Watstone was asking of his father.

"Hard to say, son," the elder man replied. "But I'd lay odds that it's on the West Side, maybe around Harrison Street or below. Maybe in the lumberyards. Three, four miles from here, I'd judge."

"Well, the river's in the way," English said, his voice seeming to relax some now, to show less concern—fear? —than it had a moment before, "and that's too big a gap for any fire to cross."

"I shouldn't count too heavily on that if I were you,

Houston," Richard Watstone countered. "I've seen fires like that before, helped rebuild after them, and when one as big as that one appears really gets to going, not even the Mississippi River is wide enough to halt it."

"You're exaggerating, Richard," English said.

"No, sir, he isn't," Howard Watstone broke in. There may have been actual fear in his voice now; I wasn't certain. "Nothing can stop a fire like that."

Having been born and raised in a world in which the danger of fire had virtually been eliminated by the use of nonflammable building materials—there wasn't enough wood left to build houses with anyway—I had really no concept of the danger and horror of a mass fire run loose in a big city. Oh, certainly, as a student of history I'd occasionally read about, studied the great fires of history: Rome, New York, Paris, San Francisco, you name it. Before the twentieth century virtually every major city had had at least one disastrous fire in its history; Chicago had had its share of them, too, I recalled. But there's a terrible difference between studying a major fire in the retrospect of history and the actuality of being there when it took place; though, despite its brilliance and the terrible glow of it, I didn't believe this to be a major fire. I thought I knew the history of Chicago pretty well—it had been my hometown—and I could recall nothing in the pages of history books about any fires during this period, other than minor ones. This one just *looked* worse than it really was. I was certain of that.

We stood there, the five of us—English, the two Watstone men, Isaac, and I—watching the yellow-red glow and seeing it grow brighter even as we gazed. Behind us Sharon and Mrs. Watstone had come out onto the porch, followed by Amanda, still in a white apron now spotted with soapy water from the washing of the dinner dishes; the women gasped in astonishment at the light that spread across the sky.

My mind was now coming out of its numbness, shutting out my wild feelings, fears, and speculations that this Deborah Watstone was the mega-grandmother of the Appointed One. The fire was coming to occupy more and more of my attention, as it seemed to be of

the others on the street, in the other yards and flower
gardens, on the other porches.

I began to search my memory of the history of Chicago again. It's October, I told myself, 8 October 1871.
Was there any fire on that date? Surely I would remember reading of one that was as big as this one looked—
and now I was not so certain that it only gave the *appearance* of a major conflagration: *it was one*. No little
lumberyard blaze or the burning of a few isolated buildings could give the kind of light this one did, could be
seen over the distance that Richard Watstone believed
lay between us and the fire.

Was there a Chicago fire on 8 October 1871? I asked
myself again. Is there anything at all I should remember
about that date?

But there wasn't. Nothing notable had happened in
Chicago on that date—this date—unless my memory of
the city's history were far more faulty than I thought.

And the fire spread.

A bit nervously, we had gone back into the house and
were finishing our brandy and lighting fresh Havana cigars.

I offered my snifter for a refill. English, as he lifted
the ornate decanter to pour, gave me an odd, questioning look, but there seemed nothing I could say in reply,
except perhaps that I felt I needed that brandy more
than I'd ever needed a drink in my life. But I didn't say
that to him.

Sharon approached me, seemed to want to broach the
subject of calling off her engagement to Howard, but
before she was able to even speak to me about it, Dr.
English pulled aside the sitting room's curtains and we
all saw, clearly now if we hadn't before, that the fire that
raged to the south of the Willow Street home was of disastrous proportions.

"Dammit," Richard Watstone said savagely, apparently forgetting the presence of his wife and Sharon, "I'd
swear that it's on *this* side of the river now."

Howard nodded agreement.

English grunted.

Mrs. Watstone looked to her husband for consolation. Sharon looked at me, puzzled and disappointed.

"Surely," Deborah Watstone said after a few moments of strained silence, "it will never get this far." There was an odd emphasis to her words that somehow gave them a hollow ring. She looked again at her husband for support. "Will it?" she asked timorously.

"No, of course not," Richard Watstone said loudly, as if all the room needed convincing, "but," he added less forcefully, "I fear that Chicago will never more be as we knew it."

"You really think it's that bad?" I asked the senior architect.

"I do," Watstone replied. "I've never witnessed a fire of these proportions, mind you, but I've talked with a number of gentlefolk who have. And I have seen what was left after one of these things burned itself out. It's not very pleasant."

"Mayhap I shouldn't say this." Howard Watstone was speaking. Like myself, he had just finished a fresh snifter of brandy, "but just think of the possibilities this holds for architects."

Sharon gave him a caustic look, flashing her eyes at me as if to say, "I'm glad I'm going to marry you and not him." I don't think she understood what he meant by the remark.

"Chicago wouldn't be the first city to be rebuilt from the ashes as a cleaner and better place," he continued.

"Rome?" Dr. English asked. "New York in the Thirties?" But I don't believe he was really thinking of Rome or New York, however. His face showed a concern that must have been directed toward his pharmacy, much closer to the scene of the fire than his home, and of other places where his money was invested.

Nor was I thinking of those two cities. Like English, my concern was with Chicago, a Chicago of 1871 as represented by lines on paper. A map of the city lay on a table near the bed in the room in which I'd been staying, a map showing the North Side of the city, the South Side, the West Side, all laid out in black-and-white and neatly labeled, the ragged "Y" formed by the branches of the Chicago River as it made its way toward the lake. I thought of the places where the fire must now be and of a warehouse off Clark Street and of the device from a future world that sat hidden there amid the dust and rats and spiders.

Oh, I'd already decided, days before, that I was going to go to the chronalcage one day and send it skipping into time, downtime, unmanned, as far as its power sources would drive it into the past, where it would be lost and buried and where whatever rust might be left of it would be ground to nothingness by the glaciers that crept over the site of Chicago thousands of years ago. I was going to do that one day. But not today. That was something to do *tomorrow*—when things were settled here, and Sharon and I were married and I was secure and satisfied in this world and had been able to reconcile myself to the fact that I would never even try to fulfill a promise I'd made, a promise that was crazy, anyway, that probably could not have been kept even if I'd tried to do it . . .

But now—now I didn't want to sever that umbilical. Not yet. I didn't want to lose the chronalcage until . . . Until what?

And history—I had to think of that, consider that, realize the full implications of that. The history I knew told me nothing of this fire. There *had been* no fire of this magnitude in the Chicago of 1871. Yes, there had been a long drought, weeks or maybe even months long, I thought, and some serious danger of fire, but later on in October, the middle of the month maybe, rain was to remove much of that danger. That was the way I remembered it: there was no fire. *Not in my history.*

But . . .

Raymond Conwell's story of the "contraptions" in Farmer McBride's potato patch came back to me: two chronalcages near the city of Chicago in August of 1871. Who? Why? And I remembered cobbler Appleyard's story of the two strangers in a tavern named Clancy's, which was actually run by a Jew, and of their accents like mine and their questions about a "friend" they were seeking.

To what lengths might Proctors and blueshirts go to find a fugitive in time?

If they knew where I was, in time and in space; if they had some means of locating me from—from what? Some kind of energy emission outside the normal framework of time that told them when/where I'd gone . . . ? If they knew that, would they burn a city of the past to smoke me out, a heretic with a stolen time machine who had fled into the past, whom they believed to be hiding then/there?

Would they?

Would they?

My God, they wouldn't be that foolish! They wouldn't dare to tamper with the past on a scale as great as that. Surely they wouldn't.

Would they?

I found myself rising to my feet, leaning on my cane, speaking. "Dr. English?"

"Yes, Eugene."

"Sir, could I borrow Isaac and your carriage for a while?"

"Good heavens, man, why?"

"I must make a trip, sir."

Startled, English looked out the window toward the blazing south. He rolled his cigar between thumb and forefinger, pondering before he spoke. "You don't mean —there?" he asked.

"I do, sir."

"Gene!" Sharon cried.

Five pairs of eyes turned in her direction. Four minds must have wondered why she showed such concern.

Then there may have been realization in some of those eyes, in those of Houston English and Howard Watstone, at least.

"I must go there," I told the surgeon.

Slowly his face came back to mine, a puzzled, worried expression on it, perhaps the beginnings of anger. But what he said was, "For God's sake, man, why?"

"I'm sorry, sir. I can't say, but I must go to Clark Street and I must go at once."

Now English merely looked dumfounded.

And so did Howard Watstone, though there was more to his expression than confusion alone.

"Is it really so very urgent, Eugene?" English asked after what seemed like a long time.

"It is."

"Very well." He sighed, looked briefly at Sharon, who now had turned to gaze into the fireplace, her back to the rest of us. "Isaac!" he called.

Silence hung heavily in the room until the butler-chauffeur entered it.

"Get the carriage ready, Isaac. I want you to drive Mr. Eugene downtown."

"Downtown, sir?" Isaac asked, seeming to doubt that he had heard correctly.

English nodded. "Downtown, Isaac." He paused, then added, "And, Isaac, it may be dangerous down there. Please take my pistol with you."

"Yessir," Isaac replied, now stoically accepting the duty as assigned to him.

"Do you know where I keep it?" English asked.

"Yessir," Isaac said. " 'Side you bed. I'll fetch it."

"Very good, Isaac," English said.

The black retreated from the room. Moments later, I heard him speak a few brief words to Amanda in the kitchen. I don't know what he said, nor what his wife replied. I can imagine.

"Gene," Sharon broke in, now turning away from the fireplace and facing English, the Watstones, and myself again, "you shan't go down there alone. You're not well." But she realized that I'd made up my mind and that nothing she could say would alter it. She was right.

"I won't be going alone," I said. "Isaac will be with me."

"I don't mean—"

Howard Watstone fixed me with a cold, even belligerent stare, interrupting Sharon. "I should be glad to go with you, Stillman." His voice was thin, but he had forced politeness into it, if not friendliness.

"That's very good of you, Watstone," I said, the words sounding foolish in my mouth, but there seemed nothing else to say.

"Think nothing of it." Still polite. Still not friendly.

Isaac came back into the room carrying my frock coat and porkpie hat and handed them to me without speaking. I nodded him thanks and recalled the image I'd seen of myself in the mirror become coming downstairs: a nineteenth-century gentleman in his late thirties, bearded and with sideburns, leaning on a cane; an old tintype; a faded photograph in some half-forgotten archives. Who was it I reminded myself of now?

"Well, let's go," I said suddenly, turning and giving Sharon a look that I hope showed love rather than pain.

She shook her head and turned away.

I don't think she expected me to return.

17

When we left I wanted to kiss Sharon good-bye, to promise her that no matter what happened down on Clark Street, there at that old warehouse, there in the shadows and flame, there where might be waiting for me men who had come downtime to take me back to a future world where I was a criminal, an outlaw, a heretic—that no matter what happened to me, I would come back to her. Circumstances as they were, I couldn't quite do that. I could only take her hand briefly and give her a kiss with my eyes and try to say, with them, "I love you, Sharon."

Then I hobbled out to the waiting carriage, to Isaac and his pistol and the white horse and the black horse, Howard Watstone following me, his eyes dark and brooding.

Sharon and her father, Richard and Deborah Watstone, and Amanda-whose-last-name-I-never-learned all came out onto the porch and stood in the lurid, garish light of the fire and of a sky that had turned to yellow in the night, a yellow tipped with images of blood and destruction, with reds, crimsons, carmine—sanguine colors that matched the feelings inside me.

How much a part of the nineteenth century *had* I become?

I gave Sharon another kiss with my eyes as Isaac said, "Gitty ahp!" and the horses clopped out of the driveway onto the hard-packed dirt of the street. Neighbors looked at us strangely, stepping out of the way as Isaac urged the horses forward.

We drove away from the English home in silence and,

hours later, it seemed (though I'm certain it was only a matter of minutes), reached North Clark Street and turned south. Here the gaslights were out; somewhere the flames or the efforts of firemen or God-only-knows-what had interrupted the flow, and the lamps beside the streets were no longer functioning. But the city was not in darkness: the flames, for an hour or more now, had been sufficiently bright to light Chicago far better than it had ever been lighted by gas, better than it would be lighted at night for another hundred years, perhaps, though this was a low-lying light that cast long, horizontal shadows down the streets, creating grotesque images of buildings, and people, a hellscape out of the works of some demented medieval master, an undiscovered perspective gone wild in a sick mind.

The nighttime city was alive, full of a kind of distorted, frenzied life, people in the streets running to and fro, some silent in wonder, some angry that the fire had not been halted, cursing the fire department and the police, the mayor and the city fathers. Some were predicting that, finally, God's wrath was descending on this wicked Babylon of the Midwest and that those who had sinned would now and forever pay for their defiance of God's holy law. Carriages darted through intersections; a man called to a loaded hack that would not stop to pick up another passenger. Dogs barked and yelped in their excitement; a tiny white bitch fornicated with a massive bulldog in the middle of the rutted street, nearly being run over by a milk wagon fleeing from the scene of the fire. The air was filled with noises: the voices of people, horses, dogs; the rumblings of carriages, wagons, hacks; the ringing of a distant fire bell; the angry yells of a respectable burgher awakened from his well-earned sleep by the unseemly commotion; and off at a very great distance, as yet hardly audible over the other sounds, a noise like a remote waterfall.

The fire had awakened the sleeping city to a premature dawn, the sky lighted by a sun that was on Earth and not in its proper place in the heavens.

Our horses clopped on south, into the teeth of a wind that had blown with an almost gale-like force all day and that now fanned the fire we moved toward. Isaac carefully navigated a path through the fleeing crowds that came in clusters to nearly block the streets.

Finally Howard Watstone spoke. "Will you tell me what's going on, Stillman? Between you and Sharon, I mean." There wasn't anger in his voice, but a coldness I found very unpleasant.

"I think you already suspect, don't you, Watstone?"

"Then she's going to give me the mitten, as she would put it?"

I nodded.

"Are you going to marry her?" Still no anger, just chill. He knew, somehow, that the relationship between his fiancée and me had been far more than platonic, that Sharon was not now the virgin he had hoped to marry.

"Yes."

He nodded. "There's no changing Sharon's mind?"

"You'd have to talk with *her* about that," I told him. "But I don't think so."

He nodded again. "I saw her eyes," he said. "She hasn't given me a look all evening, God knows."

"I'm sorry it turned out this way, Watstone. For your sake, I mean. Honestly, I never meant for anything like this to happen."

He shrugged, but I think it took a good deal of effort for him to do it, and I fully realized how wrong my initial judgment of him had been. Whatever else Howard Watstone might have been, he was a gentleman. In an earlier day he might have challenged me to a duel, but he would never raise his voice in anger.

"It happens . . ." he said. Paused. Spoke again. "You seem like a decent sort, Stillman. Be good to her. She's a dandy girl."

"I know, that, Watstone. And I will."

He tried to smile but didn't quite make it. "Well, I judge I should give you my congratulations. Chums, my dear fellow?"

"Chums, Watstone!"

He offered me his hand, and like nineteenth-century gentlemen, as we were, we shook on it. And it was a good hand he offered me, a firm hand; I thought that

under other circumstance I could have come to like
Howard Watstone.

"Sharon was going to tell you this evening . . ." I began, but didn't complete the sentence. He knew that,
too. What more was there to say?

A few blocks farther on, Watstone told Isaac to stop
the carriage and then climbed down to speak to a man
whom he apparently knew, a man in coveralls coming
out of the pandemonium, the blackness of soot and ash
on his clothing, his beard and hair singed. I couldn't
hear the words—a maddened horse was screaming as it
struggled to escape an overturned wagon—but I could
see the man's dramatic gestures as he looked back toward the glowing south, as his hands waved in the air
sketching the outlines of disaster.

A pistol shot rang out as someone killed the screaming horse.

A man with a whiskey bottle in each hand staggered
southward against the flow of the crowd.

A lost child cried for its mother.

Watstone came back to the carriage, visibly shaken as
he seated himself beside me. Isaac glanced back. Watstone nodded. Slowly we moved forward again.

"Get out de way," Isaac called ahead. "Please, folks,
get out de way."

"Appears that it started on the West Side," Watstone
related as the horses plodded on, Isaac skillfully piloting
the carriage through the thickening crowds. "In the area
of Jefferson and Dekoven Streets. There be some crazy
story going around about a cow kicking over a lantern in
some woman's barn, or something like that. Damned
crazy story, but, who knows? It may be true."

I grunted. I doubted that a cow or careless boys smoking in a hayloft had started this fire. More than likely it
was a man in a blue shirt and blue trousers with a white
cross above his heart and a 4mm needle pistol tucked
into his waistband. Or a Proctor who had put aside his
dark vestments for the costume of nineteenth-century
Chicago, though I found it hard to believe that even a
Proctor would be so cruel as to start a fire like this . . .
unless he wanted me *very* badly.

"Seems now that it's crossed the river," Watstone was saying. "That's no surprise to me. Those damned bridges are as much tinderboxes as the rest of the city, except perchance for the one on Randolph Street and mayhap one or two more." He paused in reflection for a moment. "Father's been trying to get them to build more of the new structural-steel bridges, you know, but they keep telling him that they're too expensive and Chicago's bridges are adequate for the present time. Adequate! In a pig's eye! Now they'll see!"

Justification rang in his voice. I rather felt that the architect in Howard Watstone was glad to see the eyesores of Chicago being razed. What followed, to him at least, might even be worth the cost in dollars and loss of lives.

"How far has it gotten so far?" I asked, the black-and-white city map in my mind again.

"Can't say for certain. How far must you go?"

"On down Clark Street. I can't tell you the number."

"We can try it. I trust this is as all-important as you say it is, Stillman."

"It is, to me."

As we moved farther south, passing firemen going north, seared and scorched and fleeing in disarray from defeat by the blaze that was now far beyond their ability to control—it had already cut off much of Chicago's none-too-liberal water supply—we saw evidence of a disorder that now *preceded* the fire, that moved before it like a vanguard sweeping out from its perimeter: shops had been broken into, looted, their doors and windows smashed in an orgy of criminal acquisition before the flames consumed everything.

A drunk lay in the street near an open tavern door, smashed bottles around him, half a case of fine bourbon spilling onto the ground. Not far away was a pile of abandoned clothing, loot from a ransacked clothier, thrown aside when something more attractive was sighted.

We heard a distant gunshot as a policeman tried to halt a looter who fled from another building, leaped around the drunk, went on. I think the policeman had called for him to stop, but I wasn't certain. The looter hadn't stopped, or even slowed down, when the officer fired the first shot into the air above his head.

"Halt!" the policeman now called out as he lowered the heavy revolver in his hand, brought it to aim.

For an instant the looter was silhouetted in the middle of the street, a running darkness against the red-yellow hell still blocks away.

Then the revolver discharged for a second time, kicking the policeman's hand up slightly. As the pistol's roar reverberated above the lesser noises, the looter paused in mid-stride, seemed to try to catch himself, to plant both feet firmly on the street; then he pitched, jerked forward, his arms thrown wide, dropping the packages and bottles he had clutched. He slapped to the pavement and ceased to move, a huddled bundle of ragged clothing, dark in the flames' long shadows. The policeman still held his pistol ready as he ran to his side.

"Dammit, I told you to stop," he said.

There was almost a sob in his voice. For an instant I saw the officer's face in the firelight, saw how young he was.

Isaac urged the horses forward again.

I wondered how long it would be before they called in the Army to help maintain order, and to restore order when it finally collapsed. Not long, I thought. And wasn't Philip Sheridan, of Civil War fame, now in command of a garrison nearby? I wondered.

"Isaac," I said suddenly, realizing why English had suggested that he bring a revolver, "how good a shot are you with that gun you've got?"

"Ain't none too good, Mista Gene," he said, barely glancing back over his shoulder. It was taking all his considerable strength and all his concentration just to maneuver the skittish horses now.

"I used to be pretty fair with a handgun," I said. "Would you let me have it?"

He seemed to want to relinquish the weapon, but duty was a stronger force. "Docta English, he tol' me t' take it. He didn't say nothin' 'bout lettin' you have it, Mista Gene."

"It will be okay, Isaac. Let me have it. I'll explain it to Dr. English."

I was concerned now with something I considered a far more serious threat than mere looters and drunks. More than ever, I was convinced that this was no fire of the history I knew. This hadn't happened in the Chicago of *my* past. I knew my hometown well enough to be certain of that. And this could mean only one thing: Proctors or blueshirts. Here. Now.

"Let him have it, Isaac," Watstone called, unexpectedly agreeing with me. "I'm certain it would be acceptable to the doctor."

"Yessir," Isaac said, pulling the revolver out of his belt and handing it to me with a sigh of relief.

In the light of the raging fire I could see that it was an old-fashioned, even ancient sort of weapon, a single-action Colt .44, long-barreled, though not quite as big and bulky as the ones they'd used a few years before, in the War, but still larger and heavier than most such weapons I'd been accustomed to when in the Army. Still, it was a weapon, a firearm, and I could use it—and I *would* use it if it came to that, and I didn't much doubt that it would . . .

The fire was close now, too damned close. It was no longer a distant flicker glimpsed occasionally at distances down the street, a remoteness that still had an unreality about it. Now a wall of fire stood, not many blocks before us, roaring like a great avalanche of water, devouring everything in its path: a huge, vibrating wall of yellow-red force like some superweapon from a science-fiction HV show about the yellow monsters from the Orient out to destroy the holy Church/State of America, only to be thwarted at the last moment by our square-jawed hero and his virginal, virtuous, blond-haired and blue-eyed sweetheart. The noise of it drowned out all others now and I realized we had been almost yelling to hear each other above its roar. Buildings and puny men and feeble horses—all paper cutouts in some kind of pantomime show—were silhouetted between it and us, so fragile, so ineffectual against the elemental force that swept irresistibly forward. Captain

America, where are you now that we need you? I wondered.

The horses whinnied and screamed in their fear, and struck the street in anger with their iron-shod hooves, refusing to obey Isaac's commands.

Bright sparks fell around us like a rain in Hades.

Somewhere a man laughed, shrill and hysterical.

"Dammit, is it much farther, Stillman?" Watstone demanded.

"A block, I think, maybe two."

"Then, belike, we'll have to go it on foot," he said. "The horses aren't going to take us very much closer."

"I know."

"And we'd better hurry. Whatever it is that you want isn't going to be there much longer."

I grunted but didn't speak, grasping my cane in one hand and dropping the heavy revolver into one of the pockets of my coat.

Watstone began to climb out of the carriage.

"Stay as close as you can, Isaac," he said to our driver. "Back up when you must, but don't go too far afield."

Isaac grunted an affirmation.

I was glad that the carriage wasn't going to be far away. *If* I came back to it, I didn't want to have to walk very far. I didn't think I was yet up to much walking.

Then I climbed down after Watstone, my left leg heavy and painful, seeming not to want to work for me. I would force it to work.

I wished for a moment that I had some of the pain-killing drugs English had given me during the early days of my recovery, drugs I'd taken but briefly and then given up for fear of addiction. A lot of people of this time —uncounted numbers of wounded soldiers on both sides during the Civil War—had become addicted to the opiates that were used as anaesthetics during that period, and I hadn't wanted to become one of them. But right now . . .

"Which way?" Watstone asked, and I pointed.

I thought I could remember the gutter, the alley, the

buildings across the street from the alley, the warehouse entrance at its end.

Yes, I said to myself as Watstone slowly walked forward toward the approaching wall of flame and I hobbled after him, there's the barroom, the furniture store, a block and a half away. I was *right* about where we were, but then I'd studied the map of here-and-now Chicago pretty carefully.

"Let's go, then," Watstone said.

I knew that, somewhere before us, perhaps the very men I now saw silhouetted against the garish light, or perhaps some hiding in the long, dark shadows cast by the yellow flames, Proctors or Lay Brothers of St. Wilson were waiting for me, waiting to return me to the world of 2032 or to kill me on the spot and make certain I could never again interfere with the course of historical time—although their own damage to the fabric of history might already be beyond reckoning. Had they considered that? I wondered.

Before, when I had first realized the enormity of the fire, the magnitude of the disaster that was sweeping across Chicago, I'd suspected that they were there, that they were behind it, that they somehow knew that I was in the city at this time. But that had been a suspicion held in a cold, intellectual way, a product of reasoning. Now my awareness was something more than that. I *knew* that they were there, in some manner apart from reason and intellect; I felt it, knew it in my guts . . . and I was afraid.

Was the chronalcage worth it?

Why not let the damned thing be consumed by the flames? When it's over, there'll be nothing left but slag and melted glass, I told myself, and no one of this time could ever guess from the ruins that it had been a device for time displacement from a world a hundred and fifty years hence. It would end up on some junk heap along with a lot of what had been Chicago not so long before, and would be lost, forgotten; and I could continue to live here, marry Sharon, carry out the plans she and I had made during our warm, beautiful nights together.

But somehow I just couldn't do that, and I wasn't certain why.

A dryness, a taste of hot metal came to my mouth, a weakness to both my legs that made it almost impossible for me to stand fully erect, to walk after Watstone. I felt coming over me again all the malarial symptoms of whatever sickness I had, whatever it was that I'd brought back through time with me: chills and sweating, disorientation and headache. Yet I hobbled on behind the young architect, looking, perhaps, something like one of mankind's early ancestors who hadn't quite yet mastered the art of walking on two legs and still needed the broken branch of a tree to help him along.

Then, only moments later, the worst of the sensations left me and I recovered some semblance of composure, though I felt limp and moist like a wrung-out rag.

But the revolver was a cold and heavy weight in my coat pocket, a mass of metal that seemed to slow me even further, and I found myself wondering whether I would be able to aim it correctly if—when!—the time came to use it, as I was certain the time would come, and soon.

But I'd felt that way before, I remembered, back there in India when I'd been little more than a scared kid who had been rushed through basic infantry training and then strato-rocketed halfway around the world with a bunch of other scared kids and thrown down to stand before the Imperial Chinese and fight back or get our asses blown off. And when the chips had been down, when my life had been on the line, well, I'd done what I had to do to stay alive and come out of it in one piece, more or less. And I had, back there in the cold Pleistocène. I would again, I hoped. I didn't want to kill anyone; I detested the thought of it. But I didn't want to be killed either, and I suspected there was, somewhere deep within the more primitive portions of my brain, in genes that harked back millions of years to half-ape ancestors of mankind, some killer instinct that would come to my aid as it had before.

I hurried on, trying to overtake Watstone as he

pushed forward into a horrid hellscape of firelight and shadow, noise and smoke.

A column of flame burst into the sky before us, for a few moments doubling the brilliance of the fire. Then it subsided, but as it did the rain of sparks and embers grew heavier.

Then a building a few blocks away seemed to explode, casting debris, sparks, fragments of burning wood high into the air in all directions. Flaming embers from the explosion, or violent collapse, landed on buildings nearer us, setting them aflame as well, advancing the fire farther toward the north. The air around us was thick with smoke, thin of oxygen, difficult to breathe and bringing coughing to us as we brushed against the weary firemen who retreated from the blaze, defeated as earlier firemen had been, unable to halt the advance of the wall of yellow force. Even several blocks away from the flames themselves, the heat was intense and I felt sweat beginning to form under the heavy clothing I'd worn against the chill of October. And there now seemed to be a steady wind blowing not from the southwest as it had earlier in the day, but blowing in from outside in all directions toward the center of the fire, feeding its ever-growing demands for more oxygen with which to consume.

I thought about the winds that a fire like this could, itself, cause: how the flames could create a semivacuum in their center as they burned away the oxygen, how gales could be drawn into the area of lowered air pressure, destructive gales that would further fan the flames like a great bellows; how, out of it, the wind and the heat, a great storm of fire could arise, a ball of superheated flame that wouldn't look much unlike that of a thermonuclear weapon and that could be every bit as destructive. Fire storms had been known to arise in burning cities like this. Would Chicago be another?

"Watstone!" I called over the roar of the fire and the rumblings of another collapsing structure, "Be careful!"

He paused for a moment to allow me to catch up with him, brushing glowing sparks from the sleeve of his coat.

"I'll go on alone," I said. "It's dangerous."

"I damned well know it's dangerous, Stillman," he answered, an expression that I couldn't read revealed by the firelight on his face.

"It's more than the fire," I told him between gasps for air. "There'll probably be someone there waiting for me. An enemy."

"Why?" he asked.

Now we were no more than a half a dozen meters from the entrance to the alley. The vanguard of the fire had reached to within a block or so of it; buildings here, abandoned by the firemen, were beginning to burn. The heat was almost unbearable.

"Why?" I repeated his question. "To kill me, I suspect. You'd better go back."

"I'm not doing this for you, Stillman. I'm doing it for Sharon, though I suppose I'm a damned fool for doing it."

I had neither the time nor the inclination to argue with him, nor to question his logic. The cage would be engulfed by the flames soon . . . and something inside me still told me I couldn't allow that to happen. I had to get the cage away from the fire. But exactly why, I couldn't then have said.

Hobbling on my cane, my bad leg, my good leg, I went on, Watstone beside me, and we reached the entrance of the alley, deep in shadows, dark, long, empty. I drew the revolver from my coat pocket with my right hand; it felt no lighter now that it had in the pocket, pulling the coat down, out of shape, and putting me even further off balance.

"That way?" Watstone asked, pointing into the alley.

I nodded, grunted, hobbled forward into the shadows as I heard, from somewhere behind me, a voice just barely touched with an accent foreign to the Chicago of here-and-now, yelling: *"That's him!"*

I wondered how they could be sure; I, with a newly grown beard and in the garb of this time and place, Prince Albert, porkpie, my new and specially made shoes, could not have looked much different from the "natives." But somehow someone had recognized me—

as somehow they'd been able to locate the time and place I would come back into, though they hadn't been able to locate me precisely without (perhaps!) setting this raging fire to smoke me out. Yet they must have known exactly where the chronalcage was . . .

I plunged deeper into shadows, urging Watstone to follow me. "It's not far," I said.

Would I let him see the cage? Would I reveal to him what I was? I didn't know at the time.

In the alley's shadows, between the weathered boards and flaking paint, open above revealing the glow of the fire and the smoke of it, I could see almost nothing, could only recall how long the alley had seemed before. It couldn't possibly have been *that* far from the street back to the wooden doorway that led into the warehouse, a back entrance or something.

Halfway to the warehouse, maybe more, I glanced back toward the street, the rutted street, once muddy, now dry and dusty, with its planking sidewalks; and beyond it the barroom, now empty of customers, probably sacked of its whiskey and beer as well; and the furniture store, it, too, with broken windows and doors. And in the lurid yellowish light that illuminated the street and the buildings, I saw men who looked as much a part of this time—plaid trousers, plaid vests, starched shirts, Prince Albert coats—as I thought I did, but whom I was now certain were *not,* no more than I.

"Against the wall," I whispered loudly to Watstone, fumbling with my thumb at the revolver's knurled safety. I half knelt in the alley's rubbish, cradled my right wrist with my left hand to steady the gun, pulled back on the trigger and—BOOM!

The report of the nineteenth-century pistol was savagely loud in my ears, confined as it was by the alley's wooden walls, reverberating back; and the kick of its recoil was far greater than I'd expected. But satisfaction lay in seeing one of the approaching figures stagger back in astonishment, grunt angrily, savagely.

There was a furious animal pleasure in me: the killer instinct had had its way.

"Hurry," I gasped to Watstone, finding my way to my feet and stumbling toward the rear of the alley.

The other two silhouetted figures had taken cover in shadow and, although I knew they couldn't see us in the alley's darkness, began to fire. Still a lucky shot could—

"Gaaa!" Watstone gasped, or made a sound very like that, then staggered, stumbled forward beside me, beyond me, flailing his arms helplessly in the air.

I called his name. He didn't reply. Pistols, of the same vintage as mine, continued to fire into the alley. I returned the fire—one, two more rounds at men I couldn't see.

Watstone crashed heavily against a wooden wall, moaned, clawed at flaking paint in an effort to hold himself up, then slid down the wall, his fingernails making a rasping sound on the wood, and came to earth with the heavy, dull, sickening sound of a collapsing sack of rotten potatoes.

I fired again at the invisible men, the fourth round of the six the revolver held. I was counting them carefully: two more, then there would be none. Unless I could get to the chronalcage, get a weapon from the lockers there or find the needler I'd lost.

I reached Watstone and knelt beside him. In what little light came into the alley from the approaching flames, I could just see the glistening of blood on his left shoulder where the cloth of his overcoat was ripped, sodden now with a steady stream of it. He wasn't dead: he moaned and stirred to prove it. But he was badly hurt and—

More shots rang out, going *chunk!* as the slugs hit wood along the sides of the alley.

"Goddammit! Goddammit! Goddammit!" I whispered to myself.

What the hell was I going to do now? A hundred thoughts, a thousand fears raced through my mind. Already the Proctors—or maybe the Lay Brothers of St. Wilson: it seemed more likely that they would do something this damned stupid—had tampered with the fabric of Time more than I'd ever considered doing; they'd set a blaze in Chicago to smoke me out that had now become a holocaust. It would probably rage for days, with the city as dry as it was, and would fundamentally alter the future of this city, possibly of this nation, perhaps of the whole world.

The history of Chicago subsequent to 8 October 1871, as I knew it, would never be the same.

Now, in a frightening moment, an instant during which the blood seemed to freeze in my veins, when the universe around me seemed to lose rationality and coherence, I realized somewhere within the core of me that *it is possible to change the past.*

Now the fabric of Time was torn, ripped; and with each passing moment the rip would grow wider, the changes in Tomorrow would be greater and greater. I didn't see how it would be possible for the fabric of the continuum ever to reknit itself so that its pattern would again be exactly as I had known it.

Hadn't those bastards realized what they were doing?

Had they thought they could get away with casually destroying a major city in the nineteenth century and expect that city to be as it had in the twentieth and twenty-first centuries without that historical destruction? Didn't they realize that they were destroying themselves just as certainly as if they were putting pistol barrels in their mouths and pulling the triggers?

A more immediate thought now came to me: Howard Watstone was injured, Watstone might be dying, and he just might be, could be, had to be, an ancestor of the Appointed One. If *he* is dying, I thought . . . If *he* is dying . . .

I crouched in the shadows of the alley, beside the weak and moaning figure, beside the man whose blood was gushing from a ghastly wound in his left shoulder, listening to the insane ragings of the approaching fire, the rush of wind blowing in to fan it to greater fury, the avalanche-like roarings of its insatiable consumption, the yells of men fleeing from it; and I waited for another shot to come down the alley toward me.

If Howard Watstone were to die, I was thinking, if he

were to die here and now, there was no chance that he could ever father a child by Sharon or by anyone else, no chance that his line would be carried on, no possibility that eighty years from now a new Deborah Watstone would be born and that a century from now she would become pregnant while a student at Loyola and marry another student named Robert Dover, no chance that her son would be born and be given the name Allen Howard Dover and go on to become the fanatical religious leader called the Appointed One, who would upset the world and whose followers would eventually establish a theocratic dictatorship in the United States of America. All I had to do to fulfill my promise to Melanie was go on and let Howard Watstone die here.

I was sick to my stomach when I came to my feet, glanced back down the alley, saw a silhouette of movement, fired, missed.

"I'm sorry, Watstone," I said, "but . . ."

Hugging the alley's wall, I moved on and found the door, opened it. A loud creak rang from the rusted hinges and brought two pistol shots that narrowly missed me.

With what speed and grace I could muster, I moved into the interior of the warehouse, now hardly darker than the alley had been outside. Light from the approaching fire fell through chinks in the walls, between the boards that covered the windows, glittered dully from the bars of the chronalcage, which sat exactly where I had left it.

Men were running in the alley now. No more than two, by the sound of them, I thought. They were coming close, nearing the door through which I'd just come.

I waited until the first of them reached the doorway, waited until I was certain that I could see him, again a silhouette against the lighter darkness of the alley, then fired the last round from the .38. While the echo of the pistol's shot rebounded through the warehouse's interior, I saw the man stagger backward, drop his weapon, bend forward and grasp his bleeding stomach.

I staggered across the littered gulf that separated me

from the cage, my left leg throbbing stabbingly, and wished again that I had some of Dr. English's medicine to take for the pain.

Apparently the other man—for I was certain only one was left unwounded—had not been counting my shots as carefully as I had and was deterred from attempting to enter the warehouse because of the accuracy of the shot I'd fired at his companion. But I heard him yelling at me, and I recognized his voice.

"Stillman, you don't have a chance. You'd better give—"

It was Deacon Carl Fulford again, and I wasn't going to listen to anything he had to say.

The floor was lumpy under my feet, dusty, dirty, littered with a decade or more of trash, and I stumbled, often half falling as I made my way across it, wondering what I was *really* doing, what I had already done, still wondering just how mutable the past was, how mutable time was, wondering what were the consequences of the actions of myself and of Fulford and his fellow blueshirts, and what kind of a world would await me at home. Home? Would there even be a *home* for me, uptime? Wasn't my home here now, here in 1871? Or had that somehow changed, too?

I reached the bars of the cage, dropped the useless empty pistol, grasped the bars with both hands and pulled myself up and in. Nearly falling to the deck, I righted myself, swung around the main console, and threw myself into the bucket seat.

"Fulford'll be coming in in a minute if I don't fire again," I said to myself, but I didn't dare take time to try to find the needler I thought I'd lost in the warehouse before or to search for another weapon in the locker behind me. If I were to save the cage, I had no time for anything but getting it going. Maybe not even time for that.

As I brought the generator to life and waited for the warning lights to turn from red to green, as I adjusted controls that would bring up the potentials required for displacement, I briefly considered throwing myself downtime just a few minutes, back to where I could as-

sist my previous self and Howard Watstone. I supposed
that I could go back and prevent his death, perhaps, but
if I were right . . . well, if Watstone were an ancestor
of Debbie Watstone and her son Allen Dover, better to
let him die here and now . . .

But did he *have* to die to prevent that sequence of
events? Would not my merely being here to marry Sharon alter things enough, prevent *her* being an ancestor of
the prophet? And if that were the case, maybe it
wouldn't be necessary for me to have Watstone's blood
on my hands—

There was too much to think about, too many things
to consider, too many ramifications to work out, and
now I hadn't the time to do it. I needed the time to think
—but first I had to survive Carl Fulford's intent to kill
me.

I set the chronal controls to displace me downtime
just a short period—a few weeks, three months or so—
here in this warehouse prior to my coming out of time
before. Then I could think.

Carl Fulford entered the warehouse. His gun wasn't
empty.

He fired a warning shot. Maybe he still wanted to
take me alive for some reason, but I doubt it.

"Stop, dammit!" he shouted as he passed through the
doorway. "You can't get away this time, Stillman."

But all the right lights were turning green and in no
more than a few heartbeats the potentials, all of them,
would be right and I could displace the cage and myself
downtime a few weeks.

My hands were on the controls, the switches. The yellow light falling through the chinks in the walls and the
boarded windows was bright now, and the warehouse
was filling with smoke, hot and growing hotter. The beginnings of flames could be seen near the ceiling; the
warehouse was catching fire and in minutes it, too,
would be consumed by the holocaust.

Then I was flipping the row of toggle switches and the
eerie, mad sounds of displacement were growing around
me.

"Stop it, Stillman!" Fulford cried, running across the littered floor toward me.

Then there came to me, through the noise of the approaching firestorm, above the roaring and crackling of the flames, a second mad sound of chronal displacement, somehow seeming to heterodyne with the sounds of my machine.

Another cage arriving now/here?

I suddenly had the sensation of being outside of Time, of being displaced not into the future or the past, not vertically in time, but horizontally. I felt that I wasn't in one continuous path of Time, but standing just before a branching road that led to a multitude of possible futures. It was as if I saw a discordant world, like two music boxes each playing its separate tune, notes tinkling out, one against the other, and neither of them making any sense.

As quickly as it had come, the sensation passed, and Carl Fulford was pausing just long enough to bring the barrel of his pistol up, to take an accurate aim with both of his hands wrapped around the weapon.

Maybe another cage was arriving here, amid the flame and smoke, but I didn't have the time to find out who was in it or why it was coming now/here. My fingers were coming to the end of the row of switches.

I thought I heard gunshots, though they were not Fulford's, and yet I thought I was looking right down his pistol's barrel when it fired, when I saw the flash, when—

The chronalcage displaced.

Whap!

And Carl Fulford and the burning warehouse and the early morning of 9 October 1871 were gone.

18

I was still in the warehouse, but now it was quiet and empty except for me and the chronalcage. It was warm, fetid, smelling of rot and decay and rat droppings, but there was no smoke, no flame, no threat of immediate destruction. The fire that would destroy the warehouse was now some weeks, months, in the future, though exactly how far in the future I didn't really yet know. I hadn't had time to set the calibrations that finely, though I was quite certain that I was safe, and that my previous self wasn't due to arrive for a while yet—three or four weeks, perhaps.

I sat in the cage quietly for a long time, almost unmoving, allowing my heart to slow to its normal pace and my lungs to cease heaving. The air here might not be too pleasant to smell, but it was rich with oxygen and satisfying.

I wished for a cigarette, a shot of whiskey, someone to talk with, but none of these things was available. I would just have to do without.

Now I was safe and now I had time to reflect, to ponder, to review the events of the past few months, real months and subjective months back to the time I came out downtime somewhere in the Pleistocene and during all the events that followed. I had time to regret my forgetting of my feelings toward Melanie, to regret my killing of Welles Kennedy, to feel guilt about leaving Howard Watstone to burn to death in that alley—no matter *what* some remote descendant of his might do, Watstone himself hadn't been guilty of anything.

I now knew that the past was mutable. That what is done is not necessarily, in the final analysis, really done at all. The past can be undone. The future can be undone. The present . . .

In the quiet of reflection I had a feeling of power, a sense of forces contained within the consoles of the chronalcage that *I* could control. *There were things I could do.*

Maybe, I thought—and at first the thought frightened me—maybe I could go back and undo some of the things that had happened. Maybe, for example, I could go back to the Pleistocene and assist myself: maybe I (number-one me) could go back and sneak up on Welles Kennedy and knock him in the head while I (number-two me) distracted him by coming out of the woods with the rifle. Maybe I could assist myself in stealing this/that chronalcage without it being necessary for Welles to die in the process and getting my previous self shot up doing it.

And maybe—and again the thought thrilled and frightened me—I could kill Carl Fulford there and then, downtime in the Pleistocene, and prevent him from somehow going uptime and getting help and coming back and setting 1871 Chicago afire.

Maybe I could even prevent Howard Watstone's death and yet also see to it that from his descendants the Appointed One was never born.

Maybe I could set right what had been done wrong, not only by myself and Carl Fulford and his blueshirts but by the very workings of history itself. Maybe I could see that there was a world in the twenty-first century that was worth living in.

I shuddered at the thoughts passing through my mind. Could a man, a mere human being, really do things like that? I asked myself. Wasn't this something only gods were supposed to be able to do? Or could even gods change history itself?

What arrogance I felt!

Yet . . . maybe I could do it. Maybe I should try.

I sat there for a long, long time, excitement and fear whirling in my mind.

Or I could just swing back uptime, bring the chronal-cage out in, say, 10 October 1871, somewhere safe out of Chicago, and go back to Sharon and help her and her father and the others rebuild Chicago when the fire had finally burnt itself out. Maybe I could do something there in 1871 to help make a better world, and all without trying to play at being some kind of a god with powers over the workings of history.

Yet could I do even that?

Fulford might come out of that fire himself and go to his cage, wherever it was, and using whatever devices it contained to track me down again, do more damage to the world, to time and history . . .

I wanted Carl Fulford dead.

And I didn't want to see Welles Kennedy dead.

After a while I searched out some of the rations Welles and Fulford had brought with them from 2032 and found them much more palatable than the emergency ones that had been in the cage I'd originally had. While I ate, I considered doing a little backtracking with the cage's computer. If nothing else, I could find out when/where we'd been in the Pleistocene and . . .

Another thought crossed my mind, but I didn't want to consider it then, not yet.

After eating, I began to ask the computer questions and it began to give me answers, flickering greenishly on its CRT.

My current chronal location was 2:30 A.M., 13 June 1871.

I had departed from 1:43 A.M., 9 October 1871.

Prior to that, the chronalcage had arrived from out-time at 4:04 A.M., 3 July 1871—that was when I'd arrived in the warehouse, bleeding all over myself. Where had I been before that? How far back in time into the Pleistocene?

I keyed the computer for the next back reading, but it wasn't exactly what I'd expected.

It also read 3 July 1871, but the time was 2:41 A.M. and the geo references weren't *quite* the same as those of the warehouse—close, but not quite the same. The cage had apparently only remained at those references a

short time—the elapsed-time records indicated that—
and then had geo'ed into the warehouse and uptimed a
little over an hour.

Did that make any sense? I couldn't remember anything like that, but, well, I hadn't been in very good
shape then.

I had the computer backtrack again, and it read not
at all like I expected: 3:39 A.M., 2 August 1871.

And that didn't make any sense either. I recalled no
such thing. I'd come from the Pleistocene to July, 1871,
Chicago, hadn't I? When I asked for geo references, the
computer gave me readings that worked out as a location some twenty-seven kilometers southwest of Chicago.

The cage had arrived at those geo references about
two elapsed hours previously, 1:20 A.M., had remained
there a little over two hours, and then had *downtimed* to
3 July and geo'ed into Chicago, but not quite to the
warehouse.

Crazy!

Nothing like that had happened. Or at least I didn't
remember anything like that happening. But like I said,
at the time I hadn't been in very good shape.

I had the computer backtrack again and give me its
previous reading; and this was the one I'd been expecting to get before.

Its previous date of departure downtime was to 3 September 86,159 B.C., its geo references some several
hundred kilometers to the east and slightly to the south
of Chicago.

That made sense, at least.

But if the computer were right, I hadn't come directly
from the Pleistocene into the 1871 warehouse—a place
that was just too damned lucky for coincidence, as I realized when I thought about it. I'd come out a month
later, August, then downtimed a month to July, geo'ed
into the Chicago area but not into the warehouse, and
then finally geo'ed into the warehouse itself.

How the hell had I done all that?

The sense of god-like power I'd had only a few minutes before evaporated. Chills went through me even in the heat and humidity of the warehouse.

How could a man expect to remold history to suit his own purposes when he couldn't even account for his own past? When he couldn't explain to himself how he'd gotten from one time place to another?

Something crawled up my spine that would have probably been fear if I'd been able to give it a name.

I sat there in the cage for a long, long time.

Faint light began to seep in through the chinks of the walls and between the boards over the windows as the sun rose on the morning of 13 June 1871.

I had a very strong desire to just get up and walk out of the warehouse and lose myself in the city of Chicago and wait for 8 October to come and burn it away. Then I could go to Sharon when it was safe, and pick up where we'd left off.

But I knew I couldn't do that.

I got out of the cage's bucket seat and went back to the lockers and found that Welles and Fulford had come back for me loaded for bear: enough weapons were packed in those lockers to support a revolution!

I belted a pistol around my waist, a big, ugly 9mm automatic, and hoisted a 7mm carbine and slung it over my shoulder; then I went back to the seat, where I strapped myself in, still dressed in the anachronistic costume of 1871, and with the aid of the computer began setting the cage's controls for 1:00 A.M., 2 August 1871, geo references southwest of Chicago about twenty-seven klicks.

I'm not certain that I was altogether sane right then, or later, but something inside me had to know why the cage had come out then/there and had then gone on into Chicago, downtiming to July, missing the warehouse the first time, then arriving there.

Most of all I was frightened.

In a few minutes I'd completed the self-imposed countdown and everything was ready and my hands made the trip across the row of toggles and . . .

Whap!

It was dark, but not so dark that my eyes couldn't soon adjust. When my eyes adjusted I unbelted myself and climbed out of the cage, planting my feet on the earth.

It was a warm, dry night, too warm for the October clothing I wore, but I didn't remove it. I wasn't sure when/where I might be going next. Hell, the English language isn't adequate for talking about travel through time.

There was the smell of life and growing things in the air, the odor of vegetation. And I heard the sounds of insects around me, the distant call of a night bird.

I was standing in the middle of a cultivated field—I didn't know what the plants around me were, low and rich-leafed, but I had a strong suspicion they were potatoes—and at some distance, against the faint light of the sky and its stars, I could see the silhouettes of distant trees. Nearer to me than the trees, maybe half a kilometer across the cultivated fields, stood a small house, a blockish blackness in the night, no doubt the home of Farmer McBride and his wife and his three lovely daughters. From one window spilled a faint light, dim and yellow, partly obscured by the curtains, I thought: a light left on by Mrs. McBride to guide her husband home after his card game.

I knew who the characters in Conwell's story were now: two of them were me.

I looked around me again, walking a complete circuit of the cage, and saw nothing that seemed out of place in this, a nineteenth-century farm in Illinois not far from the burgeoning city of Chicago. McBride was one of the many who sent his produce to feed the massive numbers of people who were now coming to the city, the metropolis of the Midwest.

Had McBride seen me yet? I wondered. Where was he? Crouching somewhere in the brush to my left? Wondering what I was, and how I and this "contraption" had come to be there in his potato patch?

What *was* I doing there? The *I* of this Now, and the previous one who'd come here before?

I went back into the cage and let the computer tell me that by local standards it was now 1:09 A.M.

I ought to be coming out of Time to this time/place in another eleven minutes.

Out of a fear I couldn't define, I unslung the carbine and checked its magazine and waited, my breath coming slow and uneven, my hear throbbing too loudly within me.

Time passed very, very slowly.

Then, at last, came a sound that I was certain would awaken Mrs. McBride and her daughters in the distant farmhouse, but which didn't, though it must have frightened the hiding McBride half out of his wits, the unmistakable wail of the generators of a chronalcage in the act of chronal displacement, the scream of the stuff of this universe when it finds itself thrown out of its normal place in the flow of time and into another temporal location.

A chronalcage came into being in the cultivated field no more than five meters from where I stood, and if I'd had any doubts about who was in that cage and what its occupant's condition might be, those doubts were instantly dispelled, despite the poor light of the August night. The cage was occupied by Eugene David Stillman, wearing a heavy parka and a few days' growth of beard, unconscious from shock and very likely bleeding to death from a wound in a shattered left leg.

Fearfully and with a sense of awe—I remembered the old German stories about meeting your doppelgänger— I slowly approached the cage and saw, in the dim light from the sky, snow and ice melting from the cage's base. The man in the cage stirred only once, moaned, would have fallen from the seat had he/I not been held in place by the belts that crisscrossed his/my body.

I stood for long moments looking at my former self, the 7mm carbine in my hands, hands that trembled and didn't want to retain their hold on the weapon. I half feared that somehow Carl Fulford would come out of time in another cage to capture or kill both of me— though I hadn't wondered *until that moment* how Fulford had ever gotten out of the Pleistocene in the first place so that he could come to 1871 Chicago to try to track me down. There'd been no other operable cage back in 86,159 B.C. for him to use, had there?

It would be impossible for me to say how long I stood there, waiting for I didn't know what, fearing to move, to act. Anything I did now would be tampering with *my own* past, and now I found myself terribly frightened of doing that.

Apparently when I'd left the Pleistocene, when I'd set the controls while weak and in shock from Welles' wound to my leg, I'd come out during the dark morning of 2 August 1871, some twenty-seven or so klicks from the warehouse off Clark Street.

What had happened then?

How had I bandaged and splinted my leg, reset the controls for approximately a month back downtime and twenty-seven kilometers northwest in geo terms? The *me* I saw in the cage didn't look as if he/I were in any shape to do any of that. And even if he/I *were*, how had he/I known exactly where that warehouse was, that safe place where the cage could be left and . . .

For long, dragging minutes I stood there, watching my own blood, black in the darkness, seeping from the shattered leg, soaking through torn trouser fabric and dripping down to the cage's metal deck. It wouldn't take much of that for a man to bleed to death. And yet I was still fearful of acting, fearful of altering the past as I thought (from Conwell's story) I knew it, my own personal past—yet beginning to realize that if I didn't act, I just might be watching my own death. Though was that possible? Could a *previous me* die and the current me still be alive? Even in the insane terms that seemed to govern the workings of chronal maneuvers, that seemed impossible.

But . . . I slowly said to myself, but maybe if I *don't act* I'll be altering the past, letting myself die—my past persona and my present one.

Maybe there was some truth in the stories of the doppelgängers after all . . .

Irrationally, I wondered what Farmer McBride must be thinking of all this right at this moment.

Finally, feeling a strange sense of detachment, as if there were still a *third* me standing to one side and watching the *real* me—and what I thought was me was nothing more than a puppet, an automaton going through a preprogramed activity—I slung the carbine by the strap across my shoulder, mounted the cage's front porch, stepped between the bars, and approached to examine his/my leg in the dim light that spilled from the control panel.

The leg was shattered exactly as I'd known it would be, and the blood was flowing copiously. He/I would certainly already be too weak to act to save himself/myself.

I moved mechanically to the lockers behind the bucket seat, opened them, found a handtorch and with its aid located the medical supplies, bandages, drugs, an aluminum-alloy splint. Still working in a fog, I removed his/my heavy winter clothing, cut away the torn fabric of the left trouser leg, applied a tourniquet, wiped away the worst of the blood, applied a quick-setting gel to seal the wound and stop the bleeding, arranged the metal splint to hold what was left of the bones of the leg in position.

When at last I was done with this, I rolled up his/my left shirt-sleeve, jabbed an ampoule's needle into its flesh and injected a drug to kill the pain, restore some strength, compensate for the shock this body had received. Next, I injected blood restoratives that would help make up for some of what had been lost.

It was a strange feeling, even in the semidetached emotional state I was in, to know that it was myself I was tending, my own warm flesh I was touching. I half expected to feel pain when I moved the lower portion of the shattered leg, jabbed the needles into the upper arm's flesh—and maybe I did, though it could have only been a sympathetic pain.

Then I slipped the chronal-gray jacket back on him/me, remembering that I had been wearing it when I awakened in the warehouse, though I hadn't had on the parka and the other cold-weather gear.

When at last I was finished, I was satisfied that he/I was in no immediate danger of death, though further medical aid would be needed soon, and a long recuperation—the tender mercies of one Dr. Houston English and his daughter, Sharon. I almost envied the injured man in the cage's bucket seat: Sharon would be waiting for him, though even she didn't yet know it.

Still, I knew that he—this previous me who was yet unconscious and would remain so for some hours—would not be able to operate the cage, to set its control to throw it downtime to 3 July 1871 and across geo space to the warehouse. But, if *I* were to do that, the present me, that would be some gross violation of . . . of what? Whatever it was that I feared to violate, whatever gods or laws of chronal time I feared offending, I must have already done so merely by saving my own life.

God, talk about your paradoxes!

This one *was* impossible. And yet . . .

I went over and checked briefly with the computer of *my* cage, satisfied myself of the chronal/geo references, keyed them into the controls of *his* cage, leaped out of the cage as the whine came screaming out of it, and it . . . displaced downtime a month and to safety, to the place where I had been when I'd awakened, the place from which I'd staggered out into the alley, to the street, falling into the mud, lying there until Dr. English stopped to help me . . .

God, it was crazy. It couldn't possibly have been that way.

But if I *hadn't* done it . . . If I *hadn't* done it, he'd/ I'd have died there in that field before the passage of very many more hours. And it had happened this way. Farmer McBride had seen it, hadn't he?

Then, still stunned by the enormous impossibility of it all, unable even to attempt to find some rational explanation for this sequence of events, the loop wherein I'd been the instrument of my own salvation, I went back to my cage.

As I seated myself and began keying controls, I remembered the discrepancy.

The cage hadn't geo'ed directly from this spot into the warehouse, not according to the computer's memory. I'd missed the warehouse by a few blocks and had gotten into Chicago first at 2:41 A.M., not 4:04 A.M. Had I made a minor error, now (and *then*), in setting the controls of his cage? Would he miss the warehouse as *I* had? It must have happened/would happen that way . . .

I had the computer again call up its memory of the cage's first appearance in Chicago and then set my controls accordingly, realizing how easy it would have been to transpose a digit in the sequence and subtly alter time/place of arrival. Before doing anything else, I wanted to see where his cage went from here.

My cage skipped downtime to 3 July, the early morning, outside the warehouse.

It was dark and quiet in the city, a few gas lamps at a distance illuminating the streets, the wooden buildings. The air was warm and damp and had in it the smell of the lake mingled with a stench coming off the stockyards and the slaughterhouses.

I released my belts and awkwardly climbed down from the cage, stepping to the hard-packed dirt of a vacant lot not too many blocks from the warehouse. Had it been daylight, I could probably have seen it from where I stood.

Though there was little traffic and movement in the city at this early-morning hour, someone would probably see the cage if it remained here long. I didn't plan on being here long enough for it to be seen and to encourage a series of strange stories. Then there was that terrible whine that I thought would waken the sleeping city, but didn't. But there in the middle of the street, not ten meters away, was the other cage, the *previous* cage, with him/me in it, still unconscious from the bullet wound in his/my leg.

I limped toward the cage.

A carriage, a wagon, some horse-drawn vehicle was moving not far away, on another street. I heard the horse whinny, the driver mutter to it in a coarse but friendly way.

The man in the second cage, *me,* stirred, opened his/my eyes, looked at me for a brief, uncomprehending moment, then slumped back into unconsciousness. Yes, I remembered this . . .

I went to the cage, climbed in, felt his pulse—he/I was weak, but would make it now. I reset the cage's controls: one hour or so ahead, a few blocks into the warehouse.

When I climbed down and went back to my own cage, when his cage screamed and displaced, I was satisfied that it would go into the warehouse *this time* and the sequence of events as I remembered them would begin.

I tried not to think of all the paradoxes.

Now, in the warm July night in 1871 Chicago, I began keying a new set of chronal/geo references into the cage's controls—or, rather, an old set of chronal/geo references.

I was going back to 86,159 B.C. There might be some other things that I could do there.

19

I don't suppose that it would be correct to say that what happened subsequently was insane, but now few of the occurrences seem to be wholly rational.

I key the cage to go downtime to 3 September, 86,159 B.C., to a place some several hundred kilometers to the east and slightly to the south of Chicago, hoping to come out just shortly after the arrival of Welles and Fulford and before my attack on Welles. Maybe I can stop Fulford there, prevent Welles' death, prevent Fulford's somehow leaving the Pleistocene—someone else will have to come back for him—and thereby prevent his going forward to raze Chicago. But over long chronal distances like that, precise times of coming out are difficult to determine. I may have to time-hop a bit to find just the time I want.

Still the carbine's ready in my hands, safety off, when the wail of displacement comes, and its jolt. I'm almost thrown out of the seat—I haven't strapped myself in. I want to be ready to move fast if I have to.

And then . . .

Snow and ice, a cold blue sky, a white Earth.

Two other chronalcages sit in the clearing in the Ice Age forest. A man lies sprawled on the snow, his blood red against its whiteness, a man whose face I can't see but whom I know to be Welles Kennedy.

A red swath is drawn across the snow, coming from beyond Welles' body and leading to one of the cages, the one which doesn't look damaged, which isn't half covered with snow; and in that cage, at the termination of that red swath, a man whose left leg is shattered and bleeding fights to bring the cage's controls into displacement mode.

A third man, uninjured, has been running across the clearing, has come to a stop, a big, ugly rifle smoking in his hands. He had been looking at the cage in which the wounded man struggles to displace, but turns, his face showing astonishment, when my own cage materializes out of time.

I don't think he really has time to think, to realize exactly what's happening, to recognize me, bearded and strangely garbed as I am. Yet there is a killer instinct in him. He's a Lay Brother of St. Wilson and he has been conditioned to seek out and destroy enemies of the Church/State; and some basic element of his mind must know that I'm precisely that. Or perhaps it's just an instinctive reaction, a reflex. The rifle in his hands swings toward me, the me in 1871 clothes, and fires.

He couldn't have aimed that well, but his shot is good.

I'm kicked back against the seat, the 7 mm slug ripping into the flesh below my left nipple, passing through ribs and lung tissue below my heart, somehow missing major blood vessels (really critical ones), then exiting through more ribs, tearing out flesh and bringing with it a spew of blood that showers the seat behind me as the blunted slug tears through fabric and lodges, flattened, against the seat's metal ribs.

The shock doesn't knock me out. It should, but it doesn't, though I lose my grip on the carbine and it clatters to the cage's deck.

Then he turns to fire at the other cage, the one that now whines insanely as it rips itself out of the Pleistocene and throws itself forward, uptime, to 2 August 1871.

There's no pain in me yet. There will be. It will come later. Now there's only numbness and shock, the knowledge that I've been wounded again, and this time far worse than before. And there is in me a cold determination to kill Carl Fulford before I die from the wound he's just given me.

I try to tell the cage to go downtime again, just a couple of hours, to when I can again come in on Fulford, but before he will be standing ready to do battle with a rifle in his hands.

How I key controls that quickly, I don't know. How I key them at all, I'm uncertain. But I do. I key them and my hands, moving again like those of some hominoid machine, traverse the toggle switches.

Fulford has fired at the vanishing cage, and turns to fire at me again when my own generators whine once more, having hardly ceased their previous whine, and . . . *Whap!*

Snow and ice, a cold gray sky, clouds and a distant threat of snow, a white Earth below, a clearing in the prehistoric forest.

I've overshot. This I dimly realize, for there are no cages *here,* neither the damaged one in which I'd originally arrived nor the one Welles and Fulford had used, the one I now command.

I haven't come here yet.

Wondering how much might be left of the medical supplies in the lockers behind me, I drag myself from the seat, stumble across the deck, shivering with a chill that settles over me.

Passing almost into unconsciousness and then out of it again, I open my torn frock coat and shirt, apply gels and gauze pads to the wounds in my chest and back, managing to stop the flow of blood; then I give myself injections that I hope will prevent the coming of pain, or at least slow its coming, and will reduce the effects of the shock, will keep my head clear, for a while longer at least.

I inject myself with far more of those drugs than I know it wise to use, but I'm desperate now. I have to get back uptime again. I have to! Back to where I can again get medical attention. Get help. Get to Dr. English and . . .

When I finally move into the seat again, I see that in my movements I've splattered blood across the deck, blood that ran and dripped before it froze, that made small, red craters in the snow that will remain behind when the cage is gone. That will be discovered by another Eugene Stillman when *he*—

My mind spins within my head, does crazy things despite the drugs I'd hoped would keep me conscious and rational.

Once again I key the chronalcage's controls, aiming for a date in 1871.

It will have to be *before* the fire, I'm telling myself; I can't go in afterward. But if I get there before, a day or two, I'll be safe and then I can try to get myself help. Maybe someone other than English. Maybe I can work that out: maybe I won't have to further complicate things by staggering, bleeding, into the English home while an earlier me is still there convalescing from still earlier wounds. Maybe I can find a doctor and a safe place, and then return to Sharon after the fire. Maybe I can't prevent the fire now, can't prevent it and Howard Watstone's death and all that, but maybe I can still make some kind of a life for myself there. If I don't die from this wound in my chest first.

God, what a mess I've—

The chronalcage whines and screams and displaces . . . leaps forward in time toward 6 October 1871 . . .

But when the cage leaps forward 88,030 years, it overshoots the target day by some forty-eight or more hours . . .

GOD, NO! I scream to myself.

The warehouse off Clark Street is still there, but it's full of heat and smoke and there's the sound of a gunshot still reverberating from its walls. Carl Fulford—damn him!—is there and he's still trying to kill me.

In the smoke and the beginnings of flame that lick across the building's ceiling, I don't think he sees me—not *this* me, the one who's just arrived with a bullet hole in his chest. He's looking at the previous me, who's trying to flee downtime to . . .

The carbine is still on the deck where it fell when Fulford shot me—when was it? hours, days, centuries, eons ago?

I don't feel the pain as I bend to grab the weapon, to grasp it in my hands and pull it up, but the pain is there even so. I still don't feel it as I flip the carbine into full automatic mode and pull back on the trigger and send a stream of leaden slugs across the room, through the heat and smoke and into the body of the Lay Brother of St. Wilson, while a few meters from me my chronalcage displaces, a few months downtime, to begin the leaps and loops that will bring me back here.

The carbine keeps firing until the magazine is empty and the firing pin is clicking into an empty chamber, brass jackets having gone *ping!* when they hit the deck. Now they are rolling across it and falling to the warehouse floor, but Deacon Carl Fulford has been been cut in half, is a mangled, bleeding, dying thing on the littered floor of the warehouse, and I don't care that the carbine's empty. I don't need it now.

I faint.

20

My mind is remarkably clear as I key controls and bring the cage's generator to life again and wait for warning lights to turn from red to green. This time I'm taking it slow and easy, for I want to make no mistakes.

I am not sane.

Or maybe I am.

I don't know.

Maybe it doesn't matter now.

But I know there's something I have to do, something that might not undo what has happened—or might. What I'm going to do just might wipe the slate clean and remove from the future the world that created me and Carl Fulford and sent us backward in time to try to kill each other. Maybe, when it's all over, neither one of us will exist, neither one of us will have ever existed.

Or maybe I will still exist, maybe I'll still have a ruined leg and a bleeding hole in my chest from Fulford's bullet, even though the world from which I am coming has never been.

I don't know.

I don't care.

And I don't care that Howard Watstone is already dead and that from him can never come the line which would have brought forth Allen Howard Dover. I'll have to make sure of that myself, that Dover is never born.

And I'm going to do that.

You can see why I doubt my sanity at this moment . . . but then maybe it isn't insanity either.

Even if I had killed Dover's ancestor, or at least seen him mortally wounded by another, that wouldn't necessarily mean that *he* would never be born. Not in the crazy universe I'm in. Hell, haven't I saved my own life by sending my unconscious self to a place the existence of which I could only have learned by being sent there by a previous self: a closed loop with no beginning, no end, no reason, no rationality to it.

I have the crazy image of God at the beginning of Time creating Himself out of nothing.

Well . . . ?

I cough raggedly in the smoke that now fills the warehouse, and I spit blood, but my hands move across the toggles and I prepare to displace myself a hundred years into the future and a few kilometers away in space.

As I've said, my mind is now remarkably clear. I remember the exact time and date and place that Melanie and the professor told me about. A September morning in 1971, Lincoln Park, Chicago. Debbie Watstone, three weeks pregnant, will be there alone in the park studying for an exam, a college student. Won't she? Will she?

She'll be waiting there for Harry Greenbaum, the father of the child she doesn't yet know she carries. But Harry Greenbaum will never show up. She won't learn until the next day that he died in a motorcycle accident the night before. And it won't be until a month later that she will meet Robert Dover, and six weeks after that marry him, later claiming that the child is his.

But . . . I still ask myself, will there be a Deborah Watstone there *now?*

Does it matter?

It's a bright September morning and Lake Michigan, already polluted, glistens in the sunlight to my right, beyond Lake Shore Drive, packed now with rushing automobiles. Around me, outside the cage, are grass and trees and paths and benches, and, beyond, a bathing beach in one direction and a golf course in another; statues and memorials stand here and there, specked with the droppings of pigeons, and there are people in the park, in clothing that somehow doesn't quite seem right, though I can't say exactly how their clothing is wrong.

Clumsily I reload my carbine and see that not far from me is the statue of Johann Wolfgang von Goethe and there should be a dark-eyed girl, a girl with strangely deep and gentle eyes, sitting beneath that statue, studying for a psychology examination.

She isn't there, though the date and time are right, and I can't get out of the cage to go look for her. I've begun to bleed again and I'm too weak to do more than hold the carbine in my lap and hope to see her, to kill her.

But she isn't there.

And maybe she never will be. Maybe there's no Debbie Watstone in this world.

And that makes sense, doesn't it?

DOESN'T IT?

Then as people turn, startled to have seen a cage-like affair seemingly materialize out of the air, I notice the Chicago skyline to the south and west of me, beyond the trees and the nearer buildings and the park. It's the skyline of no Chicago that *I* know, at least none that existed in *my* 1971, a 1971 twenty-odd years before my birth.

A historian's memory: Chicago was one of the American cities hit by the Nazi nuclear-armed jet bombers in the July Raid of 1947, their one successful attempt at getting back at the American homeland with their newly developed long-range jet bombers. Chicago was one of the northern cities hit during their suicidal sweep across the North Pole from Arctic aircraft carriers out of Occupied Russia. It wasn't a really big bomb that hit Chicago—not nearly as big as ours that later destroyed Berlin and Stuttgart and Munich—but it was big enough to reduce to radioactive slag the center of the city, most of which hadn't been fully rebuilt for nearly a decade.

And when it was, when 1971 came around, the skyline of the city was radically different from what it had been before: geodesic domes and towering pinnacles, monorails and a centralized nuclear power station. "The City of the Future," this new Chicago was called, the one in which Deborah Watstone had attended Loyola

University, a series of new and imposing structures built not far from where the old university had once been . . .

But this isn't that Chicago!

A weakness, a weariness comes over me, a sense of pain and anger and frustration, maybe something of triumph mixed with it. Now I'm certain that there'll be no Appointed One, no Church/State, no world of bigotry and oppression, no blueshirts and no Proctors, no enforced church services and no denial of natural human sexuality, no slave camps for blacks and no re-education centers for the milder heretics who could escape death by conversion. The world to which I will return, if I am to return to the future, will not be the terrible one I left.

I have set my people free.

While a crowd gathers and a police siren approaches from a distance, I use numb and unwilling fingers to re-set controls and begin the brief countdown that will throw me once more, for a time, outside Time, into displacement.

They come to watch and wonder, and what they must think I cannot guess: a man dressed in clothing a century out of style, wounded and bleeding, working the controls of a device that could have come only from the future, or from another planet.

What the newspapers will say tomorrow morning!

Then, again, I've gone down the sequence and all the right lights are green again and I nod a weak good-bye to the curious outside the cage and to the city that will never be the New Jerusalem and—

Whap!

21

There's an old argument that runs something like this: *if* it is possible to travel in time and *if* it is possible to change the past, a time machine *will not* be invented in that universe.

What?

(Please note: I said "will not"; I didn't say "never will.")

The argument goes something like this: Someone invents a time machine within the context of a universe that allows the existence of time travel, and, as any invention will do, it proliferates with the passage of time. At first, maybe, only a few people—scientists, serious scholars, etc.—go into the past, all with good intentions, merely to *view* the past, to *observe* the activities of history, but not to participate. But as time passes (in the day-after-day, year-after-year fashion), more and more people move, for one reason or another, into a (*changeable*) past; and, sooner or later, despite the very best of safeguards, fail-safes, instruction, and philosophy, you name it, something is going to happen, intentionally or by blunder, and changes will be made in the past. Given these criteria, it's inevitable. Every trip into the past opens up the possibility of further changes. And each time a change takes place, minor or significant, *all subsequent history* will be altered to some degree, in some fashion. Each new alternative future will have some differences between it and the world that "preceded" it, differences great or small. Perhaps an almost endless variety of "future worlds" would come into existence and then pass away, with still more changes in the past.

With me so far?

Okay, given *Time* and *times,* and given enough changes in the past, sooner or later the "future" course of events would lead to a world in which, for some reason or other, the time machine was *not* invented. *Not ever.* In short, a universe in which time travel never happened in the first place!

I think I've found it.

Oh, I'm back in 2032. Back home . . .

But there's a difference, a terrible difference, a difference so great, perhaps, that this is the last of all possible worlds.

The chronalcage is here. Now the people here have a time machine. I could have said, "a working time machine," but that isn't quite so. I suppose—I'm certain—that the chronalcage is still operable. I have no reason to believe that it isn't. But the people here don't know what to do with it—and I can't tell them.

The cage is back in the Now—the ultimate *Now* from which it cannot leave without an enormous amount of power, power that could only come from controlled thermonuclear fusion or something comparable, and the people here don't have controlled thermonuclear fusion. They've never had it—not *controlled*—and probably never will have it. It's very unlikely they will.

You see: I guess you could call this place I'm in a "hospital." It's not exactly that, but the term is close enough to give you the idea of what I mean. In a world that's all hospital—what there is left of it—it's sort of difficult to distinguish one place from another.

The machines tend me and machines tend the machines. But who, pray tell, tends the machines who tend the machines?

Outside, through the glass that surrounds me, the people look in at me. They watch me. I'm a freak. They've seen very few like me. There aren't many like me in 2032 A.D., and they're growing constantly fewer. Fewer. Fewer . . .

They look at me with their long, twisted faces, some

with eyes and some without eyes—and I don't know how those without eyes can look at me, but I'm sure they do.

They watch and they wonder, like those people back in 1971 Chicago in the park, but their thoughts are more remote from me than those of the people who gazed at my cage wonder and curiosity. I can never imagine what *these* people are thinking. Maybe it's better if I never do know.

The machines tend me, have made me as well as they can, though I've been told that I will never be whole again. Perhaps I will die soon. They haven't told me that, but I have a strong feeling that I will. And those people outside, they won't mind at all if I do.

The machines have told me things: I've got the original "Typhoid Mary" beat a country mile.

Exactly what kind of viral weapons the Eco-Europeans used on us just before I displaced out of *my* 2032 the last time, I'll never know. It didn't happen in *this* world, so the machines and I can only guess. Maybe Welles Kennedy or Carl Fulford knew, but then I never really got a chance to ask them.

But we were hit with bio-weapons, I'm certain of that. And I was infected, and I carry the disease; deep down in my genes I carry it.

The disease, whatever it was, made me sick for a while, gave me those miserable days huddled in that icy cave, but that passing illness and the malarial spells that came afterward were only the mildest effects of the disease, whatever it is, though they were the only ones that immediately affected *me*. When those symptoms, the worst of them, were over and I no longer felt constantly sick and feverish, something had happened inside me, something had altered the structure of my cells, the DNA inside them . . .

The machines tell me that there are hundreds of tiny, minor growths inside my body, not exactly carcinomas, not cancers, but maybe something like them. They've given me the technical name for them, but I can't recall it. Yet, slowly, over weeks and months, as new cells replace old ones, subtle little changes are taking place.

Nothing major. Nothing I couldn't have lived with for many years if I hadn't gotten myself messed up in other ways. But that isn't the important thing either.

What *is* important is what this thing, this virus, whatever it is, did to my sex cells, my sperm . . .

I've asked the machines to tell me about the past, to do some research for me, and they've done it. The records seem to indicate that a Miss Sharon English, of Willow Street, Chicago, Illinois, U.S.A., gave birth to an illegitimate child on Thursday, 27 June 1872, and gave to it the name Eugene David Stillman, Jr.

My son?

My son!

A sickly child with a club foot, he never amounted to very much as the world measures—measured!—things; but he did marry and he did have children, and from all indications each of them was marked in some way, marked by a minor deformity, a flaw in the genes, something not quite right about them.

The line of Stillmans fades into obscurity and is hardly mentioned in the records of the machines for over a century.

Yet they carried something in their genes, these offspring of mine: that something that I had carried back with me.

It would seem, for a time at least, that the disease was almost dormant, affecting only those in my direct line. It was not a contagious disease then, apparently, except in a venereal way.

Then a nuclear war hit *this* world with a vengeance. It was a three-way war between the world's major powers, and when it was over better than half the planet lay in ruins.

The war—the radiation from the nukes, maybe a new biological weapon—did something to those viruses carried by my descendants, must have mutated the viruses again, brought them to the full strength intended by the enemy when he dusted *my* Chicago with them.

But I won't really go into all that.

I'd rather not.

I just look back at *them,* through the glass between

us, and I see what those viruses have done, how those viruses have spread across the planet and infected the genes of an all-too-large percentage of mankind.

They tell me that a normal birth is one in a million. A stillbirth is nine out of ten. And what's in between . . .

Well, I'm looking at it—them—beyond the glass, those poor people that I won't even try to describe.

And normal births grow more rare with each passing day.

The gene pool of humankind is polluted beyond hope.

No, time travel will never be invented here. It's too late for that. It's too late for anything.

Oh, Melanie, look at what I've done to help our world.

Sharon, please forgive me.